"Make yourself at home, Josey,

Gable said stiffly. "And since you're staying, maybe my brothers and I can persuade you to cook dinner tonight. With my sister out of commission, you'll probably be better at it than us."

It was, Josey decided, the most backhanded compliment she'd ever received. And the most chauvinistic. She'd let Mr. High-and-Mighty Rawlings taunt her long enough. "Why, Mr. Rawlings, you surprise me! I never expected you to admit women were superior to men. I would have sworn you were a dyed-in-the-wool chauvinist!"

She expected him to stiffen and sputter a denial, but he was too sure of himself for that. He merely arched a dark eyebrow, like a slightly bored adult amused by a child.

"Obviously your hearing isn't superior, *Ms.* O'Brian. I said you were *probably* better at cooking than me or my brothers."

Dear Reader,

There's lots of exciting stuff for you in the Intimate Moments line this month, starting off with Linda Turner's *Gable's Lady*. This American Hero title is also the first of Linda's new miniseries, The Wild West. Set on a ranch in New Mexico, it's the saga of the Rawlings family, whose children are named after movie stars. It's no secret where Gable got his name—and in the future you can look for *Cooper, Flynn* and sister *Kat*. You'll love them all.

We're starting another miniseries this month, too: Romantic Traditions. Each Romantic Traditions title will be written by a different author and will put an Intimate Moments spin on one of your favorite romance plots. This month Paula Detmer Riggs offers up a marriage of convenience in *Once Upon a Wedding*. In months to come, look for Marilyn Pappano's *Finally a Father* (a secret-baby book), Carla Cassidy's *Try to Remember* (amnesia) and more.

We've also got another new author featured in a reprise of last year's successful "Premiere" promotion. Her name's Kylie Brant, and her irresistible book is called *McLain's Law*. All this, plus new books from Heather Graham Pozzessere, Lindsay Longford and Marilyn Cunningham. It's another don't-miss month from Intimate Moments.

Enjoy!

Yours,

Leslie Wainger
Senior Editor and Editorial Coordinator

AMERICAN HERO

GABLE'S LADY

Linda Turner

Silhouette®
INTIMATE MOMENTS®

Published by Silhouette Books New York
America's Publisher of Contemporary Romance

SILHOUETTE BOOKS
300 East 42nd St., New York, N.Y. 10017

GABLE'S LADY

Copyright © 1993 by Linda Turner

ISBN: 0-373-07523-5

First Silhouette Books printing October 1993

Printed in the U.S.A.

Books by Linda Turner

Silhouette Intimate Moments

The Echo of Thunder #238
Crosscurrents #263
An Unsuspecting Heart #298
Flirting with Danger #316
Moonlight and Lace #354
The Love of Dugan Magee #448
*Gable's Lady #523

*The Wild West Series

Silhouette Desire

A Glimpse of Heaven #220
Wild Texas Rose #653
Philly and the Playboy #701
The Seducer #802

Silhouette Special Edition

Shadows in the Night #350

LINDA TURNER

began reading romances in high school and began writing them one night when she had nothing else to read. She's been writing ever since. Single and living in Texas, she travels every chance she gets, scouting locales for her books.

Chapter 1

The featured speaker for the monthly meeting of the Southwest New Mexico Cattlemen's Association droned on about the drought that had plagued the area for the past six months, but Gable Rawlings didn't hear a word. The white Western shirt he wore was too tight across the shoulders, too long in the sleeves, and fit like a hair shirt. His teeth clenched on an oath, it took all of his considerable self-control not to flex his shoulders and split the damn thing right down the back. But it was his brother's shirt, and Cooper wouldn't thank him for ruining it.

His light blue eyes, usually so cool, burned with annoyance. Owning and operating a two-thousand-acre cattle ranch was hot, dusty work, and when he and his two brothers came in at the end of the day, they were tired and gamey and in desperate need of plenty of soap, hot water and clean clothes. That wasn't a hell of a lot to ask after the long hours they'd spent in the saddle in all kinds of weather. Lately, though, they'd been damn lucky to get hot water, let alone anything resembling clean clothes. And he knew just who to blame, and it wasn't his little sister, Kat.

Not that Kat was completely blameless in this situation, Gable reminded himself with a scowl. When Alice, the family housekeeper who had mothered all of them for the past ten years, had taken a leave of absence to be with her daughter during a difficult pregnancy, Kat had volunteered to do most of the housework. Seventeen and just the slightest bit spoiled by them all, she'd handled the work better than anyone had expected... until Dr. Josephine O'Brian had moved into her grandparents' place down the road.

An outsider, a Yankee visiting New Mexico for an extended stay while she took a break from her job at a clinic in some godforsaken part of Boston, the lady doctor hadn't been content to quietly move in and enjoy her vacation in peace. Oh, no, he thought cynically. Her kind never did anything quietly. A diehard women's libber who had probably sold her femininity for a career, she'd started stirring up trouble the minute she met Kat.

"Josey said there's nothing in a man's genetic makeup that prevents him from doing housework as well as a woman."

"Josey said a woman has to stand up for herself or the men in her life will take advantage of her."

Gable winced as his sister's familiar litany echoed in his ears. He knew keeping house for three bachelor brothers had turned out to be more work than Kat had expected, and she'd no doubt led the new neighbor to believe that her insensitive brothers worked her to the bone. But, dammit, the woman should have realized that Kat was a rebellious teenager who was enjoying martyrdom for the moment. She should have just sympathized with her and minded her own business. Instead she'd incited Kat to open anarchy, encouraging her in a series of strikes that had turned the usually well-ordered ranch upside down.

And her timing couldn't have been worse. Spring—and the annual roundup—was always hectic, but this year he had another worry gnawing at him. The final payment on a loan he'd taken out ten years ago, after his parents were killed in a car accident.

The memory, aching and bittersweet, tugged at him, softening the unrelenting set of his mouth. He'd had the best parents in the world, but no one had ever accused them of being sharp when it came to business. They'd been land rich and dirt poor, and, Gable had discovered when he'd taken over management of the ranch, in danger of going under.

At twenty-two, and newly married, he'd found not only the responsibility of the ranch thrust onto his shoulders, but also that of his teenage brothers and seven-year-old Kat. He'd almost panicked before he'd done the only thing he could to save his heritage—mortgaged the ranch to the hilt to finance the necessary improvements needed to make the Double R a viable, successful cattle company. That decision had saved the ranch, but it had, in the end, cost him more than he'd expected to pay—his marriage.

His mouth thinned, faded images of Karen swimming to the forefront of his memory. Whatever he'd been stupid enough to feel for her once had died a long time ago, but he'd never forgotten the lesson she'd taught him. A city woman full of ambition, with her eye trained unwaveringly on her career, was a woman to be avoided. He hadn't met one since that hadn't turned his blood cold, and he didn't expect Josephine O'Brian to be any different. The sooner she returned to Boston, the better.

Jerking his attention back to the podium, he tried to show an interest in the speaker's boring facts as he droned on and on, but, as usual, Gable found his mind wandering back to the upcoming loan payment. It was never far from his thoughts these days, which wasn't surprising. When he'd taken out the loan, the bank had been only too happy to accept as collateral one of the largest ranches in the state. So if the last large balloon payment wasn't made when it was due in six weeks, they'd lose the ranch. With that weighing on his mind, who could blame him for not noticing that the dishes weren't washed or that Kat hadn't done any grocery shopping and the cupboards were nearly bare?

But his brothers had noticed, and when they'd complained to him about Kat's shenanigans, his first instinct had been to laugh. After everything else he had to worry about, a few dirty dishes seemed a minor annoyance. But he had talked to Kat, appealing to her loyalty, pointing out that they all had to sometimes do things they didn't like. She was really helping out the family by taking over Alice's duties. Tears in her eyes, she'd agreed with everything he'd said.

That should have put an end to Josey O'Brian's influence then and there. And for a while it had. He hadn't heard a word of complaint out of Kat in more than a week. Then, this afternoon, he'd been running late, rushing into the house to change for the cattlemen's meeting, only to discover that Kat had gone on strike again without warning, this time refusing to wash any clothes. The only clean shirt in the house had belonged to Cooper.

Suddenly he was no longer amused by her little acts of defiance.

Dammit, it had to stop!

Which meant he had to confront the instigator—Dr. Josephine O'Brian. Up until now, he'd gone out of his way to avoid her because he had more than enough problems to deal with at the ranch and he'd heard enough about the Yankee doctor to know she was the kind of woman he wanted nothing to do with. An interfering busybody with a chip on her shoulder where men were concerned, she was the kind of trouble he had hoped would go away if he just ignored her long enough. That obviously wasn't going to happen. It was high time someone told her to keep her nose out of other people's business, and he was just the man for the job!

Snuggled up against the very base of the craggy cliffs that formed the first ridge of the mountains that rose out of the western edge of the valley floor, the O'Brian homestead overlooked miles and miles of empty, sun-drenched desert. In the rocks behind the old farmhouse, oak and piñon and ponderosa pine grew in the higher elevations, but to the east there wasn't a single tree in sight. The only relief from the stark glare of the sun was the measly shade offered by the long, thorny branches of the ocotillo and the wispy leaves of the scrub mesquite that occasionally dotted the landscape.

Deep in the shade of the porch that stretched across the front of the house, Josey settled sideways in the old wicker porch swing and propped her bare right foot up so she could paint her toenails. Her skin fresh and still cool from the tepid bath she'd just taken after spending most of the afternoon in her garden, she sighed in contentment, the nearly soundless murmur hardly casting a ripple on the surface of the silence that engulfed her.

When she'd first made the move to New Mexico, she'd been in no shape to appreciate the silence that dogged every step she took through the empty rooms of the old house that was all she had left of her grandparents. She'd grown up in the city, thrived on the sights and sounds and smells of it. Grocery stores were around the corner, not forty miles away; neighbors were people who would come running when you called for help, not strangers a mile or more down the road who wouldn't hear you even if you yelled your head off. Lonely, intimidated by the barrenness of the landscape, she hadn't been able to get used to her alien surroundings and had found herself waking in the middle of the night, her heart thumping wildly in her breast, her ears painfully listening for the familiar sounds of honking horns, screaming sirens and the cries of babies on the dark air. But there'd been no traffic, no ambulances, no people, only the occasional far-off cry of a coyote and the soft whisper of the wind as it skimmed across the sloping foothills, rustling bear grass and murmuring secrets older than time itself. More miserable than she'd ever been in her life, she'd repacked her bags half a dozen times in the first week alone, determined to go back to Boston where she belonged.

But she never got past the front door before she changed her mind. She couldn't go back, not yet, maybe not ever. For the past four years, she'd worked in an OB/GYN clinic in one of the worst neighborhoods in the city, living out her dream of providing prenatal care for expectant mothers who normally couldn't afford the medical attention they and their unborn babies needed. But working too hard and caring too much had taken its toll. She'd developed an ulcer and was so stressed out, she had trouble sleeping. Her own doctor had warned her she was pushing herself too hard, but she was desperately needed and she hadn't listened. Then Molly, one of her favorite patients, had come into the clinic late one night, dilated and ready to have her baby any second.

It should have gone smooth as silk. She'd delivered dozens of babies without a single problem, and Molly had done everything asked of her during the pregnancy. She was in excellent health, but no one could have predicted a prolapsed cord. The baby hadn't had a chance.

Pain squeezed Josey's heart, the memory still too fresh, too agonizing, to be taken out and examined without tearing her apart. Self-doubt lurked in the shadows, the what-ifs waiting to jump out and claw at her the minute she dropped her guard. Stiffening, she reminded herself that she wasn't God, and it would have taken a miracle to save the baby. But it didn't help. Nothing did. Pushing back the bruising images, she drew in a long, calming breath and tried to focus on the beauty of the land spread before her.

Stark. Empty. Tranquil in its simplicity. The sun had sunk behind the mountains to the west, casting long, quiet shadows, while more than a thousand miles away in Boston, commuters had already fought their way home in bumper-to-bumper traffic that would begin all over again in the morning. Here there was only the peace of day's end and the ever-present murmur of the wind whispering in her ear, speaking to the hidden recesses of her soul. Like a soothing balm, the quiet slipped past her taut nerves, relaxing her, easing the stressful memories that threatened to tie her in knots.

Dipping the brush back into the bottle of blushing pink nail polish, she was delicately applying color to her big toe when a black pickup truck suddenly shot up the drive from the highway like a bat out of hell. Startled, Josey glanced up... and promptly dragged a streak of pink nail polish across her toe.

"Smart, Josey," she muttered, reaching for a tissue. "You'd think you'd never had any visitors before."

Well, she hadn't, only Kat. But she drove a red Jeep and never dropped by this time of day. Absently wiping at the mess she'd made of her toe, she watched the truck draw up in a cloud of dust, its driver only a shadow behind the vehicle's dark, tinted windows. Kat had told her living in the wilds of New Mexico was a heck of a lot safer than the crime-ridden streets of Boston, but Josey had never been this isolated in the city, and her heart was already starting to pound. Forcing herself to sit still, she cast a quick glance at the front door, gauging the short distance from the swing. If she needed to, she could make it inside and shoot the dead bolt in three seconds flat.

"I'm looking for Josephine O'Brian. Have you seen her?"

The low snarl snapped Josey's eyes back to the truck in time to see an irritated giant of a man emerge from the cab. He was whipcord lean and tall, the type of rugged outdoorsman who looked good in worn jeans, scuffed boots and a black cowboy hat. At any other time, Josey might have appreciated his square jaw and tanned, chiseled face, the crow's-feet that years spent in the sun had attractively carved at the corners of his light blue eyes, but her gaze never got past the furious set of a mouth that could have been incredibly sensuous if it hadn't been pressed flatter than a pancake. She'd dealt with a few angry men before, but never one so riled she could practically see the steam spilling from his ears. And she'd never seen him before in her life!

Rising cautiously to her feet, she held her ground and gave him a cool stare, drawing her title around her like a shield. "I'm Dr. O'Brian."

If Gable hadn't been so mad, he might have laughed. From her accent, she had definitely come with the other woman from Boston, but if she was a doctor, he'd eat his Aunt Fanny's drawers! He may not have ever laid eyes on Josephine O'Brian, but he knew he'd know her when he saw her. He'd drawn a picture of her in his mind, one of a stiff, unyielding women's libber, a city woman who oozed sophistication and coldness and wouldn't warm up to a man in a blizzard. The girl standing in front of him was nothing like that.

The day had been a hot one, a forewarning of the summer to come, with a wind that was still dry and gritty, yet she looked as fresh as the desert after a dawn shower. Small and delicate, her skin was of the palest cream, soft, touchable, her hair a black wavy mass that fell unbound and free past her shoulders. For a moment, he was distracted by the bare expanse of her legs exposed by the thin pink shorts she wore with a white tank top, but he couldn't quite drag his gaze away from her face. Vulnerable. There was something about her...perhaps in the soft curve of her mouth or in the dark green bottomless depths of her eyes...that spoke of a delicateness, a softness that could be easily bruised.

Gable felt a tug of awareness all the way down to his gut and bit back a curse. He wasn't looking for a woman, especially one connected with Josey O'Brian, and it was high time he remembered that. All he wanted to do was give the nosy doctor a piece of his mind and get out of there.

His mouth curled cynically. "I don't know who you are, sweetheart, but I haven't got time to play games. Go get the doctor before I lose what little patience I've got left."

What patience he had left! she thought indignantly, her eyes flashing at his condescending tone. Who the hell did he think he was? All five-foot-four of her stiff with outrage, she looked coldly down her pert nose at him from the superior height of the porch. "Look, cowboy, I'm not your sweetheart and I don't take orders from you. I've told you who I am. If you can't accept that, that's your problem. I'm certainly not going to pull out my diploma and prove I'm a doctor to you.''

It wasn't what she said, but the way she said it, with her chin lifted as regally as any queen's and chips of ice chilling her green eyes, that had Gable stopping in his tracks, his eyes narrowed in disbelief. *This was Josephine O'Brian?* The termagant who had made his usually well-ordered life a living hell for the past few weeks? The nosy, interfering, hard-line defender of women's rights who had filled his sister's head with nonsense and caused a rift in his family without a thought to the damage she was doing? This soft, beautiful slip of a woman was Josey O'Brian?

Suddenly furious, it took all his self-control not to charge up the porch steps and shake her until her teeth rattled. ''Lady, you've got a hell of a nerve! I know you're a Yankee and a city woman to boot, so I'm going to give you the benefit of the doubt and assume you don't know how we do things around here. Let me give you a little bit of friendly advice. Quit sticking your nose into things that don't concern you. You got that?''

''No, I don't,'' she retorted, stung. ''In fact, I don't even know what you're talking about. Who *are* you?''

For half a second, Gable was almost taken in by her confused innocence...until he remembered the trouble she caused every time she saw Kat. Whatever this woman was, she was no innocent. His teeth ground on an unprintable oath, he glared at her with acute dislike. ''Don't pretend you don't know me. You've interfered so much in my life over the last three weeks that by now you damn well ought to know the color of my shorts! Because of you, I'm stuck wearing a shirt that's as tight as a straitjacket, and it's got to stop. Do you hear me? If you've got to stir up trouble while you're here, you find someone else to do it with. Stay away from Kat!''

He watched the comprehension finally dawn in her eyes and gave her a tight smile. ''That's right. I'm Gable, Kat's oldest brother *and* her legal guardian. And I'm ordering you to leave her alone. She doesn't need a friend like you.''

His cold words hurt, but Josey didn't even flinch. So this was Gable, the oldest of the four Rawlings siblings, all of whom were named after their mother's favorite movies stars of the forties. She should have known. From the day she'd first met Kat, quite by accident, at the row of rural mailboxes down on the highway, she'd done nothing but talk about her brothers, especially Gable. And her comments hadn't always been flattering.

Domineering. Arrogant. Chauvinistic. At first, Josey had thought Kat was exaggerating slightly, but now she could see she hadn't been. He ran the ranch and the family—especially Kat—with an iron hand, unfairly expecting Kat to do all the housework for three grown bachelors just because she happened to be the only female in the bunch. No wonder her young friend was so miserable! He was every bit as bad as Kat had said he was, the typical man of the West who had more respect for his horse than he did the women in his life.

And Josey didn't doubt that there were plenty of women. Even with a scowl on his face and wearing a shirt that was at least one size too small, Gable Rawlings was one good-looking devil, the kind of man who would never lack for female companionship. He probably only had to crook his finger....

Josey's delicately arched brows drew together at the thought, irritation flattening the usually generous curve of her mouth as she dispassionately studied him from the top of his black cowboy hat to the scuffed leather of his boots. She didn't care if he was as handsome as his namesake, no man snapped his fingers at her and expected her to fall in line . . . not if he knew what was good for him.

Looking him straight in the eye, she gave him a cool half smile that was guaranteed to set his teeth on edge. "Don't you think it's time to ease up on the apron strings some, Mr. Rawlings? Where I come from, a seventeen-year-old girl is old enough to pick her own friends."

"Then I suggest you go back there," he snapped, "because if you keep causing trouble, lady, you're going to have to deal with me. And nobody causes trouble in my family and gets away with it. Consider yourself warned."

Josey opened her mouth to tell him what he could do with his warning, but Gable never gave her a chance. Shooting her one last threatening glare, he pivoted on his heel and strode quickly back to his truck. Reaching the driver's side, he jerked open the door . . . and promptly split his shirt right down the back.

Josey gasped, her hand flying to her mouth to suppress the sudden grin that tugged at her lips. But it was too late. Gable's narrowed eyes flew to hers, the scorching heat of his gaze burning her from fifty feet away, before he muttered a curse and climbed into his truck. Seconds later the motor roared to life and he raced down the drive to the highway, leaving a trail of hot dust in his wake.

For a long timeless moment, Josey stared after him, shaken. Quiet descended again as if it had never been disturbed, the murmur of the wind a soothing balm. But all Josey could hear was the pounding of her heart. Gable Rawlings would be back. She knew it as surely as she knew he meant every word of his warning to leave his sister alone. But Kat was a young woman living among men; she didn't have a single woman to talk to, to confide her troubles, her dreams, to. Josey couldn't just turn her back on her when the girl needed a friend. If her brother couldn't understand that, that was his problem.

The torn shirt rubbed against Gable's back, mocking him all the way home. Josey O'Brian had had her little laugh, but he'd made his point—he'd seen the knowledge in the lady's bewitching green eyes. If she kept pushing, he'd give her more trouble than she could handle, and she knew it. So the matter was settled ... at least with the lady doctor. Kat was another matter.

His face stony, he pulled into the circular drive in front of the house and cut the engine. The evening sky was already starting to darken, and the long windows of the Victorian farm house that had been built by his great-grandfather when the Rawlingses first moved to New Mexico were lit with a welcoming glow. But tonight he was in no mood to appreciate the peace he usually found in his home. The torn shirt molding his shoulders like an irritant, he strode up the front steps to the veranda that wrapped all the way around the house. The screen door banged behind him, his booted feet angrily proclaiming his presence as he made his way down the hall to the kitchen.

Just as he expected, the rest of the family had already sat down for supper and were discussing the day's work over steak and potatoes. Cooper and Flynn, seated across from each other and still wearing the clothes they'd worn in the saddle all day, had obviously only taken time to wash their hands and face and throw some water on their hair before hurrying to the table to eat. Between bites, they argued good-naturedly over who was going to get a rare day off now that roundup had started, not even noticing his presence in the doorway.

Kat, however, saw him the minute he stepped through the door. Seated in their mother's spot, her resemblance to her was uncanny. Tall and willowy, with sapphire eyes and a smile that could knock the local boys out of their boots if she only knew it, she was, at seventeen, a pretty girl. With time and maturity, she would be breathtaking...and a handful for any man who dared take her on. Just thinking about it gave Gable gray hair.

A forkful of potatoes halfway to her mouth, she started to smile when her gaze suddenly dropped to the ragged shirt he wore. Her eyes widened, a telltale blush climbing into her cheeks as her fork fell with a clatter to her plate.

"What the—" Flynn turned to her in surprise, then followed the direction of her gaze to take in Gable's disheveled appearance in a single glance. A slow grin spread across his boyish face, teasing speculation dancing in his blue eyes. "Well, the prodigal finally returns...looking like he's been in a cat fight. Where you been, big brother?"

Cooper, seated with his back to the doorway, pivoted in his seat, frowning. "What do you mean, where's he been? He went to a cattlemen's meeting—hey, that's one of my best shirts! What the hell have you done to it?"

"Ruined it," Gable replied flatly as he pulled out his chair at the head of the table and sat down. "Believe me, I'm not any happier about it than you are. I felt like a fool going to town in it, but I was running late and couldn't find anything else to wear. It was the only clean shirt in the house."

"What're you talking about?" Flynn demanded, half rising out of his seat to go check his own closet. "Kat washes every Monday, and today's just Friday. There's got to be something clean somewhere. I'm going dancing tonight!"

"No, you're not," Gable retorted. "Not unless you're planning on wearing the dusty clothes you've got on. Everything else is dirty."

Cooper abruptly pushed back from the table, his chair scraping on the floor. "If this is your idea of a joke, it isn't funny," he told Gable. "I've got a date with Mary Lou Henderson tonight, and I'm not standing her up. You know how you are when you're looking for something— you couldn't find your feet if they weren't connected to your legs. Just because Kat didn't have time to hang our clean clothes in each of our closets doesn't mean we don't have anything to wear. Did you look in the laundry room?"

Gable nodded, his eyes on his sister's guilty face. At any other time he would have laughed, which was one of the problems. They'd spoiled her, he and his brothers, and now they were paying the price. Headstrong and full of mischief, she'd always known how to get her way with them by teasing them out of their anger and drawing a laugh from them. Well, no more.

"Would you like to tell them why their closets are empty or shall I?" he asked her quietly.

The heat intensified in her cheeks, but her eyes didn't waver from his. "I've got a research paper due next week in history. I g-guess I just forgot."

"Forgot?" Flynn exploded. "How am I supposed to go dancing when I smell like a damn horse?"

"Take a bath and put on plenty of Brut," she retorted. "The women will love it."

Gable fought back a grin. What was he going to do with her?

Cooper, on the other hand, only snorted at that bit of impudent advice. "That might be okay for the skirts he picks up at the Rusty Spur, brat, but Mary Lou is a mite more particular. If I get within ten feet of her smelling like the range, she'll have a conniption, and you know it."

Unperturbed, Kat propped an elbow on the table and rested her chin in her palm, her smile an irritating mixture of smugness and laughter. "Then maybe you need to learn how to operate the washing machine. I'm sure you can push the buttons as well as I can. Course, you'll have to hurry if you're going to wash and dry a shirt tonight," she added, blue eyes dancing. "Everybody knows Old Timex doesn't like to be kept waiting."

Flynn groaned, drowning out Cooper's muttered curse. "Oh, God, not again! If you mention that O'Brian woman's name one more time, I'm not going to be responsible for my actions." Turning to Gable for help, he demanded, "Can't you do anything with her? This is getting ridiculous!"

"I agree," he said grimly, "which is why I stopped by the O'Brian place on the way home and told our new neighbor to quit sticking her nose into things that don't concern her. I don't think we'll have any more trouble with her."

Kat paled as if he'd struck her. "Oh, Gable, how could you! She's my friend—"

"She's a grown woman," he cut in firmly, "who has nothing in common with you. I've told you before, you need friends your own age, now I'm going to insist on it. From now on, you're to stay away from Josey O'Brian."

"But—"

"No buts. Josey O'Brian is not the type of friend you need. The matter is closed."

Hurt, Kat would have given anything to argue further, but he had that stubborn look on his face that warned her his mind was made up. She knew from experience she'd have more luck arguing with a rock than she would with Gable once he made up his mind about something. And right now, she couldn't afford to get on the outs with him.

Not when she still needed his permission to go to the spring dance in three weeks.

Swallowing her frustration, she struggled not to let her resentment show, but it wasn't easy. Her brothers had always been able to read her like a well read book. "I do have friends my own age," she said quietly. "I think there's even a couple of boys who would ask me to the spring dance if they weren't so afraid of my protective older brothers."

"Afraid? Who's afraid of us?"

"What kind of boys you going to school with? Any man worth his salt wouldn't be scared off by anyone, least of all older brothers!"

"A decent boy doesn't have to be afraid of asking you out. He just has to come out here and meet us before he takes you any place."

Kat almost groaned. "Why don't you ask for references while you're at it and a financial statement? Nobody's going to ask me out when they know you three are going to put them through the third degree. Which is why I've decided to take matters into my own hands."

Gable scowled. He didn't like the sound of that at all. "What are you talking about?"

She lifted her chin proudly, her jaw set stubbornly. "I want to go to the dance, and since no one has the nerve to ask me, I'll do the asking."

"You'll do no such thing!"

"You're too young to even be thinking about dating!"

"A woman doesn't ask a man out!"

She flinched at the roars of outrage that hit her from all sides, hot tears stinging her eyes. Josey had told her to talk to them, to reason with them and try to explain how caged-in she felt, but Josey didn't know them. They watched over her like a mother hen, and talking to them did no good.

She didn't know why they didn't just lock her up in her room until she was thirty and be done with it!

Pain squeezing her heart, Kat pushed her hardly touched food away from her and rose to her feet, glaring at her three wardens. "Forget it. Just forget the whole damn thing!"

Whirling, she headed for the back door. Cursing, Gable demanded, "Where do you think you're going?"

She didn't even look back. "To a friend's house to study. I—I have a big test tomorrow." Grabbing her purse, she was out the door and racing for her Jeep before anyone could think to ask which friend she was visiting.

When Josey opened her front door to her five minutes later, the set of Kat's jaw was mutinous, her eyes filled with hot tears. "They have no right to treat me like a child!" she stormed by way of greeting. "It's not fair!"

Josey didn't have to ask who "they" were. Only Kat's brothers could bring that glint of angry hurt to the younger girl's eyes. Pushing the screen door wide, she ushered her inside, her gaze slipping past her to where her Jeep sat in the drive in the gathering darkness. She half expected to see Gable come rushing up any moment. "I take it Gable told you he paid me a visit this afternoon. Does he know you're here?"

"No," she sniffed, and flopped down onto the old-fashioned, chintz-covered couch that gave the room such a homey feeling. "I told him I was going to a friend's to study."

For the flash of a second, Josey almost cheered. *That* would show Gable Rawlings what he could do with his orders! The man was high-handed and rude and overbearing, and she was still fuming over the way he had talked to her. He might be a dictator on the Rawlings's spread, but nobody came on her property and told her what she could and couldn't do! If he thought he had problems now, he'd better not push her. Just a few well chosen words dropped in Kat's ear—

But she couldn't use her friend to strike back at Gable, she realized, regardless of how much she disliked the man. That would be placing Kat in the middle, and she would be the one who would suffer. Sinking down into her grandfather's easy chair, Josey frowned in concern. "Honey, are you sure you want to do this? He's going to be furious if he finds out you disobeyed him."

"I don't care," she cried. "He won't be any madder than I am right now." Unable to sit still, she jumped up to restlessly prowl the length of the room's braided rug. "The three of them are ruining my life," she fumed. "They treat me like a six-year-old, tell me where I can and can't go, who I can be friends with—and that doesn't include you," she added, shooting Josey an indignant look. "I can cook and clean and wash for them while they do what they want to do, but I can't go to the spring dance because nobody's asked me. And why haven't I been asked? Because any boy who would even think about looking twice at me is scared to death of my brothers. And God forbid I should do the asking!

"'A woman doesn't ask a man out'!" Mimicking Gable, she snorted in contempt. "What a bunch of garbage. They're living in the dark ages, and I'm the one paying the price for it. At this rate, I probably won't be able to date until I'm forty. I'll be the oldest living virgin in America!"

Josey bit back a grin. Seventeen-year-olds could be *so* dramatic! "I take it you told them you were going to ask Matt to the dance."

At the mention of the boy she'd had a crush on for six long weeks, Kat nodded, the anger that had supported her until now giving way to distress. "They all three had a fit. You'd have thought I had just told them I was going to ask Matt to take me to a hotel. Oh, Josey, what am I going to do? I'll be the laughingstock of the school if I'm the only girl who doesn't get to go to that dance!"

If Gable Rawlings had been there at that moment, Josey would have taken great delight in giving him a piece of her mind. The man obviously didn't have an ounce of sensitivity or he would see how his overprotectiveness was hurting his sister. Did he have to be hit over the head before he realized that the tight rein he was keeping on Kat was only going to push her into doing something crazy?

"You're not going to be a laughingstock," she said quietly. "If your brothers haven't realized your worth through the strikes, then maybe it's time to try something different."

"Like what?" she asked sullenly.

Josey grinned. "Haven't you heard that the way to a man's heart is through his stomach? Since Gable is the one you answer to, he's the one you've got to work on. Sweeten him up with his favorite dessert, then when he's feeling mellow, ask for permission to go to the dance. Only a rat would turn you down after you've gone to so much trouble for him."

"I don't know if he's a rat or not," Kat grumbled, her dimples flashing for the first time since she'd arrived, "but sometimes he can be a real jackass. All right, I'll try it. But it better work. The dance is three weeks away and I'm running out of time."

Giving Josey a big hug, she hurried out to the Jeep, promising to keep her updated on her progress. From the deep shadows of the porch, Josey watched her leave, her eyes following the red taillights as Kat headed toward home a mile away. Josey didn't have to see the house to picture Gable there, the lord of the manor. Kat hadn't followed his orders and neither had she, but she didn't think he would have any more complaints about her friendship with Kat. Starting tomorrow, he would be eating like a king, and he'd never have to know that she and Kat were still friends.

Chapter 2

Flynn stormed into the ranch office at midmorning the next day, fury etching his usually boyish face in hard lines. "Sonofabitch!" he growled. "Miller, Thompson and Guerro just quit!"

Gable, on the phone long distance with a rancher in Montana that he was interested in buying some purebred breeding stock from, swore under his breath and motioned Flynn to silence. "I won't be ready to buy until next month, Bill, but if you could send me a tape showing me what you've got, I'd really appreciate it. I've heard your Brangus are second to none, and that's just what I'm looking for. Thanks."

With the breeder's promise to get a VCR tape of his best stock out to him in the morning mail, Gable hung up and glanced up at his brother. Usually the easygoing, slow-to-anger one, Flynn prowled back and forth in front of Gable's desk like a fighter struggling with the need to hit something. Gable's dark brows snapped together in a single line over the bridge of his nose. "What do you mean, they quit? The roundup's just started and they're three of the best wranglers we've got."

"You'd better make that three of the best wranglers we *had,*" Flynn tossed back in disgust, "and you'll be closer to the mark."

"You mean, they've already left?"

At his brother's incredulous look, Flynn nodded grimly. "That's right. They're gone, vamoosed, out of here...just like that!" He snapped his fingers with a sharp jerk of his hand. "No warning, no notice, no nothing."

"Dammit, that doesn't make sense!" Gable swore. "Miller's been working for us going on five years, and Guerro and Thompson have bummed around enough to know they've never had it so good. We pay better wages than any outfit in the state, and a cowboy doesn't walk away from that without a damn good reason. Surely one of them said something."

Flynn only shook his head. "Nope. Nothing. They just turned in their mounts, got their stuff together out of the bunkhouse and left without looking back."

Leaving them shorthanded when they had a hell of a lot of work to do, and at a time when every rancher in the state was signing on every good cowboy he could get his hands on. He spat out a curse. How were they supposed to finish the roundup and make the loan payment when they didn't have enough decent, dependable men to work the cattle?

His jaw as rigid as the rocky ridges that formed the ranch's western boundary, Gable grabbed a VCR tape he'd promised to return to a rancher in Texas and tossed it to his brother as he rose to his feet. "Mail this while you're in town—"

"Town? But—"

"With three less men, we're going to need a hell of a lot of luck to make that loan payment. We've got to find someone to replace them."

Flynn didn't voice another protest, but Gable could see the doubts clouding his eyes. They both knew that any hand worth his salt looking for seasonal work had already been snatched up. By now only the dregs were left, the barflies and troublemakers who created more problems than they were worth, and their kind had never been welcome on the Double R. But what other choice did they have?

The weight of responsibility heavy on his shoulders, he sighed wearily. "See what you can find, and get the best of the lot. At this point, beggars can't be choosers. While you're doing that, I'll ride over to the north range. Cooper and the others will need an extra pair of hands."

"Okay," Flynn said with a shrug. "You're the boss. I'll be back as soon as I can."

Grabbing his black hat, Gable headed for the barn to saddle Zeus, the midnight black cutting horse that was the envy of every cowboy within seven counties and his pride and joy. He was still trying to get a halter on the spirited beauty when he heard a vehicle drive up in the yard and recognized it as Cooper's from the screech of the brakes. Frowning, he moved into the open barn doorway, not having to ask if something was wrong as his brother's long, thin body unfolded from the truck. Even when they weren't shorthanded, there was so much work during roundup that no one came back to the house before sunset unless it was an emergency.

"What's wrong now?" he asked sharply.

Cooper didn't waste any words. "The fence between us and Carl Hamilton's place is down. His herd is crazy for fresh water and streaming through the break like it's a personal invitation to drink at our springs. I've already pulled everybody off the roundup to fix the mess, but it's not enough. We're going to need Zeus.''

Gable swore a blue streak. The springs gave the Double R the best water in southwestern New Mexico, but his neighbors weren't as lucky. The drought had been hell on Hamilton's tanks, and they'd been dry for a week. Gable had tried to help by trucking in water to him, just as he had to other ranches in trouble, but evidently the shortened rations hadn't been enough for Hamilton's cattle. If they got back in the rocky canyons that the springs wound through, it would take days to cull them out of the canyon's thick cottonwood trees, cedar and undergrowth. They didn't have any time to waste.

''Hitch up the horse trailer,'' he threw over his shoulder as he quickly turned back into the shadowy interior of the barn. ''It won't take me a minute to saddle him.''

It took a heck of a lot longer, however, to straighten out the mess caused by the downed fence. The Hamilton cattle didn't take kindly to attempts to force them away from the sweet, fresh water they craved, and they fought and bawled and charged anyone stupid enough to get in their way on a slow horse. But they were no match for Zeus. With Gable comfortably settled in the saddle and giving him his head, the horse dodged and feinted and cut off every wily cow that made a break for the springs.

But it was still almost sunset by the time Hamilton's cattle were back on his side of the boundary and the fence was repaired. Nothing short of a Sherman tank would come through it any time soon. Bone-weary and too tired to talk, Gable and Cooper headed back to the house on one of the hundreds of pitted gravel roads that crisscrossed the ranch, linking pastures and range for as far as the eye could see.

Gable knew he should have been satisfied with the day's work. And relieved. They'd only lost one day and tomorrow the roundup would pick up again without further interruption. But he couldn't stop thinking about how he'd checked the fence bordering the Hamilton place just last week and he hadn't noticed a single weak spot. How could he have missed a sagging fence post?

Beside him, Cooper stirred, his eyes on the small rise in the distance where the house sat like a king upon his throne in the gathering twilight. "Uh-oh, looks like Kat is up to her tricks again."

Lost in his thoughts, it was a moment before Gable could figure out what he was talking about. Then it dawned on him that the house was dark. Usually by this time of day, Kat was busy cooking supper in the kitchen, the warm glow of lights that spilled from the windows guiding them home through the thickening dusk. The minute they hit the yard, the scent of cooking meat would tantalize their senses, sending them rushing into the house like a bunch of starving buffalo. But tonight there wasn't a single light on in the entire house, and he didn't have to be within smelling distance of the stove to know that there would be no enticing aromas to greet them when they rode up.

A muscle ticked along his jaw. Obviously his little talk with her the previous evening had gone in one ear and out the other. "I thought she was smart enough to know when she was pushing her luck," he muttered. "Looks like I was wrong."

Vowing to lay down the law once and for all, he stormed into the house shouting for Kat at the top of his lungs while Cooper took Zeus to the barn. But the place was as silent as a tomb. Flynn hadn't returned from town, and a quick search revealed that Kat was nowhere to be found. The books and homework that she usually dumped haphazardly on the table in the entrance hall weren't there, so she obviously hadn't come home after school. Normally, Gable would have been worried about her, but remembering the mutinous set of her jaw when he'd ordered her to end her friendship with Josey O'Brian, it didn't take a genius to figure out where she was. Swearing, he pivoted on his heel and headed for the back door.

Cooper was just coming up the steps of the back porch as the screen door slammed behind him. Cooper stopped in surprise, looking past him through the screen door to the empty kitchen. "Did you straighten her out already? What's for supper?"

"Nothing. She's not here." Stepping past him, he started down the porch steps without checking his pace.

"Hey, where are you going?"

"To find her. She's probably with the O'Brian woman right now laughing over the thought of us having to cook our own supper." He could just see the good doctor smugly chuckling, thinking she had outmaneuvered him. "Let 'em laugh. We'll see if they're still chuckling when I get through with them."

Alarm shot through Cooper at the steely look in his brother's eyes, and with a muttered curse, he hurried after him down the porch steps. "Now don't go off half-cocked," he said hurriedly. "Kat can be a spoiled brat sometimes, but she doesn't mean any harm. She's just a kid, and sometimes kids make stupid mistakes."

"Especially when they've got someone they respect encouraging them into open rebellion," he retorted, wrenching open the door to his truck. "It's high time both ladies learned that rebelliousness has a price."

"Dammit, Gable, will you stop and think a minute? The O'Brian woman isn't going to take kindly to you charging over to her place in the mood you're in. What if she calls the law? It would be just like her—"

"Let her call 'em," he retorted as the motor roared to life and he threw the truck into gear. "I'd like nothing better than to turn her in for contributing to the delinquency of a minor."

Cooper wanted to shake him. "Will you at least take a second to think this through?"

But Gable was in no mood for cool rationale. He didn't want to think, to hesitate for even a second. This time Josey O'Brian had gone too far. He'd warned her to quit interfering in his family life; now she had to pay the consequences. His jaw rigid, he let out the clutch and sent the truck surging forward.

The O'Brian homestead, when it came into sight a few minutes later, looked much as his home should have looked . . . ablaze with light, warm, welcoming. Irritation flared, churning in his gut. Kat's Jeep was nowhere in sight, but he wasn't surprised. She'd probably hidden it in the garage in the hope that he would assume she wasn't there. She should have known him better than that.

Striding up the steps, he crossed the porch in three long strides and jammed a finger against the doorbell, holding it down until it sounded like the angry buzz of a bee. The sound of it matched his mood exactly.

Without warning, the door was wrenched open to reveal an exasperated Josey O'Brian. "What the—" At the sight of his scowling face, she groaned. "Oh, God, it's you! What do you want now?"

"My sister," he growled. Without waiting for an invitation, Gable jerked open the screen door and stepped inside. "Where is she?"

"How would I know? I haven't seen...wait!" He moved past her before she realized his intentions, forcing her to step back in surprise. By then he was halfway down the hall. Outraged, she started after him, hurrying to catch up with his long strides. "Stop! What are you doing? Get out of there!"

Paying her no more attention than a charging bull would a gnat, Gable jerked open the door to the laundry room and surveyed the freshly washed, delicate lingerie she had spread out over a drying rack. Lace, satin, the finest of cotton batiste. At the sight of the soft clouds of underwear that were no more substantial than a whisper in the dark, he was hit with the sudden image of those same bits of fluff gracing the tempting curves of the lady indignantly huffing at his side. His gut clenched, the unexpected heat in his blood stunning him, irritating the hell out of him. But the look he cast Josey O'Brian fairly dripped mockery. "I've seen women's underwear before, Doc. This ain't nothin' new."

Cursing the heat climbing in her cheeks, she gritted her teeth and told herself not to let the man rattle her. Just because he was obviously looking for a fight didn't mean she had to accommodate him. All she had to do was remain calm.

But much to her dismay, hanging on to her cool with Gable Rawlings seemed to take all her self-control. For reasons she couldn't begin to explain, the man had a talent for pushing her buttons, and there didn't seemed to be anything she could do about it. Like it or not, he made her edgy, and for the life of her, she hadn't been able to figure out why. It wasn't as if he was the first chauvinist she'd had the misfortune to run into. The medical field was full of them...arrogant men who delighted in dropping sexist remarks that were neither wanted nor invited. She'd

learned to handle them with cool, unshakable profession-
alism. So what was it about Gable that was different? She
had only to be in the same room with him to feel her nerve
endings clamor a warning.

Reaching past him, she firmly closed the door to the
laundry room and glared at him. "I don't care if you've
made a study of every pair of bra and panties worn from
here to El Paso, you can't come barging in here like you
own the place. I've already told you, Kat's not here. Please
leave."

"Not on your life, lady." Stepping around her, he
quickly moved through the rest of the downstairs, only to
find all the rooms unoccupied. "Yesterday you agreed to
quit interfering in my life, but it was just lip service, wasn't
it? You never had any intention of minding your own
business."

"I did, too! I have—"

He stopped abruptly at the foot of the stairs and whirled
to face her, his nose only inches from hers as he demanded, "Then where is Kat? Why didn't she come home
from school? Why didn't she cook supper like she usually
does?"

Startled, caught in the trap of his piercing blue eyes,
Josey stiffened, the thunder of her heart in her breast
deafening in her ears. Every instinct she possessed
screamed at her to back up, to put some space between
Gable and herself while she still could. But he was so close
she could feel the warm moistness of his breath against her
lips, so close the scent of him—all rugged man and Old
Spice—wrapped around her, teasing her, taunting her, in-
vading her senses, clouding her mind until she found it
nearly impossible to put two thoughts together. What was
the man doing to her?

Alarm bells screeching in her head, she swallowed thickly. "I don't know. Maybe she had to stay late... at school."

The curl of his lip told her what he thought of that feeble excuse. "Look outside. It's dark already. Even on days when she stays for club meetings, she's always home by now. Admit it," he ordered softly, dangerously. "You told her to keep up with the strikes, didn't you? Get 'em right in the gut—quit cooking. That's what you told her, isn't it?"

"No!"

"And now that she's done it, she's leery of coming home and facing the music," he continued as if she hadn't spoken. "And it's all your fault."

The way to a man's heart is through his stomach.

The memory taunted her, the words of advice she'd given Kat just last night still hanging in the air as clearly as if she'd spoken them aloud. She paled. She'd suggested Kat cook her brothers' favorite desserts, not go on a cooking strike. She couldn't have possibly misunderstood, or, worse yet, assumed from her words that a negative action based on that old premise was more effective than a positive one. Could she? She'd been upset, angry, looking for a way to strike out at her brothers...

And she'd obviously found one. Guilt-stricken, Josey admitted reluctantly, "She could have twisted something I said, but I never intended her to do anything like this. I was trying to help."

Her eyes were big and green and so full of contrition a saint would have had a hard time not being moved by her. And God knew, he was no saint. But he was also a man who had learned a long time ago not to trust the wiles of a woman... any woman. Especially one as dangerous as Josey O'Brian, who could switch from an outraged

woman defending her home to a vulnerable, seemingly
wronged innocent in the blink of an eye. But the defini-
tive word here, Gable reminded himself, was "seemingly." A woman who had caused as much trouble as she
had in the short time she had been in New Mexico couldn't
possibly be as innocent as she appeared.

Hardening himself against her, he looked down at her
with dislike. "Save the act for someone who appreciates it.
Where is she?"

"I don't know. I haven't seen her. I haven't!" she cried
when he started up the stairs, but she might as well have
saved her breath. Following at his heels, she watched him
check the three upstairs bedrooms and bath, the temper
coloring her cheeks deepening with every step he took.
She'd never met such an infuriating man in her life! He'd
all but called her a liar in her own home!

"I told you she wasn't here," she said tartly when he
came out of the last bedroom without finding a thing.
"She probably stopped off at a friend's house on the way
home and lost track of time, but hey, don't take my word
for it. Search the attic. And the garage. And don't forget
all the closets. She might be hiding behind the sheets in the
linen closet."

Gable's eyes turned icy at her sarcasm. "If I were you,
lady," he said silkily, "I'd watch my mouth. You're the
one who started all this."

"Me? All I tried to do was be a friend to your sister, who
in case you hadn't noticed, doesn't have a single woman to
turn to for advice."

"She has a family to come to if she needs to talk. She
doesn't need anyone else."

"Oh, really? And when was the last time you or your
brothers actually listened to her? Actually took her seri-

ously when she voiced an opinion? She might as well be the maid for all the attention you pay her feelings.''

Her words struck a nerve like a needle hitting bone. Good God, was that what they'd been doing? Shrugging off her complaints because they all still considered her just a kid? She should have said something—

But she had, his conscience reminded him. And he hadn't listened. So she'd gone to a stranger instead.

''She shouldn't have taken family problems to an outsider,'' he said stiffly, ''and *you* shouldn't have interfered. You encouraged her rebelliousness—''

''I encouraged her to do whatever it took to get you to finally listen to her,'' she cut in heatedly. ''It's not my fault you're so hardheaded!''

''Hardheaded?'' he choked incredulously. ''Lady, I've got nothing on you.'' Suddenly making a snap decision, his hand whipped out to grab her, his fingers wrapping around her wrist like a shackle. ''Come on.''

The heat of his touch shimmered up her arm like a ripple of summer lightning. Startled, Josey felt the echoing warmth of it streak through her and was hit with the overwhelming need to run. But before she could so much as move, his steely fingers tightened around her wrist and he tugged her after him toward the front door.

Alarmed, she tried to plant her feet and jerk free, but she was no match for his strength. He pulled her after him as easily as if she were a helpless rag doll, which only served to infuriate her. ''Wait! What are you doing? Dammit, *let go of me!*''

''Not on your life,'' he ground out grimly, hitting the screen door with the flat of his free hand and sending it reeling back on its hinges. ''You stuck your little nose into something that didn't concern you one too many times, so now you have to pay the price. While me and my brothers are tracking down Kat, you can cook our supper. After all the problems you've caused us, it's the least you can do."

He was crazy, Josey thought, stumbling after him. "You can't be serious!"

Towing her after him to the driver's side of his truck, he jerked open the door and pulled her into the vee made by the door and the cab of the pickup. His eyes, when they met hers, were as cold as Arctic ice. "Do I look like I'm kidding?"

Josey wanted to tell him she didn't care if he was kidding or not, she wasn't going anywhere with him. Only he stood between her and escape and all she had to do was duck under his arm before he realized her intentions. But one glance at the rigid, granitelike lines of his rugged face, and any thought of making a break for it died a swift death. She knew the frustrated, furious look of a man who had been pushed too far once too often when she saw it. And Gable Rawlings was rapidly reaching that point. She wasn't afraid of him, but only a fool would keep pushing his buttons when he was obviously in no mood for logic, rationalization or reason. Without a word, she got into the truck.

But inside, she was seething. Just as soon as he cooled off, she was going to give him a piece of her mind!

Ablaze with lights and dominating the desert landscape for miles in every direction, the headquarters of the Double R was everything that Josey had heard it was. Victorian in design, complete with gingerbread trim, long windows and wide verandas both upstairs and down, it had as many bedrooms as a small hotel yet still managed to possess the coziness of a well-loved home. Any other time, she would have loved to explore every nook and cranny of it, but she was in no mood for a tour. Refusing to break the silence that had thickened the air like a fog from the moment she'd climbed into Gable's truck, she stiffly followed him into the huge, old-fashioned kitchen at the back of the house.

The fierceness of his expression relaxing some now that he had her where he wanted her and there was little she could do about the situation except walk the mile back to her house in the dark if she wanted to rebel, he pointed out where the pantry was, as well as the pots and pans and any utensils she might need. "Cook anything you want," he said imperiously. "Just make sure there's plenty of it. Cooper and I will be back as soon as we track down Kat, and Flynn should be straggling in any minute. He probably ate in town, but that won't stop him from choking down another meal before he goes to bed."

He turned to leave, insolently assuming that she was only waiting until he left before she jumped to do his bidding. Her dark green eyes snapping fire, all sixty-four inches of Josey stiffened in outrage. "You may be lord and master of all you survey on your own land, Mr. Rawlings, but nobody died and left you in charge of me. In other words, I don't take orders from you or anyone else. If you're expecting to eat tonight, you better get busy cooking."

Her words, as sharp as the finely honed edge of a knife, caught him right between the shoulder blades before he'd taken more than three steps. She saw him freeze and forced herself to stand her ground as he slowly turned to face her. "You either cook or it's a long walk home in the dark."

It was the wrong thing to say. Josey considered herself mild-mannered and easygoing most of the time, but she didn't handle ultimatums well. She had too many memories of her mother taking them from a man, weakly bending to a stronger will rather than risk the displeasure of the current male in her life. And from the day Josey's father had died when she was five, until her mother's death two years ago, there had been a lot of men. Not once had her mother stood up to any of them.

Just the thought of any man ordering her around as though she were an empty-headed bimbo grated on her nerves like sandpaper on an open wound. Throwing up her chin, she started past him. "Fine. It's a nice night for a walk."

She was going to do it, Gable thought incredulously. She'd rather face a long, dangerous trek in the dark than lift a finger to cook for him and his brothers. Muttering a curse, he stepped in front of her, cutting off her escape. "Dammit, woman, you can't—"

"I can do anything I damn well please, Mr. Rawlings—"

"Stop calling me Mr. Rawlings!"

His shout of exasperation caught him off guard as much as it did Josey. They both froze. A single foot of floor space separated them. His eyes searching hers, his throat suddenly as dry as dust, Gable stared at her in irritation, not liking the way his body was responding to the lady. He hadn't touched her, but he felt as though she'd punched him in the gut and stolen all the air from his lungs. Dammit, what was going on here?

"Hey, what's all the shouting about? I guess you found Kat...oops."

Cooper, halfway into the kitchen, stopped in midstride, the surprise that rippled across his angular face almost comical as his gaze bounced from Josey to Gable and back again. Even a complete fool could have felt the tension crackling like static electricity on the air, and he'd never considered himself a fool, especially when it came to women.

Shooting Josey a smile full of mischief, he said, "Don't mind me. If you want to shout at Gable, go ahead and let him have it. It isn't often that I get to see a woman give him hell. I'm Cooper. Have we met?"

Wishing his brother to perdition, Gable didn't give Josey a chance to answer. "No, you haven't," he said shortly. "This is Josephine O'Brian. I brought her home to cook supper for us since she's the one responsible for Kat's stupid little strikes."

His brother's tone warned Cooper that something wasn't quite right. His brown eyes swung back to Josey in surprise. "You encouraged Kat to strike, then volunteered to cook for us?"

"Not exactly," she retorted. "I haven't volunteered for anything...except to walk home. Your brother kidnapped me."

Cooper almost laughed. Who was she trying to kid? Gable, kidnap a woman? Why in the world would he stoop to that when he only had to crook his little finger to get just about any lady he wanted?

Grinning, he began, "You losing your touch, big brother?" only to stop as he got a good look at his older brother's face. Good God, was he actually blushing? He frowned. "Would someone like to tell me what the hell's going on here?"

Gable scowled, shooting Josey a hostile glare. "Nothing," he said flatly. "Dr. O'Brian is exaggerating—"

Josey opened her mouth to snap back that she was doing nothing of the kind, but she never had the chance. Outside, the harsh, staccato blare of a horn ripped through the quiet of the evening as a pickup raced up the drive, its headlights cutting a path through the darkness as it braked to a sudden halt right next to Gable's truck.

"What the—?"

"That's Flynn. Something's wrong!"

Josey forgotten, both brothers hit the front door at almost the same time, hurrying outside just as Flynn yelled, "Come and give me some help. I've got Kat with me. She's sick!"

The animosity between her and Gable forgotten, Josey hurried to hold the front door open as Gable and Flynn helped a lily-white Kat inside.

"I found her pulled over on the side of the road in her Jeep," Flynn explained. "She got sick on the way home from school and could hardly move without throwing up. She'd been sitting there for hours, too weak to drive home, waiting for someone to come by and help her, when I came across her on the way back from town."

"Oh, no!" Stricken by the images Flynn's words stirred, Josey took charge of the situation as naturally as if she'd never taken a break from medicine. Quickly finding Kat's room, she turned back the spread on the old-fashioned pineapple bed. "Easy," she directed as they laid her down. Moving to the girl's feet, she slipped off her shoes, then glanced up to find Cooper hovering in the doorway, his lean face, like his brothers', etched with deep lines of concern. "I'll need my medical bag," she told him. "It's in the coat closet in the entrance hall at my house. Can you get it for me?"

He nodded, heading for the door before the words were hardly out of her mouth. "I'll be right back."

Taking up a position on the opposite side of the bed from her, Gable asked quietly, "You need anything else?"

"Her nightgown," she replied promptly. "I'll help her change and then we'll see about getting some liquids down her. After the afternoon she's had, she's probably dehydrated."

Flynn quickly volunteered to check out the fridge and see what kind of juice they had, while Gable retrieved a Mickey Mouse nightshirt from the oak chest in the corner. Crossing back to the bed, he silently handed it to Josey. He didn't have to ask if she was a good doctor, he could see it in the caring of her hands. With a gentleness he wouldn't have expected from Josey after his run-ins with her, she tenderly brushed Kat's short brown curls back from her forehead and used her palm to test her temperature. Before she lifted her eyes to his, he knew the message he would read there. Kat was burning up. He'd felt the heat emanating from her like an electric blanket as he'd helped her upstairs, and it scared the hell out of him. Kat was never sick.

"Is she going to be okay?"

His voice was gruff, his light blue eyes clouded with worry and a guilt that mirrored Josey's. Just the thought of Kat all alone on the side of the road, sick as a dog, tugged at her heart. While she and Gable had been arguing, Kat had been in dire need of their help and they hadn't even known it. If Flynn hadn't come across her when he had stopped to investigate, there was no telling how long she would have lain there before they'd found her.

"Right now, I'm sure she feels like she's dying," she said, the smallest trace of a smile twitching at her lips, "but I don't think there's anything seriously wrong. She's probably just picked up a virus. If we're lucky, it should knock itself out within twenty-four hours."

Relief coursed through Gable, along with a gratitude that rocked him to his core. Less than an hour ago, he'd been so furious with this woman that his only thought had been to make her pay for all the trouble she'd caused him.

Given the least encouragement now, however, he'd have swept her into his arms and hugged her. He had to be out of his mind!

Abruptly moving to the door, he said stiffly, "I'll see what's holding Flynn up with that juice." He added huskily, "Holler if you need anything."

He was gone before she could so much as blink, the tense silence he left behind warning Josey that she had missed something. But she had no time to dwell on the matter. Kat stirred, shifting restlessly against the sheets. Leaning down, she touched her gently on the shoulder. "Can you sit up, honey, so I can help you get your gown on? It won't make your stomach feel any better, but at least you'll be more comfortable."

Kat groaned and struggled to comply, but by the time the two of them got her out of her jeans and T-shirt and into her nightshirt, her face was white as parchment. "Oh, God—"

Throwing back the covers, she made a dash for the bathroom that connected her room with the guest room next door. "Easy, honey," Josey soothed, holding her head until the moment passed. "It'll be better in a minute."

"No it won't," the younger girl finally choked, spent. "I feel *awful!* I don't think I'll ever eat again."

Helping her back to bed, Josey bit back a smile and gently wiped her face with a damp cloth. "I'll remind you of that in a couple of days when you're dying for a Big Mac and fries."

Perched on the side of the bed, Josey watched her close her eyes, and started to get up, but she'd hardly moved when Kat grabbed her arm. "Where're you going? You're not leaving, are you?"

Even in the poor light, Josey could see the panic in her eyes, feel it in the quick, biting grip of her fingers. The guilt that had pulled at Josey when she'd first learned Kat had spent hours on the side of the road, alone and sick in the middle of nowhere, tugged harder. She was just a kid, with no mother to baby her or care for her, only rough brothers who looked totally out of place in a sickroom. How could she leave her?

"Don't worry, I'm not going anywhere," she said soothingly, patting her hand. "Just downstairs. I'll be back in a little while with some juice and aspirin. Try to get some rest."

Chapter 3

It wasn't until nearly thirty minutes later, after Cooper had returned with her medical bag and she'd been able to get some juice down Kat, that Josey sought out Gable to tell him of her decision to stay the night. Considering his disapproval of her friendship with Kat, it wasn't something she expected him to be thrilled about, but that was just tough cookies for him. Kat had looked so miserable, she just couldn't leave her with only her brothers to care for her.

She found the three Rawlings men in the kitchen arguing over which of them was the best cook. It was a title no one apparently wanted to claim. Standing unobserved in the open doorway, Josey couldn't help but grin.

"What do you mean, *I* can cook?" Indignant, Flynn glared at Gable as if he'd lost his mind. "Did you work in the sun without your hat again or what? You know I can't boil water without burning up the pan. Let Cooper take over Kat's duties until she's back on her feet. At least he knows how to crack an egg without getting the shell in it."

"Oh, yeah," Cooper drawled. "Big deal. Any first-grader can crack an egg. Try eating it after I cook it, though. You ever tasted rubber? Believe me, a dog wouldn't eat it."

"I've eaten your eggs before," Gable put in. "They're not *that* bad."

"Neither are your hamburgers," Cooper tossed right back at him. "Even if they are burnt on the outside and nearly raw in the middle. Why don't *you* cook?"

"Because we've already got one sick person in the house. Don't you think that's enough?"

Amusement glinted in his blue eyes, giving a devilish cast to the bantering smile that curled one corner of his mouth. Stunned, Josey stared at him, unable to believe that this was the same man who chewed her up one side and down the other every time their paths crossed. He was smiling, actually smiling! And this wasn't just a perfunctory curl of the lips, but a full-blown roguish grin of amusement. It wasn't even directed at her, yet Josey could feel the heat of it wash over her like a warm wave. The strength of it almost sent her running hard in the opposite direction.

Gable Rawlings was a problem she didn't need. Not now, not ever. He was too arrogant, too domineering, and much too attractive for her peace of mind. Years ago, she'd made a conscious decision to focus all her energy on her career, knowing that the price she would pay would be loneliness and the loss of dreams that most women grow up with...a husband, children. Loneliness she could handle. Following in her mother's footsteps, letting love make her dependent and weak, was something she couldn't. She wouldn't, couldn't play the helpless female just to stroke a man's ego...even if that man was the best-looking devil she'd ever seen in jeans.

Her throat as dry as the desert floor, every instinct she possessed told her to get out of there as fast as she could, to cut and run and spend the rest of her time in New Mexico avoiding Gable Rawlings. But Kat was upstairs, expecting her to check on her a little later, expecting her to stay the night in case she needed her. How could she walk out on her when she was feeling so miserable?

A mistake, she thought, guilt jerking at her heartstrings. She wasn't ready to get back into medicine, even if the stethoscope had felt good in her hands. She wasn't ready to stay in this house overnight and deal with Gable Rawlings and the unwanted feelings he stirred in her on his own turf. She needed to go back to her grandparents' place, where it was quiet and isolated and there was no one there to make her feel things she didn't want to feel. But she couldn't. Kat needed her.

Drawing in a bracing breath, she bluntly announced to the room at large, "Kat seems to have a case of the flu. She's resting comfortably right now, but I'd rather not leave her alone tonight. She said I could use the guest room that connects to her room."

She was spending the night.

The news shot through Gable like a hot bullet, plowing into him, stunning him. Dammit, he didn't want her here, didn't want her help. The fact that she wasn't turning out to be what he'd expected changed nothing. She might look all soft and innocent and vulnerable, but there was something about the sensual curve of her mouth and the dark emotion in her eyes that warned him she was the type of woman who could make a man burn. Let her take her fireworks somewhere else and set someone else on fire. He wasn't interested.

But before he could find a way to politely decline her offer, his brothers were falling all over themselves making her feel welcome. "Hey, Doctor, that's really nice of you," Cooper said with a slow smile. "I know Kat will feel a lot better having a woman around."

"Yeah, we're not too good when it comes to sickness," Flynn confided sheepishly. "We never had to do much of that with Alice around—she's been fussing over all of us for so long we don't know how to get along without her. You don't know how we appreciate this."

His jaw clenched on an oath, Gable almost told Flynn to speak for himself. But the manners his mother had instilled in him when he was growing up were too deeply ingrained for him to mistreat a guest in his own home. He hadn't, however, forgotten why he had brought the good doctor there in the first place. "Make yourself at home, Doctor," he said stiffly. "Since you're staying, maybe we can persuade you to cook dinner tonight. With Kat out of commission, you're bound to be better at it than the rest of us."

It was, Joscy decided, the most backhanded compliment she'd ever received. And the most chauvinistic, phrased as more than a request but not quite a demand. From the corner of her eye, she saw his brothers glance at each other in surprise, but all her attention was on the man who never seemed to miss a chance to jerk her strings. Enough was enough. She'd let Mr. High and Mighty Rawlings taunt her long enough. Through no choice of her own, circumstances had thrown them together, but she wasn't going to endure another second of it without setting him straight about a few things.

Her green eyes glittering with the light of battle, she leaned a shoulder against the doorjamb and hooked her thumbs in the back pockets of her jeans. Her grin, slow and sassy, was full of mischief. "Why, Mr. Rawlings, you surprise me! I never expected to hear you admit women were superior to men. I would have sworn you were a dyed-in-the-wool chauvinist."

She expected him to stiffen and sputter a denial, but he was too sure of himself for that. He merely arched a dark brow, like a slightly bored adult amused by a child. "Obviously your hearing isn't superior, *Ms.* O'Brian. I said you were *probably* better at cooking than the rest of us."

"Why? Because I'm a woman?" she tossed back. "What has sex got to do with anything?"

Gable could have told her *"Everything!"* but bit back the word before it could slip from his tongue. Josephine O'Brian was too sharp by half, and he had no intention of admitting to her that the only reason he was having this discussion with her at all was because of sex! If she weren't so damned attractive, he wouldn't be constantly drawing lines in the sand to challenge her.

His eyes darkened, the half smile that curled one corner of his mouth tightening ever so slightly. "I'm not touching that one, lady. Most women know how to cook. Do you?"

She hesitated, then shrugged indifferently. "It depends."

Gable felt his temper slip and wanted to shake her. The woman could push a peace-loving man into committing mayhem! "On what?"

"On whether I'm being ordered to do it or asked," she replied sweetly. "I don't take orders well."

Flynn and Cooper, watching the exchange like grandstanders at Wimbledon, choked on a laugh at the huge understatement and the smug smile that accompanied it, drawing them a dark look from their older brother that didn't intimidate them in the least. Turning back to Josey, Gable drawled dryly, "Tell me something I don't know."

"*And* on whether I'm going to get some help or not," she continued without batting an eye. "Slave labor went out with the Civil War. If you want something decent to eat some time before the turn of the century, you or your brothers will lend a helping hand. I'm a doctor, not a chef."

Flynn didn't wait to hear more. "Hey, I'm outta here," he announced with a grin. "You know what they say about too many cooks in the kitchen."

Gable scowled. "Hold it!"

But Flynn only turned toward the doorway where Josey still stood. Winking at her, he eased around her and kept on walking.

Cooper chuckled. "Flynn's right. I'm sure the two of you can handle everything fine. Just holler when it's time to eat. I'm so hungry I could eat my boots!"

"Dammit, Cooper!" Gable began, but it was too late. His middle brother strolled out, too, that damn grin of his so infuriatingly smug Gable wanted to grab him and wipe it off his mouth. But there was still the woman standing in the doorway to deal with. "You wanted help. It looks like I'm it," he said shortly. "Let's get on with it."

For the span of a heartbeat, Josey almost told him to forget it. This was not what she'd had in mind! But she'd taken a stand, and she could hardly refuse his help after she'd made such an issue of having it. Damn, how had she gotten herself into such a mess?

Squaring her shoulders, she had no choice but to abandon her position in the doorway. "Let's see what we've got to work with."

They both turned toward the refrigerator at the same time and almost ran full tilt into each other. Startled, they

stopped short, blue eyes locking with green. Seconds
passed, stretching into an eternity, while the deafening silence rang with a throbbing beat neither wanted to hear.
But it was there, nonetheless, an awareness, a keenness
that stirred the senses and refused to be ignored.

Have you lost your mind, Josey? Move. Now!

She never knew how long she stood there, dazed, before the sharp voice of caution penetrated the roar of her
heart thundering in her ears. Even then, it seemed like
forever before she could force her feet to move. Heat
scalding her cheeks, she stepped back. "You check the refrigerator," she said tightly. "I'll see what's in the pantry."

The meal they all sat down to nearly an hour later was
surprisingly good—pan-fried steak, baked potatoes and a
salad—but Gable was in no mood to appreciate it. Josey
sat at his right, in Kat's place, never once looking at him
as she innocently chatted with his brothers and ate every
bite on her plate. Gable wanted to kill her. Supper was two
hours late, he'd had a hard day with little to eat, and he
should've been starving. But he was edgy, irritated, his
appetite nonexistent. He'd never again be able to look at
a steak without thinking of Josey O'Brian.

She hadn't said two words to him since they'd found
themselves alone and suddenly within touching distance,
he thought irritably. Abandoning even an attempt at eating, he set down his knife and fork to glare at her from
beneath lowered lids. She'd shied away from him like a
skittish virgin steering clear of a lecher, making sure that
she never came too close, the few comments she did deign
to make to him strictly limited to the task at hand. Yet the
minute Cooper and Flynn joined them at the table, she
opened up like a flower in the sun, laughing and talking

with them as if she'd known them forever. Not once did the path of her gaze ever cross his.

He should have been thanking his lucky stars—he could sit there in brooding silence without lifting a finger to keep the conversational ball rolling—but he didn't like being ignored at his own table. Especially by a woman he found next to impossible to keep his eyes off. She only had to shift in her chair, lift her fork to her mouth, smile over something outrageous Flynn said, and she drew his gaze as easily as Julia Roberts attracted autograph hounds.

Furious with himself and unable to sit there a minute longer and watch his brothers make idiots of themselves over a city woman, he wadded up his napkin and moved to push back his chair. "While you three are enjoying yourselves," he bit out coolly, "I'm going to check on Kat."

"No, I'll do it." Josey rose swiftly to her feet, relieved that the meal was finally over. She liked Cooper and Flynn, but focusing on their teasing banter had been next to impossible with Gable sitting at the head of the table, his disapproval barely disguised. He didn't want her there, didn't like her, didn't want anything to do with her. But though she'd tried her best to deny it, she knew he'd felt the heat between them, the tension that was as razor sharp as a surgeon's scalpel, as surely as she had. And ignoring it wasn't going to make it go away. Dear God, why had she insisted on spending the night?

Heat rising in her cheeks, looking everywhere but directly at him, she said, "That's why I'm here, remember? So finish your dinner. I'm done, anyway, and it could be a long night. I need to turn in and get some rest while I can. Good night, guys."

She escaped before he could stop her, her parting words including them all. His jaw set, unable to stop his eyes from following her as she hurried out of the kitchen, Gable watched the innocently provocative sashay of her slim hips and knew there was going to be nothing good about the night.

Cooper, watching the direction of his gaze, leaned back and hooked an arm over the back of his chair like a man preparing to have himself a good time. "I do believe that's the most interesting meal I've had in a long time. Don't you think so, Flynn?"

"Oh, yeah," his little brother agreed, devilish laughter dancing in his sapphire eyes. "Gable was a trifle touchy, don't you think? Hardly said two words all night. That's not like him at all, especially when there's a lady around."

"Course, this lady didn't fall at his feet like most of them usually do," Cooper pointed out baldly. "She's got too much spunk for that."

Ignoring his older brother as if he wasn't there, Flynn confided, "If you want to know the truth, I think she knocked him out of his boots before he knew what hit him." He grinned broadly, clearly delighted at the prospect. "Life's just full of surprises, isn't it?"

"Ain't it the truth," Cooper chuckled. "I never would have believed it if I hadn't seen it with my own eyes. Gable, smitten by a lady doctor." He shook his head in wonder. "You think we should start planning the wedding?"

"Not if you value your life," the object of their discussion said dryly, his lips twitching in spite of the nerve they'd struck. Dammit, had his attraction to the woman been that obvious? "I'm not interested in Josey O'Brian or any other woman."

"That wasn't how it looked from where I was sitting," Flynn retorted. "You couldn't keep your eyes off the lady."

"And you were damned mad she wouldn't give you the time of day," Cooper added gleefully. "Admit it. She bowled you over."

But Gable had no intention of admitting anything. "Are you guys blind or what?" he demanded with growing impatience. "I wasn't the one hanging on her every word like a lovesick teenager with raging hormones. In case you didn't notice, we don't get along."

"Because you keep fighting the inevitable," Cooper said confidently, as if he were the older brother and Gable the younger one in need of encouragement. "Can't you see that you're just wasting energy? You've met your match. Relax and enjoy her."

It was too much. With a muttered curse, Gable rose to his feet and stalked from the room, the sound of his brothers' soft laughter ringing in his ears.

The night was moonless and dark as pitch, the whisper of the breeze a murmur that barely disturbed the post-midnight quiet that shrouded the house. Lying flat on his back in the big poster bed that had been his parents', Gable stared up at the darkened ceiling and silently cursed the sleep that wouldn't come. His body was exhausted, in desperate need of sleep, his brain strained from thoughts he'd spent hours trying to avoid. But every time he came close to easing into forgetfulness, the soft, muffled sounds of a stranger in the house jerked him back to wakefulness.

The quiet shutting of a door, the murmur of voices, the click of a light being turned on, then off...with every whisper of sound, images stirred. Without closing his eyes, he could see Josey slipping through the darkness, a silent seductress in the night, the gown she'd borrowed from Kat molding sweet, tempting curves as she boldly came into his

room to join him. Her eyes locked with his, she eased the
gown from her shoulders, letting it fall with a rush to the
floor. White silk. Her skin would feel like white silk under
his hands, his mouth, smooth and hot and oh, so soft. He
only had to touch her to have her melt against him with a
cry of need . . .

His blood pounding, need tightening his loins, he stiffened, swearing in the dark. He was fantasizing, actually
fantasizing about Josey O'Brian! Had he lost his mind?
The woman was another Karen, tantalizingly soft on the
outside, hard-boiled career woman on the inside. She
might appear to enjoy the peace and quiet of the country
right now, but she wouldn't stay any longer than his ex-
wife had. Because the success women such as her thrived
on couldn't be found anywhere else but in the city.

Muttering a string of curses, he turned over and
pounded his pillow into a more comfortable position, determined to get some sleep. Closing his eyes, he deliberately tried to dredge up the face of the last woman he'd
dated—Mary Jo Barker, a redhead who was as fiery as her
hair and one hot little number. Instead, it was Josey's cool,
confident smile that taunted him, Josey's defiant green
eyes that dared him to just try and push her from his
thoughts. Clenching his jaw on an oath, he damned himself for a fool for ever agreeing to let her stay the night.

Out in the hall, a door shut quietly. Gable tensed, listening. Bare feet padded down the darkened hall, making
only a whisper of sound, but he heard it as clearly as if a
herd of elephants were stampeding through the house. He
didn't have to look outside his bedroom door to know that
it was Josey; this was her third trip downstairs to the
kitchen for some juice for Kat, and by now he was as familiar with the sounds of her movements as if she'd lived
in the house for years instead of hours.

Annoyed, he forced himself to relax. If Cooper and Flynn could see him now, he'd never hear the end of it. Dammit, what was wrong with him? If abstinence was making him this restless, then by God, it was time he got out a little more. Maybe he'd call Mary Jo tomorrow.

But long moments later, another woman was the last thing on his mind. The house was quiet, too quiet. And Josey hadn't come back upstairs.

Frowning, he told himself not to be a jackass and go rushing down to check on her like some cockeyed knight in search of a damsel in distress. He'd never seen a woman less in distress in his life than Josey O'Brian. She could take care of herself, so there was nothing to be concerned about just because she'd decided to stay downstairs for a while.

Satisfied, he closed his eyes. But five minutes later, he was still listening for the sound of her footsteps in the hall. Nothing moved. Swearing, he reached for his jeans.

On silent feet he made his way downstairs like a ghost on the prowl, gliding through the darkness with ease until he came to the swinging door that separated the kitchen from the rest of the house. He started to push it open, only to pause when he suddenly heard the familiar whine of the teakettle singing on the stove. He swore under his breath, suddenly feeling like the world's biggest idiot. He should have known nothing was wrong with her; she was just making herself a cup of coffee.

He told himself to get the hell out of there—he had no intention of having a coffee klatch with the lady in his kitchen in the middle of the night!—but before he could stop himself, he silently pushed open the door.

Just as he'd expected, the teakettle was whistling merrily on the stove, steam spilling from its spout. But it was the woman sitting at the table who drew his gaze. Slumped forward and as still as death, she had her head down and her face buried in her folded arms.

Gable's heart jerked in his chest. In the next instant he was at her side, worry etching his brow. She still hadn't moved, hadn't even heard him enter the kitchen. Was she sick? The dark curtain of her hair concealed most of her face from him, allowing him only a glimpse of a flushed cheek. Did she have a fever? Frowning, he leaned over her and laid his palm against her forehead.

She came awake at the first touch of his hand. He should have backed off then and there, but her eyes, startled and confused with sleep, flew to his just then, and he found himself trapped in the bottomless green pools. Fascinated in spite of himself, he could only hover over her and watch her slowly become aware of her surroundings.

"Are you all right?"

The words, revealingly hoarse, came from his throat with no conscious thought and shattered the spell that held them in its grip. Josey abruptly pulled back, forgetting that she wore nothing but the Garfield nightshirt she'd borrowed from Kat until she realized Gable was in a similar state of undress. Barefoot and shirtless, he'd tugged on jeans and nothing else. With a will of their own, her eyes measured the breadth of his strong shoulders, the tanned expanse of his hard chest, the dark shadow of hair that trailed down past his navel and disappeared beneath the faded fly of his well-worn jeans. As a doctor, she'd seen her share of naked male chests and more during her years of medical school and internship, but no man had ever backed up the air in her lungs the way Gable did.

Suddenly realizing that she wasn't the only one doing her fair share of looking, heat flamed in her cheeks as his smoldering gaze dropped down the length of her. She was completely covered, she told herself. There was nothing to be embarrassed about. The nightshirt was hardly seductive and concealed every curve. Yet she could feel the touch of his gaze on her bare skin as surely as if he'd stripped her and stroked her with his hands.

Her breath tearing through her lungs, she felt as if she was suddenly standing on the edge of a cliff with no idea how she'd come to be there. What was wrong with her? It wasn't like her to go all breathless just because a man had given her a hot look. She was thirty-two years old, for God's sake! Surely she could look him in the eye and act as if it didn't bother her that he'd caught her dressed for bed. After all, what did she care what he thought of her? He meant nothing to her and their chances of running into each other after tonight were slim to none.

But when push came to shove, she didn't have the aplomb or sophistication she needed to carry off nonchalance. Feeling like the seventeen-year-old whose gown she wore, she folded her arms across her breasts and faced him defensively. "Of course. Why wouldn't I be?"

Even to her own ears, her voice sounded husky. She winced, but he didn't notice. "I heard you come downstairs," he said stiffly. "When you didn't come back up, I thought you might have caught Kat's virus."

Which would explain why she'd awakened to find him leaning over her with his hand pressed to her forehead. "I'm fine," she assured him quietly. "Just tired. Over the last few weeks, I guess I've gotten used to going to bed with the chickens. Late nights never were my cup of tea, anyway. If I don't load up on caffeine, my pilot light just seems to go out after midnight."

It was the first attempt at friendly conversation either one of them had made, and the timing couldn't have been worse. It was three in the morning, they were both half naked and she was the last woman he wanted to get friendly with in the broad light of day, let alone the middle of the night. He was too aware of her, too aware of the way the soft material of the nightshirt molded the enticing curve of her breasts. But he couldn't force himself to walk out on her.

Moving to the stove, he removed the teakettle from the burner and carried it to the table, where he poured a steaming stream of water into the mug she'd added a teaspoonful of instant coffee to earlier while she'd waited for the water to boil. "Then you'd better drink this," he said gruffly, holding it out to her. "You were dead to the world when I walked in here. How's Kat?"

Josey had no choice but to take the mug, though she had no intention of sitting down in nothing but her gown and drinking coffee with a bare-chested Gable Rawlings! "Better," she replied stiffly. "She's still nauseous at times, though her fever seems to have broken." A quick glance at the clock on the wall was the only excuse she needed to cut their little tête-à-tête short. "I hadn't realized I'd been down here so long. Looks like coffee break's over."

She started to set the still full mug down when his hands suddenly closed over hers, molding her fingers back around it. Later, she swore her heart stopped in midbeat. Eyes wide, she lifted her gaze to his only to discover that he was just as stunned as she by his action. With a muttered curse, he released her.

"Take it with you. It'll help keep you awake."

Her senses humming, Josey nearly choked on a laugh that bordered on hysteria. Dear God, did he really think she was going to have a problem staying awake after this? Her fingers were still tingling from his innocent touch, her pulse hammering. How could she even think about sleeping when she felt as if she'd just stuck her whole arm in a light socket?

"Th-thank you." She turned away, her only thought to get away. "I'll try not to wake you if I have to come downstairs again."

She should have realized he wasn't a man she could easily walk away from. He made no move to come after her, but he stopped her at the door with one last question. "Do you think Kat's kicked the worst of this?"

Her hand poised to push open the swinging door, she didn't misunderstand what he was asking...not when would Kat recover, but when would *she* be leaving. Glancing over her shoulder, her eyes met his. "Probably. She was able to keep down the last juice I gave her, which is a good sign. She won't feel like running a marathon any time soon, but by this afternoon, she should be able to eat some soft foods."

He only nodded in acknowledgment, but just for a moment, she could read his thoughts as clearly as if he had spoken aloud. With Kat on the road to recovery, Josey's presence at the ranch would soon no longer be necessary and she could go home.

The time couldn't pass quickly enough for either of them.

"Can't you stay a little longer? Plee-ase, Josey," Kat wheedled. "I'm sick. If you leave, I'll be here all alone... helpless...a shadow of my former self," she continued dramatically. "There's no telling when the guys will come in from the roundup. What if I get hungry? I'm so weak, I could fall down the stairs trying to get to the kitchen."

Josey laughed, shaking her head. For someone who was *so* sick, Kat was looking remarkably better. She was still pale, but her eyes had that old spark back in them, and it had been hours since her stomach had so much as twinged in protest. "I don't think you have to worry about going hungry," she said with a grin. "Gable said he would come back in at lunch to check on you. I'm sure he can manage to fix something for you when you're ready to eat."

She'd expected Kat to make a less than complimentary comment about her brother's abilities in the kitchen when she surprised her by turning serious. Her eyes troubled, Kat said quietly, "That's why you want to leave, isn't it? You want to be gone before he gets back."

It was on the tip of Josey's tongue to deny it, but she'd never been any good at lying to herself or anyone else. "He hasn't exactly made it a secret that he doesn't like me, honey. We managed to work out a truce last night because you were sick, but now that you're better, it's time for me to get out of here. I'm not a masochist. I don't stay where I'm not wanted."

Kat winced. "I can understand why you feel the way you do, but he hasn't always been so infuriating. When I was little, he was wonderful. Then Karen . . ."

When she hesitated, Josey lifted a brow inquiringly. "Who's Karen?"

The younger girl cast a quick look toward the open door to her room, as if she expected her brother to appear any moment. "His ex-wife," she confided grimly. At Josey's look of surprise, she explained. "He met her at a cattlemen's convention in Dallas and fell like a ton of bricks. The next thing the family knew, they were married and leaving for their honeymoon. While they were gone, my parents were killed in a car wreck."

"Oh, my God," Josey whispered.

"It was ten years ago, but I can still remember it like it happened yesterday." Her eyes dark with pain, Kat stared into the past and a hurt that hadn't eased any with the passage of time. "Our lives turned upside down overnight. My parents were gone, and everything fell on Gable's shoulders. It couldn't have been the easiest way to start a marriage. Not only did he find himself in complete charge of the ranch for the first time, but he had me and Cooper and Flynn to take care of. They were teenagers and could help him a lot, but I was just a kid.''

It must have been a nightmare, Josey thought, her heart breaking for all of them. Gable couldn't have been more than a boy himself, even though he'd been old enough to marry. In spite of that, she couldn't picture him not being able to cope. He had an air of confidence that said he could handle just about anything. So what had happened to his marriage?

She hadn't realized she'd spoken her last thought aloud until she saw anger flare in Kat's eyes. ''Karen was all wrong for him. She was a legal secretary with her eye out for number one. She thought we had a lot of money and married Gable so he could support her while she went to law school. Then Mom and Dad died and she found out we had more land than money. She wanted Gable to sell the ranch and move us all to Dallas, and when he refused, she divorced him.''

''My God!''

''She was a real witch,'' Kat said flatly. ''And Gable's never been the same since she walked out on him. He dates a lot, but he'll never trust another woman again.''

Too late, Josey wanted to cover her ears, to block out any reasons why she should cut Gable Rawlings any slack. She didn't want to admire the stance he'd taken, sacrificing his marriage for his sister's and brothers' heritage, didn't want to find any reason to like him. She just wanted to escape to her house and forget that she'd ever met him, forget how he'd touched her hand last night in his kitchen and just that easily set her heart thumping in her breast.

"That still doesn't change the fact that he doesn't want me here," she said huskily. Feeling as if she was running but unable to stop the panic coursing through her veins, Josey leaned down to the bed to give Kat a quick hug. "I've got to go. Call me if you need anything."

"But how are you going to get home? You don't have your car."

"I'll walk." The way she was feeling now, she could have run the entire mile to her grandparents' place without stopping to take a breath.

Later she told herself, if she'd have left ten minutes earlier, she would have made it. But just as she pulled open the front door, Gable drove up much as he had yesterday, gravel flying out from the wheels of his pickup as he braked to a bone-jarring stop. Her heart jerking at the sight of him, she opened her mouth to tell him she was just leaving.

"Thank God you're still here," he said before she could open her mouth. "I just brought in Cooper and Flynn. They've got Kat's virus."

Chapter 4

Seated at the kitchen table, the sound of Josey's footsteps echoing mockingly overhead as she prowled the hallway between Flynn's and Cooper's rooms, Gable stared broodingly at the cup of coffee growing cold between his hands. He could castrate a young bull, patch up a dog that had tangled with a pack of coyotes, put down a horse with a broken leg when it was the humane thing to do. But don't ask him to hold somebody's head when they are violently ill... not unless you want him sick, too. He just couldn't do it, and he made no apologies for it. So when he'd seen Josey standing there on the porch when he drove up with his two moaning brothers, he'd wimped out and asked her to stay. Hell, he thought in disgust, he'd almost begged her!

If she'd have asked him for the moon in return, he would have given it to her, but she hadn't. Instead she'd calmly directed him to help them to their rooms, then she'd taken over, just as she had with Kat.

That was more than six hours ago. He'd left Flynn and Cooper to her care and gone back to work, throwing himself into the hard, physical labor of the roundup. Flynn hadn't been able to find a soul in town yesterday to replace Miller, Thompson or Guerro, so now they were short five men. And the due date of the final loan payment was drawing closer with every passing day. He didn't want to ask what was going to go wrong next—he was afraid fate would show him.

Shouldering his brothers' load as well as his own, worry burning like an ulcer in his gut, he'd convinced himself he had too much to do to give Josey a second thought. He couldn't have been more wrong. The minute he'd stepped outside, all he'd been able to see was Josey. Josey leaning over his brothers . . . fussing over them, making them feel better . . . touching them.

Six hours, he fumed. For six long hours he'd fought a jealousy he had refused to acknowledge and just barely managed to keep in check. But now that the workday was over and he had nothing to concentrate on, it slammed into him. He swore, a short, pithy oath that threatened to turn the air blue, and shoved his chair back from the table, rage burning in his eyes. Had he lost his mind? The woman wasn't interested in Flynn or Cooper; she was a doctor, for God's sake! And even if she wasn't, he didn't give a damn who she touched.

Unbidden images came to mind . . . Josey slipping down the hall to his room, to him, her fingers cool and knowing on his hot skin as they moved over him, teasing him, haunting him, driving him over the edge—

Suddenly realizing what he was doing, Gable stiffened, but it was too late. His blood was hot, his body tight and crawling with need. He wanted to throw something, or better yet, ram his fist through a wall. Loss of control had never been a problem with him before; he knew how to put a lid on his desires and his temper. But there was something about that woman that made him as itchy as a randy teenager who suddenly had more hormones than he knew what to do with.

His jaw as rigid as granite, he stalked over to the sink and dumped out his coffee. Another twelve hours or so, he thought, grasping at the time limit as if it was the only thing that stood between him and desperation. Surely he could manage to get through the rest of the evening and night. All he had to do was avoid Josey as much as possible.

But the minute he turned from the sink, he knew that was going to be impossible. The house was big and sprawling and if they both set their minds to it, they could have stayed out of each other's way for days. But there was only one kitchen, and she stood there in the doorway.

The emotions he'd been struggling with all afternoon twisted in his gut. She had that look on her face of the tough, big-city doctor who could handle whatever crises were thrown at her, but there was something in her eyes that reminded him of a fawn who had stumbled unaware across the hunter before she'd thought to run. Didn't she know what it did to a man when she looked at him that way? he thought irritably, his hands balling into fists. He wanted to reach for her, to hold her, to protect her...

You're losing it, Rawlings, a voice drawled in his head. *The lady's about as helpless as a rattlesnake. You make the mistake of falling for those soulful eyes of hers, and you're gonna get bit.*

Not bloody well likely, he thought grimly. He'd already been bitten once by a woman and had the scars to prove it. It wasn't a mistake he intended to make again. Standing his ground, his gaze locked with hers, the width of the room as wide as a canyon between them. "How are the boys doing?"

The "boys," as he so aptly called the two grown men stuck in bed upstairs, were two of the worst patients she'd ever had. Talk about babies! From the way they'd moaned and groaned for most of the afternoon, you'd have thought they were dying. She'd lost track of the number of times she'd crossed the hall between their rooms to wipe a brow, offer comfort, assure them they would indeed live through this.

Amused by their antics, she wanted to share them with Gable, but his cold, shuttered expression didn't encourage the intimacy of shared laughter. Which was, she realized soberly, probably a good thing. The house might be crowded with his sick siblings, but they were just as alone now as they had been last night.

Awareness, like the heat that thickened the air before the breaking of a storm, seemed to spark between them, setting Josey's pulses throbbing. She was in trouble and she knew it. Right that moment, she should have been dredging up memories of her mother and all the reasons why she couldn't let down her guard with him, but all she could think about was the way he made her pulse skip without once having lifted a finger to touch her. God help her if he ever decided to kiss her.

Pushing back the breath-stealing image, she said stiffly, "They're a couple of sick puppies, but Kat, I think, had the worst of it. Though you'd never know it to hear them tell it. Flynn was all set to call the family lawyer this afternoon to make out his will."

Just for an instant, she thought Gable's lips twitched, but the smile was gone before it could catch hold. He turned abruptly toward the refrigerator and jerked opened the door to study the well-stocked shelves. "Flynn's never gotten sick yet that he didn't think he was dying. Did you come down to get them some fruit juice?''

''There isn't any.''

Bent over to retrieve an apple from the fruit tray, Gable jerked up, his gaze immediately going to the shelf where there was usually some kind of juice. The bottle of grape juice that had been half full that morning was gone. ''I'll get some from the pantry.''

He moved toward the walk-in closet where the canned goods and staples were kept. Josey could have saved him the trip. She'd checked everywhere, including the freezer, and there wasn't another drop of juice in the whole house. ''There isn't any,'' she said. ''I checked earlier. There's not any canned soup, either.''

Unperturbed, Gable dug in his pocket for his keys and tossed them to her. ''Take my truck and run down to the Quick Stop and get what you need.''

She caught the keys but didn't budge. ''Is it a standard?''

He frowned. ''What? My truck? Of course. Why?''

Josey should have known. Every vehicle on the place was standard shift! ''Because I never learned how to drive one,'' she said simply, and tossed his keys back to him.

''Then make a list, and I'll go get what you need.''

Josey would have liked nothing better. But he had to drive right by her house to get to the small drive-in grocery fifteen miles away, and she was in definite need of a change of clothes. She could have told him where to find her jeans and T-shirts, but she could just see him pawing through her drawers, his big, rough hands catching on her delicate lingerie, and the words wouldn't come.

''I'll go with you,'' she said finally, when she could trust her voice to be steady. ''I didn't exactly come for an extended stay, and I need some things from my house. We can stop on the way.''

By the time they left her house, the small canvas bag that held her clothes stashed behind the truck's bench seat, Josey knew she'd made a mistake. Sunset was still an hour away, but the sky had been overcast all day with the threat of rain, and the darkness of the night was already creeping over the barren landscape, claiming it. Heavy, damp air rushed in through the open windows as shadows gathered in the cab of the truck, pressing in on them, intensifying their isolation. Studiously clinging to her side of the bench seat, she only had to glance out the corner of her eye to see the strong planes of Gable's profile outlined by the last, lingering traces of dim light that hovered over the mountains to the west. Instead she anchored her swirling hair at her nape and stared straight ahead at the long ribbon of road that uncurled ahead of them.

Silence engulfed them, as thick as smoke, while in the distance, the lights of the Quick Stop sprang on like beacons in the night. Josey knew they'd be there in only a matter of minutes, but the silence was tingling with an awareness that grated heavily on her nerves, making her as jumpy as a scalded cat. Common sense told her to hold her tongue—the only time she and Gable weren't arguing was when they weren't talking. But she couldn't stand the quiet that seemed to echo with the drumming of her heart. Before she could stop herself, she began to chatter.

''The first time I stopped at the Quick Stop, I thought it was just like any other Circle K or 7-Eleven back home— you know, beer and sodas, candy and chips, that kind of thing. I couldn't believe it when I saw they carried everything a real grocery store does. But then, I guess they have to with Lordsburg so far away. Of course, the prices are higher, but who wants to go to town for a quart of milk when they can pay a few cents more and get it almost right around the corner? If it hadn't been for the Quick Stop, I would have had to make the trip to Lordsburg a half dozen times the first week alone.''

Gable only grunted in reply, her words flowing over him like a rush of warm water. She was nervous. He'd have given anything not to have noticed it. He could hold his own with her when she was angry, indignant, looking coolly down that pert little nose of hers as if he'd just crawled out from under a rock. But when her nerves were jumping, her voice not quite steady, her eyes avoiding his, he had this insane desire to touch her, to draw her close to see if her heart was thundering as badly as his.

His hands tight on the steering wheel, he muttered an expletive under his breath and glared at the lights in the distance, his booted foot on the accelerator pushing the speedometer well past the legal limit. How had he ever gotten himself into this mess? He knew what the lady did to him—she twisted his gut in knots just by walking into a room—yet here she was, so close he could almost feel her softness next to him. And every time he inhaled, that subtle, sexy, *maddening* scent of hers teased his senses, making a mockery of his efforts to ignore her.

A muscle jumping in his rigid jaw, he stared at the lights up ahead and tried to judge their distance. Ten more minutes, max, he told himself fiercely. It seemed like forever.

The rain that had held off all day started to fall five minutes before they reached their destination. At first it was just an occasional drizzle that the truck's intermittent wipers easily took care of, but by the time they pulled into the Quick Stop's brightly lit parking lot, the drizzle had turned into a light but steady downpour.

For a long moment after Gable cut the engine, neither of them moved. Fat raindrops danced on the cab roof and slid down their quickly rolled-up windows, glistening like liquid diamonds in the light from the store. At any other time Josey would have found peace in the soothing patter of the rain, but no woman with any blood in her veins would have been able to sit next to Gable in the thickening shadows and find peace.

Casting a quick look between the store's overhanging roof and the dark, heavily laden sky, she reached for her door handle. "This isn't going to let up anytime soon. I might as well make a run for it before it starts coming down harder."

"Wait!"

For the life of him, Gable didn't know what possessed him, but before he'd realized his intentions, he'd pushed open the driver's door and quickly come around to her side of the truck. Wrenching open her door, he took off his black cowboy hat and plopped it down on top of her head. "There," he said huskily. "That should protect you some."

Just that easily, he stopped time and blocked out the rest of the world. Other pickups pulled up at the store, doors slammed, thunder rumbled in the far-off distance, but Josey saw nothing but Gable, heard nothing but the rush of her blood through her veins. He stood within the vee made by the open door and the body of the pickup, so close she could see the raindrops misting his dark hair and eyelashes. Her heart missed a beat and stumbled into a run. Gallantry, she thought, touched in spite of herself. She'd never expected gallantry from him. He didn't even like her! Yet there he stood, his head bare and his broad shoulders shielding her from most of the rain, getting soaked while he waited to help her from the truck.

Something in her melted, something she should have been guarding with the utmost care. But it was already too late. Trapped, unable to move, to think, she ached for his touch in a way that staggered her. "Gable . . ."

His name was hardly more than a whisper on her lips, a hoarse, faint, sensuous cry that he had every intention of ignoring. All he had to do was take a step back and give his head a chance to clear. It was that simple.

No one was more surprised than he when he reached for her.

"Damn."

Before she could do anything but gasp, before he could hear the voice of reason roaring in his ears, he had her right where it seemed he'd been burning to have her ever since he'd first laid eyes on her—in his arms. With nothing more than a tug of his hand, he pulled her out of the pickup and wrapped her close, his mouth hard and hungry on hers.

He felt the stunned surprise that rippled through her as she instinctively clutched at him, her fingers curling into the wet cotton of his shirt as his hat tumbled from his head and fell unnoticed to the ground. The rain pounded down on them, someone whistled, but the thunder was in his blood now, the heat from the lightning curling into his stomach, firing his loins. *Let her go!* The need was there, stronger than the rest, urging him to release her while he still could, while he still wanted to. But no woman had ever felt so good against him.

"Oh, God!"

Shaken, her head spinning and mouth throbbing, Josey suddenly jerked back, her eyes huge in her suddenly pale face. The kiss couldn't have lasted longer than a heartbeat, maybe less...just long enough for desire to stir to life and tempt her to stay in his arms and let him teach her all

there was to know about a kind of passion she couldn't
begin to imagine.

Panic pulled at her; tears threatened, horrifying her.
Dear God, what was she doing? "I h-have to...the
juice—" Unable to manage the rest, she flushed and
pushed past him, beating a hasty retreat into the store.

His hard face wet with rain, Gable watched her flee as
if the hounds of hell were hot on her heels. It took no
bragging on his part to admit that he and his brothers were
three of the most eligible bachelors in the state, and he'd
been chased by enough women in the years since his di-
vorce to know when one wanted him. A moment ago,
Josey had wanted him. Yet he would have sworn he'd
tasted innocence on her lips, which was ridiculous. The
woman was in her early thirties, a doctor, a city woman
who was no doubt very experienced when it came to men.
So what the hell kind of game was she playing?

Through the store's wide plate-glass window, he followed her movements through the aisles until she disappeared behind a large display at the back, not liking the
suspicions that stirred in him. Tricks. He thought he'd seen
them all, from subtle come-ons to out-and-out brazen-
ness, but no one had ever tried innocence before. And for
a moment there, it had damn near worked. Her shyness,
the surprise that had shimmied through her when he'd
pulled her close, had caught him off guard, delighting him,
seducing him into forgetting where they were, who she was,
what she was—the wrong type of woman.

A plot, he decided in disgust. Had her friendship with
Kat, the trouble she'd stirred up, been nothing but a plot
all along to get his attention? Damn, what an idiot he'd
been! Cursing himself for ever reaching for her, for kissing her, for ever needing her so much he forgot common
sense, he snatched up his soaked hat from where it had

fallen into a puddle and knocked the water from it. Caught up in his anger, it wasn't until he climbed back into the truck to wait for her that he realized he was as wet as his hat. With an impatient hand, he pushed back the wet hair that kept dripping in his face, fury burning in the cold depths of his eyes as he glared through the windshield at the first lady who had ever been able to make him forget his physical comfort. And she kissed like a sixteen-year-old. Hell!

The store was busy—other shoppers had seemed to come out of the woodwork with the rain—but Josey hardly noticed. Standing in front of the shelf that held a surprisingly varied selection of canned soups, she blindly stared at the labels and tried to regain her composure, but she was still too shaken, her thoughts too scattered. She'd wanted him to kiss her, and he had. And she hadn't realized what she was inviting until it was too late.

Passion. With nothing more than the slow glide of his tongue, he'd given her a taste of passion. And suddenly she knew why her mother had lost her identity in the men she'd loved, why she'd dressed for them, worn her hair the way they liked it, why she'd cooked and cleaned and did everything to please them. Because for one fleeting, heart-stopping moment when Gable had stirred a sweet, melting need in her, Josey almost turned to putty in his hands, his for the molding.

No!

Denial echoed in her ears, unspoken. She hadn't come to New Mexico for this, didn't want it, never had. She had a career to worry about, decisions to make that had nothing to do with Gable Rawlings. And she'd made a vow, she reminded herself, that she'd never stake her happiness on a man, never take a chance and drop her guard long enough to follow in her mother's footsteps. Thanks to the career she'd chosen, keeping that vow had been easy. Medical school and her residency, then the long hours she'd put in at her clinic, hadn't left much time for romance. Not that she'd noticed. No man had ever tempted her enough to make her feel the loss of what she'd been missing.

Until now.

She was thirty-two years old and had less experience than a sixteen-year-old. God, how he'd probably laugh if he knew—if he hadn't already guessed. Put her in the middle of a medical catastrophe, even in an operating room, and she was calm and cool and in control. But this . . . this she wasn't ready for. Oh, she'd been kissed before, but the few times she hadn't been able to avoid such embraces, they'd been nothing but quicksilver, unemotional brushes of lips that were broken off immediately and forgotten just as fast. Gable had probably never kissed a woman that way in his life.

Remembering the hot, hungry pressure of his mouth on hers, heat suffused her in a slow tide that burned all the way to the tips of her toes. No, there was nothing unemotional about Gable's kiss, nothing about it that would be forgotten minutes, hours, *days* later.

And she didn't like it! She wasn't used to not being in control, to not knowing where she was headed at all times. Nothing shook her. Nothing! Yet here she was hiding behind the potato chips in a convenience store like a ninny just because Gable Rawlings had dared to shake her normally unshakable confidence with a kiss! Lord, what was she going to do?

Face him and act as though nothing out of the ordinary has happened, a voice in her head ordered sternly. It was, after all, the only choice she had.

With fingers that weren't quite steady, she dropped half a dozen cans of soup into the small basket she'd picked up at the entrance, then moved on to the juice selection. By the time she reached the checkout stand at the front of the store, she had enough food for an army of sick patients and she was once again in control of her emotions. But walking out to the truck without blushing like a schoolgirl was one of the hardest things she'd ever done.

The rain helped. It was no longer a gentle shower, but a heavy spring downpour, complete with a brisk wind and an occasional rumble of thunder from the lightning that flashed on the horizon. While she'd been inside, the temperature had dropped ten degrees and the store parking area had taken on the appearance of a small lake. Her head down and shoulders hunched against the rain, she hopscotched over the larger puddles and reached the truck just as Gable pushed open the passenger door from the inside.

"Thank you." Avoiding his gaze, she climbed in beside him and somehow managed to keep her voice as cool as the falling temperature. But it wasn't easy. Her heart was pounding out a wild rhythm in her breast and she could feel the heat of his narrowed gaze as surely as if he'd reached out and touched her. A shudder slid through her, and she instinctively wrapped her arms around herself to hide it. It was too late. He'd seen it.

"Are you all right?"

The question was low and grating in the silence, the rough timbre of his voice searing a path down her spine like a hot brand. Josey shivered again, her teeth clamping down on an oath as she wrapped her arms tighter around herself. She wouldn't let him unravel her just because he had the kind of smoky, bedroom voice that sounded as if it came right out of a woman's most erotic fantasies, she promised herself. *She* didn't have fantasies!

"I'm cold," she said stiffly, still not deigning to look at him. "And it's getting late. We should be getting back. The others are probably getting hungry by now."

For a long moment Gable didn't move, but stared at her in growing irritation instead. The lady was some piece of work. She was soaked to the skin, her hair wet and scraggly, yet she sat there issuing orders as regally as if she were a princess and he was nothing but a horseless cowboy with stinky boots. From the look of cool aloofness on her face, the kiss he'd laid on her only moments before might never have happened.

And for some reason that he refused to examine too closely, that annoyed the hell out of him.

He'd held her in his arms, felt her surprise, tasted, just for an instant, her hunger, he thought furiously. She might appear to be as cool as a cucumber on the outside, but the lady didn't fool him for an instant. She was hot, an inferno just waiting for the right spark to set her ablaze. She couldn't pretend indifference now. Not with him, dammit! She might be able to get away with that kind of crap from the pantywaists she dated in Boston, but this wasn't Boston. And he was no pantywaist.

His jaw set, he started the truck with an abrupt flick of his wrist and pulled out onto the highway. Almost immediately, they plunged into a darkness that was broken only by the glare of the headlights and an occasional angry flash of lightning. The rain was still falling in torrents, filling low water crossings and the dips in the road, making driving hazardous. Unable to take his eyes from the black asphalt that led to the cutoff for the ranch, Gable eased the pickup through a runoff stream that hadn't been there earlier, the steady, swishing beat of the windshield wipers loud in the tense silence.

"Does it always flood like this after just a little bit of rain?" Josey asked quietly.

He didn't glance at her—he couldn't—but he knew she, too, watched the road. "The ground's baked hard from the sun and can't absorb a quick downpour. The runoff will drain away fast enough as soon as it stops. Don't worry, you won't have to swim home. I'll get you there safely."

"I wasn't worried."

If any other woman had responded so confidently, Gable would have taken it as a reflection of her faith in his ability to take care of her. But Josey O'Brian had already made it clear she didn't depend on a man for anything. Irritated, he shot her a hard look. "No, a woman like you wouldn't be worried, would she? You can take care of yourself if anything happens."

His tone was sharp, surprising her. What did he mean, a woman like her? Glancing over at him, she lifted a delicately arched brow. "Do you have a problem with that?"

"Me? Hell, no! But the man you left behind in Boston might. Of course, maybe Yankee men are different," he said with an indifferent shrug. "Out here, a man likes to think his woman wants his protection."

His woman. The chauvinistic label echoed in Josey's ears and should have instantly raised her hackles. She was no man's possession and never would be. But the thought had barely registered when it was pushed aside by images of Gable protecting his woman, safeguarding her with his body, cherishing her with his love. As a lover, he would be something right out of a woman's dreams... strong and sensuous and generous... catching her up in his passions until they both hot and aching and lost to everything but each other—

Suddenly realizing where her thoughts had wandered, she blushed hotly and thanked God for the concealing darkness. Had she lost her mind? She didn't care what kind of lover he would be if he ever let go of the past, how generous he could be, how hot. His sex life was none of her business!

"I didn't leave a man behind in Boston," she said stiffly.

"Aha! So that explains it."

His tone was so smug and knowing, Josey wanted to smack him. "Explains what? I don't know what you're talking about."

"Explains your hostility toward men," he retorted mockingly, his grin flashing in the darkness. "You're frustrated."

"I'm what!"

"I suppose it's perfectly understandable," he reflected easily, continuing as if she hadn't spoken. "You're an attractive woman, successful, too smart for your own good. Some man should have snatched you up a long time ago and kissed some sense into you, but the men in Boston are blind, and you resent it. Can't say I blame you. A woman should be kissed . . . often. How else is a man supposed to keep her in line?"

How else, indeed? Gritting her teeth, Josey just barely resisted the urge to snatch a can of soup out of the bag of groceries and throw it at his grinning head. The nerve of the man! "Thank you for that analysis, Dr. Freud," she said tightly, "but don't give up your day job to go into practice. I don't resent the lack of romance in my life."

For an instant only, he took his eyes away from the road long enough to lift a skeptical brow at her. "No? That's not the way it looks from where I'm sitting."

Oh, he was insufferable! "I don't care how it looks to you," she snapped, "I'm not looking for a man. And I'm not one of those women who's worried about her biological clock, either. I'm a doctor all the way down to my bones, and I like my life just the way it is."

If he'd been wise, Gable would have dropped the subject then and there. She'd just verified that she was everything he'd thought she was—a hard-nosed, driven career woman who was more interested in her work than having a husband or family. He should have been relieved. Instead, all he wanted to do was shake her until her teeth rattled, then kiss her senseless.

His hands tightening on the steering wheel so he wouldn't be tempted, he stared straight ahead and said grimly, "I got news for you, lady. You're a hell of a lot more than a doctor beneath your lab coat and stethoscope. You just haven't met the man who can teach you how to be a woman."

And he could be that man.

Alarmed, Josey recoiled from that thought as if it were a snake poised to strike her. He wasn't just talking about being a woman; he was talking about letting her heart rule her head, and she wanted no part of it. "If you're implying that you may be that man, you can think again," she said coldly. "You won't be teaching me anything."

If the memory of his kiss hadn't still been fresh in her mind, she might have been a little more diplomatic. As it was, she couldn't have drawn the battle lines more clearly. From the corner of her eye, she saw his jaw clamp tight on an oath, but the entrance to the ranch came into sight then, and, without another word, he turned off the highway. Josey sighed in relief as the lights to the house beckoned in the distance.

"Well, there you are! I was getting worried. I thought you might have gotten stranded between here and the Quick Stop."

Her head bent against the rain, the groceries tightly clutched in her arms, Josey glanced up in surprise to find Kat holding the back door for her. "What are you doing downstairs?"

Coming up onto the back porch behind her, Gable took one look at his sister and frowned in disapproval. "You should be in bed."

"Oh, come on, guys," the younger girl groaned. "I'm sick to death of that bed. And I'm feeling a lot better. I think I could even eat something."

Josey hesitated. Kat was still pale, and she probably had no business being out of bed just yet, but Josey didn't have the heart to send her back upstairs. Especially when that meant there would only be her and Gable at the big kitchen table for supper. "All right," she said finally. "I guess it won't hurt for you to be up for a while. I'll start you some soup—"

Gable stepped around her to take the bag of groceries from her, his hands accidentally brushing hers and sending a jolt of heat up her arms. Startled, Josey's eyes flew to his and found a mocking smile curling his mouth. "I'll start it while you check on Cooper and Flynn."

He knew, she thought, mortified. He knew what he could do to her with just a touch. And from the glint in his eyes, he was going to pick up the gauntlet she'd unthinkingly thrown down during the drive back to the ranch from the store. Heat staining her cheeks, her heart pounding, she hurried upstairs. But his brothers were both asleep, and there was no reason not to return to the kitchen. Her spine ramrod straight, she started back down the stairs, determined not to let Gable fluster her. After all, he already had an ego the size of Santa Fe. She didn't intend to add to it by letting him think even for a minute that he could shake her up any time the mood struck him.

But when she walked into the kitchen, he didn't even glance her way. Instead he was glaring at Kat, who sat at the table and didn't seem the least perturbed. "We've been over this a thousand times already. You are *not* inviting a boy to the dance. Do I make myself clear?"

He had a glare that could intimidate a rattler, but from where Josey was standing, Kat didn't seem the least bit impressed. "It's too late," she retorted. "I already did, and I can't back out now. He accepted."

"Then he can un-accept. You're not going."

His jaw was set in stone, his tone one not to be argued with. Josey knew that if Kat hadn't been sick, she would have probably snapped right back at him, but she was in no shape for a full scale argument. Stepping into the kitchen, Josey deliberately drew his ire. "Why not?" she demanded. "There's nothing wrong with a woman inviting a man out. It's the 90's, Gable. Or hadn't you noticed?"

"You're damn right, I noticed," he said, frowning. "I noticed that you're real quick to give Kat advice, but I don't see *you* asking anyone out. If you're so sophisticated, why don't you follow your own advice?"

"Because I don't know anyone to ask. I've only been here six weeks."

As far as excuses went, it was a sorry one and they both knew it. Kat's presence forgotten, he said, "That's a copout. You know me."

She froze, unable to believe she'd heard correctly. Did he actually expect her to ask him out? He couldn't be serious. But from the glint in his eyes, it was obvious that not only was he serious, he fully expected her to try to squirm out of the corner she'd neatly boxed herself into. She'd be damned if she'd give him the satisfaction!

The light of battle in her eyes, she lifted her chin. "All right. I'll ask you out if you'll let Kat go to the dance. What do you think about that, Mr. High and Mighty Rawlings?"

He grinned, his eyes alight with an expression she couldn't quite fathom. "I think I'll accept. While Kat's at the dance, you can take me out."

Chapter 5

He'd set her up!

Standing on the back veranda, steam rising from her coffee mug, Josey stared unseeingly at the outbuildings of the Double R, their eaves still occasionally dripping rain from the night before. The sky, washed clean of clouds, was cerulean blue, the air fresh and cool. From the top of a light-pole, a meadowlark sang a lilting melody, but Josey found little comfort in it. She'd spent the night trying to figure out how she could have been so stupid as to ask Gable out, but now, in the clear light of day, the answer was obvious. He'd set her up.

Her first instinct was to laugh at her own foolishness. The very idea was ridiculous. Gable didn't lack for confidence where women were concerned. If he'd have wanted to go out with her, he'd have certainly asked.

And she would have said no.

He hadn't needed to hear her rejection to know she'd have turned him down flat, she thought in growing irritation. She'd made it clear during the ride home from the store that she wasn't looking for a man. So he'd set her up by goading her until she asked him out.

Behind her, the screen door squeaked as it was pushed open, and she knew without looking that Gable had followed her out onto the porch. She'd come to know the sound of his step over the past few days, but even if she hadn't, only one man had the ability to make her pulse skip from twenty feet away.

Her gaze trained on the rigid line of the mountains that marked the western boundary of the ranch, her fingers tightened around the coffee mug she held. "Cooper and Flynn are doing much better," she said quietly. "In fact, I had to threaten to tie them to the bed to get them to agree to take it easy one more day. If they need anything, I'm sure Kat will be able to get it for them since she's just about back to her old self."

"So you're ready to go home."

She nodded. "I've already got my things together. I just need a ride back to my place. If you could get one of the hands to take me—"

"I'll do it."

Her heart stumbled just at the thought of getting back into his truck with him. "That's not necessary," she said huskily. "I'm sure you have better things to do—"

"You know, if I didn't know better, I'd think you didn't want to be alone with me," he said softly. "You haven't looked me in the eye since you asked me out. What's the matter? Change your mind?"

"No!" Chin up, color flying high in her cheeks, she whirled to face him, only to find him right behind her, a satisfied grin curling his mouth. She felt her throat go dry and couldn't do a thing about it. Lord, he was a good-looking devil! "I haven't changed my mind about anything," she said tightly. "The date still stands."

She didn't sound exactly thrilled at the prospect of going out with him, but her eyes were shooting sparks at him, and it took all his strength of will to hang on to his grin when what he really wanted to do was drag her into his arms. "Fine. Now that we've got that settled, I guess there's no reason why I can't take you home, is there?"

The man, Josey decided irritably, had a knack for getting his own way. "I'll get my things," she said flatly, and stepped into the kitchen with as much dignity as she could muster.

He was right behind her when the shortwave radio in the corner crackled to life. "Red Dog to Double R One, come in, please. This is Red Dog."

Striding over to the transmitter, Gable picked up the microphone and answered the call. "This is Double R One. What's up, Red? I thought you'd be hard at work rounding up the spring pasture by now."

A mangled cuss word came over the airwaves, followed by the angry voice of one of his oldest hands. "I was just heading over there when I passed the holding pasture. I think you'd better get out here."

Something in the old man's tone warned him he wasn't going to like what was coming next. "Why? What's wrong?"

For a moment there was nothing but dead silence before Red finally said tersely, "The yearlings are gone, boss. Can't find hide nor hair of 'em."

"What do you mean, gone?" Gable demanded sharply. "You got fifty acres of mesquite brush out there. Search it."

"We already did. There ain't nothing there." He swore again, and this time the words were clear and colorful.

"Looks like rustlers, boss. The bastards must have come in during the rain last night."

Unflinching, Gable took the news like a blow to the stomach. The holding pasture had held half the yearly calf crop; the other half, he and his men were still culling from the herd. Gone, he thought in growing fury. Half the yearlings he planned to sell to pay off the loan were gone! "I'll be right there."

Swearing, he switched off the transmitter and was halfway across the kitchen to the back door when Josey stepped into the room. "Okay. I'm ready—" She stopped short at the sight of his grim face. "What's wrong?"

"Rustlers." He spat the word out as if rustlers were the lowest life form on earth. "I just got a call from one of my men. I'm on my way out there now to check it out. I'll take you home afterward."

"Of course."

The pasture the cattle had been taken from was ten miles south of the ranch headquarters. Bordered on one side by a narrow, pothole-laden, dead-end road and the jagged rocks of the mountains on another, it was relatively secluded and safe. Which was why Gable had decided not to increase security when he'd started using the pasture as a holding pen. After all, there were no other houses for miles and no one used the road but his men. Or so he'd thought.

Staring down at the tire tracks left in the mud between the edge of the road and the barbed-wire fence that marked the southern boundary of the ranch, Gable bit out a curse. Someone with a hell of a lot of guts had driven an eighteen-wheeler in there during the night, then somehow managed to back it right up to the fence despite the narrowness of the road. Deep gouges in the mud of the pasture testified to the fact that they'd dropped a loading ramp over the fence so they could herd the cattle right into the truck. They'd even brought their own horses!

"Whoever did this took a hell of chance, boss," Red said, his weathered face as grim as Gable's as he scowled down at the deep tire marks. "If they'd have gotten stuck in the mud once that truck was loaded, they'd have had a hell of a time explaining themselves when we showed up for work this morning."

But they hadn't gotten stuck and his yearlings were long gone. Swearing, Gable lifted his gaze to the pasture that was now empty of everything but mesquite brush and an occasional cactus. What next? he thought furiously. The ranch had taken hit after hit over the past week, irritating, annoying little blows that hadn't caused any lasting damage alone. But when he put them all together, it was obvious they were in serious trouble. First, some of his best hands had quit without warning when it was too late to hire anyone else, fences were knocked down, delaying the roundup another day, then the flu had struck. And his brothers weren't the only ones who had taken to their beds. He was short-handed, behind schedule, and now this. How the hell were they going to recover from this type of financial blow when his loan payment was in the back of some rustler's truck?

Standing at the edge of the road, Josey watched the lines carving Gable's lean face deepen and found herself wanting to touch him, to soothe his furrowed brow and assure him everything was going to be all right. "What are you going to do now?"

He shrugged, a bitter taste in his mouth. "Call the sheriff so he can alert the auction barns and slaughterhouses."

"Then there's a possibility they can still catch them?" she asked hopefully. "Surely the slaughterhouses won't accept a cow with a Rawlings brand."

"Just because the bastards—begging your pardon, miss—did the stealing in New Mexico doesn't mean they'll sell them here," Red said. "We're just too close to Mexico and the state line. Unless you catch a rustler in the act, the chances are slim you'll ever see those cattle again. Why, they were probably turned into hamburger meat at some slaughterhouse in Arizona before we even got up this morning."

It was a grim prediction, and nothing less than the truth. "There's nothing more you boys can do here," Gable told the hands standing around with solemn faces. "Go ahead and get started over at the spring pasture. I'll be back to help as soon as I can. Come on, Josey, I'll take you home and call the sheriff from your place."

She wanted to argue with him—surely there had to be *something* else they could do besides just turn it over to the local authorities—but he was already striding toward his pickup. Without a word, she hurried after him and climbed into the truck.

He didn't say much on the ride back to her place, but Josey wasn't fooled. He was furious. A muscle ticked along his clenched jaw, but it was the rage blazing in his eyes that anyone with any sense would have gone out of their way to avoid. She pitied the rustlers if he ever caught up with them.

The minute they stepped into her house fifteen minutes later, she led him to the phone in the kitchen and un-abashedly eavesdropped as he talked to the sheriff. Just as he'd predicted, there wasn't much anyone could do.

"He's tied up at a trial this morning, but he'll be out later this afternoon to get a look at those tire tracks," he told her after he'd hung up. "Not that that'll do much good. But he can compare the tracks of other rustlers in the area to see if this was an individual act or a more organized one."

"You mean this is a common occurrence?" she demanded, surprised. "I thought rustling cattle was just one of those old crimes romanticized in western movies. I thought it died out decades ago."

"Not hardly," he replied. "It's a million-dollar problem and getting worse each year. For a junkie in need of a fix, or a desperate parent struggling to pay his bills when he's just lost his job, cows on a lonely stretch of road are just asking to be stolen. A good rustler who dresses the part and acts like he knows what he's doing can load a gooseneck trailer in plain sight without raising the least suspicion. Anyone who happened to pass on the road would just think an owner was moving his own cattle."

Josey thought of the lonely roads that crisscrossed just the southwest quadrant of the state alone, and lifted widened eyes to Gable. "My God, then how do you keep from losing your shirt? Your ranch must cover a hundred miles or more and there are several public roads through it."

"We're careful," he said with a shrug, then had to ruefully admit that even then, they slipped up sometimes. "Usually," he amended. "We try to cut down on the risks involved by grazing the majority of the cattle in pastures that aren't bordered by roads." The only reason he hadn't done that this time was because he'd known they would be moving the cattle soon, so he'd put them in a pasture on the little known road thinking they'd be perfectly safe. And that mistake in judgment could cost him and his family the ranch.

Worry twisted in his gut, but none of it was reflected in his face as his eyes met hers. "I've got to get back to work, but first I want to thank you for all your help over the last couple of days. I don't know what we would have done without you."

He spoke stiffly, as if she were the last person on earth he would want to thank for anything, every word dragging. But there was no doubting the sincerity of his tone or the honesty shining in the depths of his eyes. Amusement and something else, something she didn't want to feel for him, stirred, warming her. *Shrug it off,* a voice in her head advised, but when she tried, her voice was as stiff as his. "It was nothing...really. If I hadn't been around, I'm sure you would have managed just fine by yourself."

"You obviously haven't seen me in a sickroom," he said ruefully. "I'm serious, Josey. I owe you. If you ever need anything, you only have to ask."

His eyes locked with hers, silently making promises. Trapped, her heart starting to pound, it took all her strength of will to remind herself that she didn't want gratitude or anything else from him. "Kat's my friend," she said, cringing at the smoky huskiness of her voice. "I stayed because I was concerned about her...and Cooper and Flynn, too, of course. Payment isn't necessary."

One look at the determined jut of his chin and she knew he wasn't going to let the matter die so easily. Before he could say another word, she grabbed the keys to the old Jeep she'd inherited from her grandfather and gave Gable a breezy smile. "Well, thanks for bringing me home. I hate to run you off, but I know you've got work to get back to, and I need to run into Lordsburg for a while."

The city, she thought desperately. She needed the sights and sounds of the city, a town, civilization, to remind herself that her stay in New Mexico was only a short one. Her cheeks hot, she headed for the front door, where she stopped to face him, her friendly, overly bright smile firmly in place. "Can I get you anything while I'm in town? With all that's happened, you're probably too busy to run errands yourself. Anyway, there's no sense both of us making the trip."

She was chattering again, as she usually did when she was nervous. Staring down at her, a frown knitting his brows, Gable wondered what he'd done to make her edgy. He was half tempted to plant his feet and make her tell him, but she was already ushering him out the door. Talk about here's your hat, what's your hurry! The lady obviously couldn't wait to be rid of him.

"No, I don't need anything," he said, jamming his hat on his head as he stepped out onto her front porch with her right on his heels. "Just the missing yearlings. But I don't think you're going to find those in town."

The bitterness that hardened his words was there for an instant only, but Josey heard it and wanted to reach out to him, to somehow find a way to ease the anger he wouldn't allow himself to lose control of. But from the moment she'd met him, he'd warned her to mind her own business. In this, at least, she could respect his wishes.

"Probably not," she agreed quietly. "Maybe the sheriff will get lucky."

The cynical curl of his mouth told her what he thought of that empty hope, but he only shrugged and started down the porch steps while Josey locked up the house. She thought he was headed for his pickup, but when she turned from the door to follow him down the steps, she found him standing by the open garage door, his narrowed gaze inspecting every inch of her old Jeepster Commando.

When he heard her footstep on the steps, he turned, his tone accusing. "You're going to drive *that* forty miles into town?"

Surprised, she glanced at the Jeep as if it had somehow sprouted wings since she'd last driven it. But it looked just the way it always did. "Of course. Why not?"

"Why not?" he echoed incredulously. "Do you even have to ask? Look at the thing. It looks like it's held together with superglue. One good bump and it'll probably fall apart."

Josey had to admit, the vehicle wasn't the prettiest thing since Cinderella's coach. But it did have a certain panache to it that she kind of liked. Once it had been bright yellow, with white pinstriping and a white convertible top that must have looked quite sporty when her grandfather had driven it off the showroom floor. But that had been nearly thirty years ago, and it wasn't looking quite so sporty now. The paint was faded and rusty in spots, the ragtop worn thin and a dull off-white. Mechanically, it was in pretty good shape, but Josey could hardly blame Gable for thinking otherwise. She'd seen better looking cars in a junkyard.

"It's not that bad," she said defensively. At the mocking lift of his eyebrow, she conceded, "Okay, so it needs a little—a *lot*—of cosmetic work. It still runs like a top. And it's the only wheels I've got."

Gable wasn't impressed. "Speaking of wheels," he said dryly, "have you looked at the tires?"

"Tires?" Sounding like a parrot, Josey dropped her gaze to the rear tires. As far as she was concerned, one Goodyear looked just like the rest. "They're black," she replied, glancing back up at him. "So?"

"Of course they're black!" he thundered. "They're also bald as billiard balls and so thin you can practically see the air in them. You are *not* driving into town on those tires!"

It was the wrong thing to say in the wrong tone of voice. Ramrod straight, she looked down her nose at him. "I beg your pardon?"

Too late, Gable saw her back stiffen and her eyes snap fire and knew he'd handled her all wrong. Damn the woman, couldn't she see he was concerned about her? Muttering a curse, he tried to get a grip on his own anger, but he couldn't shake the image of her racing down the highway on those bald tires and having a blowout at fifty-five miles per hour.

"Just leave it alone until I can drive it in and get new tires put on it for you," he snapped, and held out his hand for the keys. "After all you've done for us, it's the least I can do."

If there had been anything within reach, Josey would have thrown it at his head. The nerve of the man! Who the hell did he think he was? "If that's the only reason you don't want me driving it, you can take your gratitude and...and stuff it!" she ground out through clenched teeth. "And the same goes for your orders, too. Your family might let you get away with being a dictator, but not me! That Jeep is mine, and if I want to drive it, I will." Her eyes glistening defiantly, she shoved the keys into the front pocket of her jeans.

He was at her side in a flash, grabbing her before she could do anything but gasp. "What are you doing? Let go!"

But Gable's temper was hot, his blue eyes narrowed with purpose. "Not on your life, sweetheart," he growled, and jammed his hand into her pocket for her keys.

At the first touch of his fingers molding the curve of her hip, heat jumped between them like the reaching flames of a blowtorch. Startled, they both froze. Desire. Josey wasn't so inexperienced that she didn't know it when she saw it etching the hard lines of a man's face. Gable wanted her...badly. Heat shimmered through her, the sudden thunder of her heart loud in her ears.

"Gable—"

His name was a plea on her lips, one Gable couldn't resist. He knew he was courting disaster, but any chance he'd had of walking away from her unscathed ended the instant he touched her. With a groan of defeat, he jerked his hand from her pocket, the keys snug in his grasp, and dragged her flush against him.

He half braced himself for her rejection, but it never came. Instead she held herself perfectly still, as if she were afraid to move, to let herself feel. Then, with a murmur of need, she melted against him as if she couldn't get close enough. Groaning low in his throat, he kissed her as he'd been dying to for longer than he cared to remember.

Heat. Hot, clawing, instantaneous. It hit him from the blind side, stunning him with its strength, intoxicating him. His head reeling, his hands tightened on her, pulling her closer until her breasts were molded to his chest, her hips snug against his hardness. The rightness of it nearly drove him to his knees. Even then, he told himself he could handle this, handle her. Then she moved against him, her tongue shyly stealing out to play with his, and the control he'd always taken for granted came close to blowing up in his face.

Her body singing with need, her knees weak, she clung to him. There it was again—the passion, the fire, the stardust streaking through her veins, setting her aglow and making a mockery of all her fine resolves. Soon, she promised herself, she would remember why she was furious with him and why she didn't—couldn't—want this. But not just yet. More. She just needed a little more of the sparks that no one else had ever been able to set off deep inside her.

She made him forget . . . everything. Her mouth hot and hungry under his, her hands blindly roaming over him, trailing fire, he struggled to clear his head. But he could feel her urgency, taste it, and all he could think of was pulling her down to the ground and losing himself in her, taking her in a raw, primitive way, claiming her in a way he'd never claimed a woman in his life.

Stunned, his thoughts reeling, Gable jerked himself back from the edge with a muffled curse and broke the kiss. For what seemed an eternity, he couldn't move, couldn't do anything but stare down into her desire-softened face. What the hell was he doing? This was Josey O'Brian he was kissing. Josey O'Brian he was in danger of losing his head over. The same woman who argued with him every chance she got and wouldn't even let him open a door for her if she could prevent it. She was a mass of contradictions, a woman of the world who kissed with an innocence that was devastating, a city woman who didn't seem in any hurry to leave the middle of nowhere. And she thought he was bossy, domineering and a chauvinist, for God's sake!

Yet he wanted her in a way he hadn't wanted any woman in a long time.

Stung by the thought, he released her abruptly and stepped back, away from temptation. Jangling her keys in front of her face, he said gruffly, "I'll keep these for now and come back for the Jeep this afternoon. By tonight you'll have new tires."

Not giving her a chance to protest further, he turned on his heel and left, the angry roar of the pickup's motor echoing in the stillness he left behind.

Her knees weak and heart still hammering wildly in her chest, Josey collapsed on the porch steps, her eyes on the trail of dust the black pickup dragged after it. He'd kissed her as if he were starving for the taste of her. And she'd kissed him right back the same way. Dear God, how he'd made her want him! She could still taste him on her tongue, still feel the strength of his arms, the hard proof of his desire. And deep inside, where no one could see, she still throbbed.

Yet he'd left her. He'd driven off and hadn't looked back once. Why should he? He'd gotten his way. He'd ordered her not to drive the Jeep, and she had no choice but to obey him. What else could she do? He'd taken her keys.

So you're going to calmly sit back and take this from him just because he melted your bones like butter with a couple of hot kisses? a voice in her head jeered. *Is that all it takes to turn you into one of those women who lets a macho man direct her life as if she doesn't have enough sense to come in out of the rain? Is that all it takes to turn you into your mother?*

The taunting words slapped her in the face, bringing her back to her senses as nothing else could. Horrified, she jumped to her feet. Had she lost her mind? She wouldn't be weak and submissive for any man, let alone Gable Rawlings! Damn him, who did he think he was, telling her what to do, then acting as though it was a given because of a couple of kisses? He wasn't her boss or her daddy, and she'd damn well do as she pleased.

Fury burning in her eyes, Josey stormed into the house and immediately went to the secretary desk in the living room. When she'd gone through her grandfather's papers the first week she'd been in the house, she'd come across a second set of keys that she was almost sure went to the Jeep. Now if she could only remember where she'd put them. Pulling out first one drawer, then another, she finally found them in a cubbyhole that held a collection of odd keys, paper clips and a couple of rusty screws. Ten seconds later, she was rushing out the front door.

The Jeep started on the first try, and with a grim smile of satisfaction, she put it in gear and turned toward town, thankful that her grandfather had had the good sense to buy an automatic. Gable had long since disappeared down the road, which was fine with her. He'd find out soon enough that she'd defied him when he came back this afternoon for the Jeep and found it sitting on four new tires. She couldn't wait to see his face!

As it turned out, she didn't have that long to wait. Tooling along at fifty-five miles per hour, she topped the small rise right before the entrance to the Rawlings's ranch and almost stopped in her tracks at the sight of Gable's black pickup pulled over on the side of the road. He was parked next to the bank of mailboxes belonging to all the ranchers in the area, standing out in the morning sun talking to the rural postal carrier.

Josey grinned, mischief dancing in her eyes. Things couldn't have worked out better if she'd planned them herself. Hitting the gas, she raced down the highway, waiting until she drew even with Gable and the mailman to honk the horn and give a merry wave. She passed them so quickly, they were little more than a blur, but she was almost sure she saw Gable's jaw drop in shock. Laughter bubbled up in her. Revenge. How sweet it was!

"Hey, wasn't that the O'Brians' granddaughter? The lady doctor who's moved into their old place for a while?" Victor Martinez asked, automatically throwing up his hand in greeting at the first sound of the horn. "I haven't met her yet, but I heard she's a real pretty woman. Must be lonely, though, living by herself way out here. She doesn't get a lot of mail, either."

Unable to believe his eyes as the yellow Jeep rapidly disappeared down the highway, Gable hardly heard him. She'd deliberately defied him, he thought in growing fury, the jaunty wave she'd given him as taunting as a red flag in front of a bull. Dammit to hell, just wait until he got his hands on her! He hadn't warned her about the tires just to hear himself talk. They were dangerous. And she was racing down the road like a bat just let loose from hell. What had she done? Hot-wired the damn thing?

"Yeah, that was her," he said grimly. "Excuse me, Vic, I've got some unfinished business to take care of."

Steaming, he took off after her, cursing her and himself all the way. The woman was a headache he didn't need. With Cooper and Flynn still out, he had work to do, dammit! Not to mention a hundred head of missing cattle and a loan payment to worry about. He didn't have time to race up and down the highway after a woman who seemed to have made defying him her life's work. Let someone else worry about her. She wasn't his responsibility.

Giving himself all the reasons why he should turn around, he pressed down on the accelerator instead, an image of one of the Jeep's tires disintegrating at any moment driving him on. If she had an accident...

He didn't even want to think about it. His jaw clenched, he raced after her, the truck's powerful motor easily eating up the distance between them. Within minutes, he was right behind her, his eyes meeting hers in her rearview mirror. Without saying a word, he dared her to try to outrun him.

Surprised to find him so close—how had he caught up with her so quickly?—Josey's heart jumped into her throat. She hadn't expected him to follow her, but she shouldn't have been surprised. He was a man who didn't handle defiance well, she thought, then almost giggled. Talk about an understatement! He was livid, his jaw set in granite, his lips pressed tight in a thin line of anger.

Jerking her gaze back to the long, empty ribbon of road that stretched out before her in a straight line, she told herself she didn't care. He couldn't kiss her one moment, then turn around and treat her like a five-year-old the next. She wouldn't stand for it. The rest of the world might jump to do his bidding, but he'd soon learn she wasn't so tractable...even if her eyes couldn't meet his without her yearning to be back in his arms. Groaning at the thought, she studiously kept her gaze trained on the highway, determined to act as if she didn't know he was right on her rear bumper.

For forty long miles, he followed her. Her eyes never strayed to the mirror again, but she knew he was right on her heels, like a runner in a marathon. Shadowing her every move, she could almost feel his hot breath striking the back of her neck, stirring her hair—and her senses, damn him—setting her heart pounding at a frantic rate.

When Lordsburg finally came into sight, she almost wilted in relief, her foot instinctively pressing harder on the accelerator. But it wasn't until she started to turn into the garage where she intended to buy tires that she glanced in the mirror again. Their eyes met, locked, spoke volumes. He was going to follow her into the garage and insist on paying for her tires—she could almost read his intentions on his face. Her jaw set, she glared back at him and dared him to try. If he so much as reached for his wallet, he was going to have a fight on his hands.

For a long, timeless moment, she thought he was going to ignore the silent message she was sending him, but something in her eyes must have gotten through to him.

With a mocking salute, he followed her into the garage parking lot, but only to turn around and head back to the ranch. With a look that spoke louder than words, he told her he had been the winner in their little tug of war down the highway. He'd watched over her whether she'd wanted him to or not, and she was getting new tires. Amused in spite of herself, she watched him disappear down the main street of town until he was out of sight.

Buying the tires took all of ten minutes; getting them put on and balanced was another matter. Told the wait would be at least an hour, Josey walked across the street to the Sagebrush Café. It was one of those old-fashioned places, with plastic gingham tablecloths on the tables, a soda bar along one wall, a row of booths along the other, with the rest rooms and coatracks at the back. The menu probably hadn't changed in forty years, obviously with good reason. It was still a couple of hours before noon, and the place was packed with locals, their trucks parked out front like horses gathered around a watering trough. The only table available was the next-to-last booth at the back.

She'd hardly sat down when a harried waitress hurried over, plopped down a laminated menu in front of her, and immediately poured her a cup of coffee. "Here you go, hon. Now what can I get you? If I don't take your order now, it'll be a while before I can get back to you. This place is a zoo this morning."

Josey didn't have to open the menu to know that the Sagebrush didn't cotton to the latest warnings about cholesterol. Giving in to the inevitable, she smiled wryly. She hadn't had anything but coffee for breakfast, and she intended to go whole hog. "Then I'd better order now. How about bacon and eggs, the eggs over easy and the toast unbuttered? And plenty of coffee. I'm having tires put on my car across the street, so I may be here a while."

"No problem," the older woman assured her with a smile. "I've been running around like a chicken with my head cut off since we opened at six, so I could use a couple of slow tables. Take your time. I'll be right back with your food."

She'd hardly left when the lowered conversation in the booth behind Josey caught her attention. At the mention of Gable's name, she stiffened, listening before she even realized she was eavesdropping.

"I told you we could do it," a gravel-rough voice rasped in what was little more than a whisper. "Gable doesn't suspect a thing."

A second man laughed huskily, an unpleasant, oily sound that sent goose bumps rippling down Josey's back. "He just thinks he's had a string of bad luck, and who can blame him? Downed fences, hands that quit without notice, rustlers and the flu. Course we can't take credit for the last, but by the time he and those brothers of his figure out someone's been sabotaging them and slowing down their work, it'll be too late."

"They'll miss the loan payment at the bank," a younger man added. "Times are tough and Fred Hawkins has already said he can't set a precedent by letting any delinquent loans slide. He'll have to foreclose, and when he does, the Double R will go on the auction block."

Horrified, Josey could almost feel the glee coming from the booth at her back, even as she told herself this couldn't be real. Why would anyone plot against Gable to make him lose his ranch?

"And we'll all be there waiting," the first, gravelly-voiced man said smugly. "Together we can outbid anyone else and finally get our hands on the Rawlings's springs. We'll incorporate, take down the boundary fences, and run our cattle with the Double R's."

"We'll be as big as the King Ranch down in Texas."

"And never have to be dependent on the Rawlings bunch again," the oily one added in satisfaction. "Their springs have never been known to run dry, but all they bother to give the rest of us is a few measly truckloads of water when the drought's so bad our tanks are dry. I'm sick of being a charity case."

"Five more weeks," the gravelly-voiced man said. "Just five more weeks and it'll be over. We'll have it made in the shade, just like we always dreamed."

The waitress returned with her food then, but Josey had lost her appetite. She heard the three plotters throw some change down on the table and start to rise, but when she quickly glanced over her shoulder to get a look at them, the waitress blocked her view. She caught only a glimpse of three men of staggered heights, cowboy hats on their heads, just seconds before they opened the door and stepped outside.

Shaken, Josey stared after them long after the door had cut them off from view, her thoughts tumbling over themselves like circus clowns. She had to tell Gable; there was no one else to do it. But, God, she wasn't looking forward to it. She already knew more of his personal business than she wanted to...she'd stayed at his home, nursed his family, argued with him, shared kitchen duties with him, kissed him. She was getting in too deep, but there didn't seem to be anything she could do about it. Every time she made a move to get out of his life, something happened to pull her back in again. If she didn't know better, she'd swear it was fate.

Chapter 6

The roundup was in full swing when Josey arrived at the spring pasture three hours later. Standing near the barbed-wire fence, she shaded her eyes against the glare of the sun and stared in wonder at the scene spread out before her. If it wasn't for the pickups parked alongside the narrow road that formed one side of the pasture, she could have easily imagined she'd stepped back in time to the Old West. Cowboys decked out in spurs, chaps, boots and hats kicked up dust as they worked the cattle on cutting horses, cutting the calves out of the herd and directing them toward a corral at the opposite end of the pasture. The smell of wood smoke floated on the dusty air, along with the bawling of cattle, the jangle of spurs and tack, the enthusiastic yells of the cowboys as they threw themselves wholeheartedly into their work.

Suddenly, without warning, a rebellious calf took exception to being separated from its mother and made a break for it. The young bull, however, had hardly taken three steps when a horse and rider darted after him, quick as lightning. Fascinated, Josey watched the cowboy slouched in the saddle sway and flow with the horse's swift-footed movements with a boneless grace that stole her breath. She's seen such things on T.V. and in old Westerns, but she'd never realized how well the two worked together. Like two pieces of a whole, each seemed to know what the other was going to do without so much as a signal of communication.

"Can I help you, ma'am? You lost or something?"

Startled, Josey dragged her eyes away from the Western ballet being played out before her to find a young cowboy on a speckled gray mare approaching her from the opposite end of the pasture. He hardly looked old enough to shave and wore a battered straw cowboy hat that seemed to be resting on his ears. Biting back a smile, Josey said, "I'm looking for Mr. Rawlings. I was told at the house that he was out here directing the roundup."

"He's over at the corral, ma'am," he said, nodding toward the small fenced-in area that butted up against a large outcropping of rock a hundred yards away. "Is he expecting you?"

"Not exactly," she hedged. "But I've got to talk to him." And without waiting for an invitation, she slipped through the barbed-wire fence as gracefully as she could without snagging her clothes, then carefully picked her way across the pasture toward the corral.

She was the only woman in sight, but she didn't draw a second look. A beehive of activity, the corral seemed to be full to overflowing with cowboys on foot and bawling calves. Captivated, she watched two ranch hands grab a calf that was nearly as big as they were and wrestle it to the ground. Almost immediately, four more cowboys were on it. Like a team of surgeons, each with their own specialty, they branded it, dehorned it, vaccinated it and castrated it in less than a minute and a half. It wasn't until the men stepped back and the unhappy little steer regained its feet and bolted away that Josey realized that Gable was one of the four cowboys.

Her pulse jumped at the sight of him. To anyone who didn't know him, he could have easily been mistaken for one of his own ranch hands. He was dirty and hot, his shirt dusty and flecked with blood, yet somehow he still managed to look wonderful. Pulling off his black hat, he wiped the sweat and grit from his brow with his forearm and laughed at a comment made by one of the others. Josey couldn't hear what was said and didn't care. She couldn't take her eyes from him. His smile, even when it wasn't directed at her, warmed her inside and out.

He was just turning back to the small campfire that held the branding irons when he suddenly looked up and found her standing at the fence, watching his every move. Surprise flickered across his face, and then something else, something she couldn't quite read that was gone in a heartbeat as he excused himself from his men and strode toward her.

Stopping at the fence, he pushed his hat to the back of his head and grinned down at her mockingly. "Well, well, if it isn't the defiant Dr. O'Brian. Here to rub my nose in your new tires, Doctor? I thought you'd already done that."

Conscious of the interested eyes on them, Josey felt heat rise in her cheeks and could have shot him. "No," she snapped. "This isn't about the stupid tires. I overheard something in town this morning I think you should know about."

He merely lifted a brow at her. "You tracked me all the way down here just to pass on some gossip? I'm flattered, but it really wasn't necessary. Whatever's being talked about in town usually makes it out to the surrounding ranches with the next morning's mail. If you'd have just waited, I'd have heard about it, anyway.''

"Not this, you wouldn't have," she replied grimly. Dreading the telling, she quickly and concisely repeated everything she had heard in the café, leaving out nothing. When she finished, his crooked grin was gone, his expression stony. "I don't know who they were," she said regretfully, "I didn't get a look at them, and they mentioned three others, though not by name. I thought you should know as soon as possible. They were very sure of themselves."

Sabotage. The word cut through Gable like a switchblade in the back, stunning him as everything fell neatly into place. Of course! Why hadn't he seen it sooner? On a ranch the size of the Double R, only a greenhorn expected to get through the day without running into one kind of problem or another. There were always fences to be mended, sick cattle to be treated, repairs on the truck to be made. But the problems they'd been hit with lately had bordered on disasters at a time when they could afford them the least. The hands that quit without notice, the downed fences—Hamilton! Remembering how he'd checked the downed fence the day before and found nothing wrong with it, he swore softly. So Carl Hamilton was in on the conspiracy. Who were the other five?

The Rawlings's springs had always been a thorn in the side of the other ranchers, a source of sweet, life-giving water that never ran dry, even during the longest droughts. He wasn't stupid—he knew there were those who resented that, in spite of the fact that he and his brothers shared the springs' largess with anyone in need. But he'd never thought his neighbors' jealousy was so great that they'd set him up to lose everything just so they could get their hands on the springs. The nerve of the bastards!

They wouldn't get away with it, he vowed furiously. Now that he knew what they were up to, he'd beat them at their own game. Obviously his cattle hadn't been rustled, in spite of appearances to the contrary. The so-called friends who were after his ranch might be devious, but they would never be stupid enough to risk arrest by selling cattle that didn't belong to them, which meant they were probably just hiding the cattle on their own ranches until he missed his loan payment. Now all he had to do was find them.

"It looks like I owe you...again," he said tightly. "Thanks for the information. I'll get right on it."

"What are you going to do?"

"Find my cattle," he retorted. Turning to his ranch hands, he said, "Red, you take over here. I've got to check a lead on the yearlings. I don't know when I'll be back."

He headed for his truck, crossing the pasture with long strides, his expression grim. Irritated that he could dismiss her so cavalierly after she'd raced out here to warn him about the plot against him, Josey fell into step beside him. "I'm going with you."

"The hell you are!"

He stopped short, scowling at her, but she just kept walking, her mind made up. "Don't look at me like that," she said, pulling open the passenger door of his truck. "Apparently you didn't even know there was a conspiracy against you until I told you. So what's going on? Those men I overheard know you. You've obviously helped them, but they sounded like they hated you and your family. Why?"

Gable hesitated. He'd tried to tell himself he didn't owe her any explanations about ranch business, but she was right. Until she'd told him, he'd never suspected his recent troubles were the result of a plot against the ranch. "Water," he finally said stiffly. "Out here, it's more precious than gold. We've been in a drought for going on six months now, and that little shower we got yesterday was just a teaser. It'll help for a day or two, but that's all. Tanks are drying up all over the county and the situation is starting to get critical. I've trucked water to those who were in the worst trouble, but obviously that's only stirred up resentment."

"But you were trying to help them!"

"Some people find a handout hard to swallow. But when a man's got thirsty cattle and no water, he gets desperate."

She could understand desperation. She could even understand a man with bruised pride striking out impulsively. But there was nothing impulsive about the attacks on the Double R. "But these men are plotting to steal your ranch, your home, for *water!*"

She sounded so shocked, he had to smile at her naiveté. "This is a rough land, lady, and not everyone plays by the rules. My ancestors were some of the first settlers in this part of the state, and when they came across the springs, they recognized their value and claimed them for themselves. We've been fighting to keep them ever since. Seems like a lot of folks down through the years haven't taken kindly to sitting by and watching their own spreads dry up and blow away during a drought while the Double R keeps prospering because there's always water."

Walking around his pickup, he jerked open the driver's door and frowned at her across the width of the seat. "That doesn't mean we stand by and let them drag us down into the dust with them. We fight for what's ours when we have to. So now that you know the whole story,

I'd appreciate it if you'd go home and let me and my men take care of this. You'd only be in the way."

If she had any sense, Josey knew she'd do as he asked. But temper flared in her eyes at just the thought of being patted on the head like a good little girl being sent home to play with her dolls. "You don't even know where to look," she argued stubbornly. "What are you going to do? Search every ranch in this corner of the state?"

"If I have to."

"But it'll take you weeks! Let me help you, Gable."

"No."

His jaw was set in granite, his mind already made up. Josey could have kicked him. Had she ever met a more infuriating man in her life? "Just because I didn't see the men plotting against you doesn't mean I wouldn't recognize their voices if I heard them again," she insisted. The rough, gravelly voice of one of the conspirators rang in her ears, only to be followed by the unpleasant laughter of another. She shivered, coldness sliding down her spine as she recalled every nuance, every inflection, as clearly as if she'd recorded it. "They were very distinctive."

"So what are you suggesting? I take you to the men I suspect are capable of this and tell them you want to hear them talk so you can see if they're the bastards who are sabotaging my ranch? Come on, Josey, it'll never work!"

"It would if you pretended you were introducing me around since the only other doctor in this area is on the other side of Lordsburg, over forty miles away, and the nearest hospital is even further north in Silver City," she countered swiftly. "No one would suspect a thing. If I recognized one of the men from the café, then you could come up with a reason to search their property, instead of every ranch in the area. It would save you a lot of wasted time."

Time he didn't have. Reluctantly Gable had no choice but to admit that she was right. But, damn, he wasn't looking forward to spending the next few days driving around the countryside with her. How was he ever going to get her out of his life if fate kept throwing them back together?

"All right," he said ungraciously. "You can go. But if things get nasty, don't say I didn't warn you."

It was a simple plan that should have worked beautifully, but by the middle of the second day, Gable was beginning to give up hope. He'd taken Josey to every neighbor he thought might be capable of plotting against him and introduced her as the new doctor in the area. He'd lost track of the number of ranches they'd visited, the number of men and women Josey had shaken hands with, the number of cups of coffee they drank and pieces of pie they'd forced down. They were invited into people's homes and showered with a friendly hospitality that would have made Gable feel guilty as hell if he hadn't reminded himself that aside from Carl Hamilton, there were five men out there who were pretending to be his friend while scheming to get their hands on the Double R. If he had to lie to uncover their identity, then he would.

But despite Josey's claims to the contrary, she couldn't identify a single rancher as one of the three men she'd overheard in the Sagebrush Café.

"This isn't working," she admitted quietly, voicing his thoughts as they drove down yet another long gravel drive that seemed to be a carbon copy of every other ranch road in the county. "I wanted to save you time, but I only seem to be dragging out the inevitable. Maybe we should just forget the whole thing."

"Don't give up yet," he said as he drove up in front of Roy Mitchell's house and braked to a stop. "You didn't dream up that conversation at the Sagebrush, so those men have got to be here somewhere. We've just got to find them. So far, we've just been narrowing down the field. C'mon, let's go see if Roy's here. You'll like him. He and my father were best friends. He might have a suggestion on what to do next."

Roy Mitchell was home, all right. They found him in the barn overhauling an old pickup that looked as if it was on its last legs. At the sight of Gable striding toward him, the older man grinned broadly and reached for a red rag to wipe his hands. "Well, son of a gun, if it ain't Gable! How you doin', boy? I heard you had that pesky flu that's been going around and wiping out every ranch between here and Albuquerque."

"Not me." Gable laughed, taking the hand he offered in a firm shake, then slapping the older man on the back. "Coop and Flynn won't be eating any peppers for a while, but I'm doing fine. Thought you might want to meet the new doctor, though, just in case you need her services. Josey, this is Roy Mitchell. Roy, Dr. Josephine O'Brian. She just moved into her grandparents' place down the road from me."

"Is that right?" the older man said, giving his fingers one last rub with the red rag before holding out a calloused hand to her. "Pleased to meet you, ma'am. Hope you'll be staying a while. We could use a good doctor in this neck of the woods."

Josey automatically held out her hand to Roy Mitchell, but in her ears rang the gleeful words of one of the men in the café who had been thrilled that Double R had been hit with the flu on top of everything else. That man's gravelly voice matched Roy Mitchell's to a *T*.

He and my father were best friends.

Stricken, Josey fought the urge to snatch her hand back. She had to be mistaken, she told herself desperately. Surely this man wouldn't plot to destroy Gable, not when his friendship with his father went back decades. Why, anyone seeing them together could easily mistake them for uncle and nephew, so affectionate was their relationship. There had to be another explanation.

But try as she might, she couldn't stop herself from comparing the rough cadence of his words now with the distinctive rhythm of the voice she'd overheard at the Sagebrush. They were the same. She was sure of it. If she lived to be a hundred, she'd still hear that voice in her head, plotting trouble.

"Actually, I'm only here for a short while," she finally managed stiffly. "Probably just until summer." Swallowing the sudden lump in her throat, she forced out the words she and Gable had agreed on as a signal that she recognized the voice of one of the men from the café. "Gable and I met when he came over to my grandparents' place looking for strays. He's been having a problem with downed fences."

Gable stiffened as if she'd slapped him, the piercing look he shot her dark with disbelief. What the hell kind of game was she playing? he wondered irately. Roy was like family! He would no more plot against him than he would have his father. She had to be mistaken.

But her jaw was set at a challenging angle, her eyes sure as they met his. Half inclined to tell her she was crazy, Gable found himself going along with her instead and couldn't for the life of him say why. "I feel like a damn fool admitting this," he said gruffly, the lie sticking in his throat, "but Josey's right. I seem to have misplaced a hundred head and the only thing I can figure out is that they slipped through a break in the fence between the Double R and your place. Mind if I take a look and see if they accidentally wandered over here?''

Surprised, the older man quickly assured him, "No, of course not. But why don't you let me call my foreman on the radio and he can get some of the boys to do it? There's no use you driving all over creation when I've already got men out in the field."

But Gable was already shaking his head. "I couldn't ask you to take men away from your own roundup to look for my cattle. The fault was mine for not checking that stretch of fence sooner. I'll do it."

"I'm just as responsible for the upkeep of that fence as you are," Roy pointed out. "At least let me go with you. I can help you look."

Guilt twisted in Gable's gut. He'd never felt more like a hypocrite. He opened his mouth to tell the older man that his help wasn't necessary, only to shut it with a snap. Dammit, this man was a friend! How could he decline his offer without offending him? After all, they were on Roy's ranch and he could do whatever he wanted.

Shooting Josey a hard look that warned her she was dead wrong about her suspicions, he shrugged. "Sure. I can always use another pair of eyes. Let's go."

With Josey sitting in the middle, the three of them piled into the cab of Gable's pickup. Within minutes they were bouncing over the rough terrain of the ranch, riding the fence line that formed the outer boundary of the property. Roy, totally at ease, talked of the old days and the way trucks and helicopters and propane-fueled branding heaters had tried to change roundups, but how, a hundred years from now, there'd still be a need for a cowboy with a good horse and fine roping skills. If he was the least bit apprehensive about missing cattle being discovered on his spread, he didn't show it.

His hands biting into the steering wheel, his mouth pressed into a grim line, Gable fought with the knowledge that his presence there was an accusation in itself, even though Roy had no way of knowing that. If his father, God rest his soul, could somehow see what he was doing, he'd turn over in his grave.

"Well, I'll be damned."

Jerked out of his musing by Roy's muttered exclamation, Gable glanced over at the older man to find his eyes trained on the pasture they'd just entered by driving over a cattle guard. Following his gaze, Gable sucked in a sharp breath. They were miles away from any shared border with his ranch, yet there were at least thirty head of cattle with the distinctive brand of the Double R blazed into their hides peacefully grazing in the buffalo grass.

Stunned disbelief dropping like acid into his stomach, Gable braked to a bone-jarring halt, unable to drag his eyes away from the cattle, *his* cattle, on another man's land. A man who, if asked, he would have sworn he could trust with anything he had, including his life. *Why?* he wanted to cry. *Dammit, why?*

The growing silence, already tense, darkened with a suspicion that was almost tangible, but Gable would have cut off his tongue before he'd allow himself to throw out a single accusation. Instead he forced himself to go along with the charade he and Josey had developed earlier, a charade he'd never seriously thought he'd have to act out in real life.

"I knew old Bossy led those young cows through that fence," he said with a disgusted humor that didn't quite ring true even to his own ears. "She can wiggle through a picket fence when she puts her mind to it."

"I don't know what to say," the older man replied sheepishly, rubbing his palm against his whiskered jaw. "I swear to God, I had no idea your cattle were on my land, son. You know I would have rounded them up and trucked them over to your place if I had. I'm as surprised as you are."

To someone who didn't know him well, his shock might have come across as genuine. But Gable had played poker with Roy for years, and he'd always been a lousy gambler. He'd never been able to bluff his way through a poor hand in his life. And right now, he was lying through his teeth.

"Don't sweat it," Gable gritted out, his smile a grimace that never reached his eyes. "These things happen. Next time I'll just have to be more careful."

The older man, not knowing when to shut up, wouldn't let it go. "Still, I feel responsible. I can't imagine how your cattle got through the fence and miles from your place without any of my men noticing. As soon as we get back to the house, I'll have my foreman and some of the boys load them up in the gooseneck and take them back to the Double R. Everything will be back to normal and we can both forget this ever happened."

Gable only looked at him, bitterness crawling through him. He had no intention of forgetting anything. Damn, what a fool he'd been! Until now, he'd only checked the ranches of those men whose ethics were less than spotless. He'd never thought he needed to suspect a friend.

Turning away, he told Josey, "Come on, let's go. I just remembered some other neighbors I want you to meet."

They left without a backward glance, silence stretching between them as Gable drove to the ranches that until now he had not thought it necessary to check—those of his closest friends.

It took them two more days, but by the time he drove Josey home at the end of the fourth day, he had three more names to add to Carl Hamilton's on the list of conspirators. Playing out the same scene they had acted out at Roy Mitchell's, they found cattle from the Double R on John Stinson's and Ben Hopkins's ranches. And each time, friends—men Gable had grown up with and thought he knew as well as he knew his brothers—looked him right in the eye and pretended surprise with an ease that infuriated him.

There were still two unknown conspirators unaccounted for, but he wouldn't know as much as he did if it hadn't been for Josey. Once again he was indebted to her, he thought as he parked behind her Jeep. He didn't like the feeling any better now than he had earlier. Every time he thought he had her figured out, she confounded him by doing the unexpected. He would have sworn she didn't like him, wanted nothing to do with him, yet she'd gone out of her way to warn him about the mischief brewing right under his nose. Even then, after she'd told him about the plot against him, she could have turned her back on him and let him discover who his enemies were on his own. Instead she'd insisted on helping him without once throwing an "I told you so" in his face, even when he'd deserved it.

Cutting the motor, he sat unmoving, staring at the dark windows of her house, cursing the awareness that made him attuned to her slightest movement as she shifted on the seat next to him. Blast the woman, he couldn't figure her out! She challenged him at every turn, never letting him get away with anything, yet every time their eyes met, the kisses they'd shared were there between them, throbbing. He couldn't remember the last time a woman had jerked his string so easily, and he had to do something about her. But he was damned if he knew what. And that scared the hell out of him. He'd never been so unsure of himself with a woman in his life.

"Well, I guess I'd better be go—"

"I don't know what I would have—"

They both spoke at the same time, each jumping to fill the awkward silence that threatened to rage out of control the second the engine died. Startled, they both froze, stilted words hanging in the air between them like bombs waiting to explode. With a will of their own, their eyes met, then dropped to lips still parted in speech. Hearts thundered, and still the silence grew.

Heat climbing into her cheeks, it seemed an eternity before Josey was able to drag her gaze from his and think clearly enough to speak halfway intelligibly. Her purse clutched to her breast like a shield, she said thickly, "I'm glad you found your cattle. Now you should be able to make your loan payment without any problem."

It wasn't going to be that easy—the recovered cattle represented only half of the payment and they still had the roundup to finish—but Gable only nodded. "Thanks to you. I owe you. Again."

Gratitude. He was talking gratitude, but it wasn't that emotion that she saw in his eyes, heard in his voice, felt in the air. It wasn't gratitude that had her reaching for the door handle while she still could, before he tempted her to forget all the reasons why she wanted nothing to do with him. "You owe me nothing," she said huskily, and pushed open the door.

One touch, and Gable knew he could have stopped her. But some last shred of self-preservation warned him if he reached for her now, he might not be able to let her go. Ever. So he sat back and watched her flee from him as if she couldn't get away fast enough. And all the time, he wanted her.

Chapter 7

"I hope you don't mind taking this as payment, Doctor. My husband hurt his back last month and he just hasn't been able to work none. The last thing we needed was another doctor's bill, but what was I supposed to do when my boy fell and broke his arm? I couldn't stand to see him suffering and everybody said you were real understanding about things like that. I sure appreciate your help. Why, I don't know what I would have done if I'd have had to drive Jimmy all the way to the hospital in Silver City. He was suffering so, I just wanted to cry."

Josey smiled and accepted the casserole Sylvia Petty pushed into her hands. Since Gable had introduced her to nearly all the area ranchers five days ago, the news that there was now a doctor in the area had spread like wildfire, and she'd known it was only a matter of time before the sick and injured came looking for her. She hadn't come to New Mexico to practice medicine, but she'd known she had to be prepared in case of an emergency, so she'd applied to the state for a license. Luckily she had also made a trip to Silver City for supplies, because total strangers soon found their way to her house at unexpected times of the day and night, wanting her to treat them for everything from the flu, which seemed to be scouring the countryside, to tetanus shots from run-ins with rusty barbed wire.

Even then, the first time she'd opened her door to a would-be patient, she'd taken one look at the cowboy with the dislocated finger and had almost told him she wasn't practicing medicine for the duration of her stay. And her specialty was obstetrics, not general medicine. But the instinct to help had been too strong, and she hadn't been able to turn him away when he was obviously in pain. So she'd patched him up and sent him on his way, and it had begun. Other cowboys had followed, along with other children such as Jimmy, as well as elderly patients complaining of arthritis...she'd taken them all in...all except the expectant mothers.

She knew she was wrong to refer them to a doctor in town. She couldn't keep running from the past; it would continue to haunt her until she delivered a baby again. But she couldn't. *She just couldn't!* She still dreamed of Molly and her poor baby, still woke in the middle of the night in a cold sweat, her face wet with tears, horror at her own inadequacy that fateful night choking her. And try though she might, she couldn't make herself take the one step that would end the nightmare.

Once she'd realized that it was the pregnancies she wanted to avoid and not medicine in general, she'd thanked God for sending her that first hurt cowboy. She hadn't realized how much she'd missed medicine. And a rural practice, she was discovering, was a lot more laid back than the one she'd left in Boston. Perhaps it was because the area was sparsely populated and there weren't many opportunities to socialize, but people tended to treat her more like an old friend instead of a doctor, always taking time to gossip a little with her, making her feel as though she'd been a part of the community forever, before going on their way. It was, she admitted to herself with a smile, nice. Some paid with money, but others, such as Mrs. Petty, who were short on cash, had heard from someone at the Double R that cooking wasn't her forte, so they settled their bill with creamery butter, yard eggs, fresh cream and sometimes full meals. Amused and touched, Josey graciously accepted whatever they chose to give her and admitted to herself that there were unexpected benefits to being a country doctor. She hadn't had to cook for herself in days.

"I'm glad I could help, Mrs. Petty," she said sincerely, setting the covered dish on the desk in her grandfather's study, which she was slowly converting into a combination office and examining room. "Jimmy should be fine now. Just make sure he doesn't get the cast wet. And try to keep him out of the hayloft until that arm's healed."

"I will, Doctor, but you know how boys are," she said, fondly ruffling the five-year-old's sandy hair as they stepped out onto the front porch. "I turn around and he's gone. Thanks again for your help."

The minute they left, the silence that invariably filled the house whenever Josey was alone fell like a shroud, but she knew it wouldn't last long. Kat had started dropping by on her way home from school, usually to share some interesting gossip or just chat. Josey loved her company, but she didn't need to know that all the Double R cattle were back where they belonged or that Gable had called Sheriff Denkins to tell him what was going on only to be told that there was nothing the law could do until a crime was actually committed. And that cattle wandering onto neighboring ranches was not a crime. She didn't need to know that the sheriff's lack of interest infuriated Gable—she could almost see his steel blue eyes blazing in anger and hear him rage to his brothers how he wasn't surprised. Roy Mitchell, John Stinson and Ben Hopkins had been instrumental in getting the sheriff elected, and the good ol' boys protected their own. The Rawlingses could expect no help from Denkins or anyone else.

No, she didn't want to think about Gable, his problems, or the date she'd so foolishly asked him for, she decided. Hopefully, he'd forgotten that, which would be just fine with her. He was finally leaving her alone, and she had almost convinced herself that that was just the way she wanted it. The less she saw of him, the sooner she would forget the kisses that seemed to fill her thoughts whenever her hands got too idle or the silence too heavy.

Determinedly, she switched on the stereo to low and let the soothing sounds of soft jazz wash over her as she cleaned up the study. She was still there twenty minutes later when Kat walked in from school looking so glum, Josey had to bite back a smile. No one could look more depressed than a teenager having a fit of the sulks. Without a word, she hustled her into the kitchen and set out some of the chocolate cookies one of her patients had made for her. "Here, maybe this will cheer you up," she said, pulling out a chair at the table and motioning her to sit. "What happened? Have a bad day at school?"

"No, it's Gable. He is the most unreasonable man who ever walked the face of the earth!"

Josey almost groaned. "What's he done now?"

"He said if I want a new dress for the school dance, I either have to buy it in Lordsburg or Silver City." With a snort of disgust, she picked up one of the cookies and bit off a healthy bite. "I may as well stay home," she grumbled, swallowing. "That's probably what he's hoping for, anyway. The only reason he agreed to let me go in the first place is because you tricked him into it."

Josey could have told her that *she* was the one who'd been tricked, but she doubted if Kat would agree with her in her present mood. "The Boutique has a pink dress in the window that you'd look nice in," she said, mentioning Lordsburg's only dress shop. "Of course, Silver City will have a bigger selection but—"

"But I didn't want to look nice!" Kat cried, then blushed crimson when she realized what she'd said. "You know what I mean. I wanted to knock Matt's socks off. And I can't do that with a dress from town or Silver City! Only Tucson carries something like that."

"Tucson! But—"

"Oh, please, Josey, will you talk to Gable?" she begged. "*Plee-ase?* He'll listen to you, I know he will. I'm just a kid, but you're a woman of the world, and you can make him understand how important it is to have the right dress for your first dance."

Josey paled. "Oh, I don't know, Kat—"

"Please? If you don't help me, I'm sunk. I can't wear just any old dress. I need something special and I can only get that in Tucson. Please say you'll talk to Gable."

It was the last thing Josey wanted to do. Couldn't Kat see that she'd already stuck her nose into the Rawlings's family business too much already? Gable wouldn't appreciate her interference in a matter he'd already said no to. "Why don't you talk to him? Tell him what you've just told me and I'm sure he'll understand."

The younger girl's shoulders slumped in defeat. "No, he won't. He doesn't know what it's like to be a seventeen-year-old girl going to your first big dance. You do."

Unfortunately she was right, and Josey couldn't stand to see her so depressed. Knowing she was making a mistake but unable to stop herself, she sighed. "Okay, I'll talk to him. Just don't blame me if he still says no."

With a squeal of delight, the younger girl jumped up to hug her. "I won't. I promise! I knew I could count on you. You're the best!"

But later that evening, after supper when Josey drove up to the Rawlings's Victorian home, she didn't feel like the best. Every instinct she possessed told her to turn around and go home. What was she doing here? She'd spent the past five days trying to put Gable out of her mind, trying to forget the stupid date she'd asked him out on. Bringing up the dance would only remind him of it. Why had she let Kat talk her into this?

Because she *did* remember what it was like to be seventeen and full of dreams and wanting a perfect dress for a dance more than anything else in the world. And she'd promised Kat. Sighing in defeat, she cut the ignition and climbed out of the Jeep. There was no help for it. She might as well get it over with.

"Hey, Josey, how you been? I was just on my way out to go dancing. Come on in." Pushing open the screen, Flynn greeted her with an engaging boyish grin. Dressed in neatly pressed Levi's, a starched Western shirt, his short hair combed and his square jaw freshly shaven, he looked like every young girl's dream and every mother's nightmare—trouble in boots and a cowboy hat, with a twinkle of mischief dancing in his eyes. "You looking for Kat? I think she just went upstairs—"

"Actually I'm here to see Gable," she admitted reluctantly. "But if he's busy, I can talk to him another time. Maybe I should have called first—"

"Don't be ridiculous," he assured her. "He's just catching up on some paperwork in the study. Go on in. It's the last door on the left at the end of the hall."

He motioned her on, giving her no choice but to square her shoulders and knock softly at the study door. But, oh, how she was tempted to call the whole thing off when Gable growled for her to come in. Why hadn't she had the sense to just call him and discuss the matter over the phone instead of meeting with him face to face? Cursing her thundering heart, she pushed open the door and stepped inside.

Expecting Flynn, who had bugged him all during supper to go into town with him and get away from the ranch for a while, Gable looked up with an impatient scowl. If he said one more word about going dancing, he was going to tell him to stuff it. There was only one woman filling his thoughts right now—

And she was standing in the doorway looking as fresh as a spring morning in white cotton pants and a flowered blouse. Pleasure shot through him at the sight of her, rocking him back on his heels, annoying him no end. The past five days had been a blur of activity, one task bleeding into another, until his mind was so numb with exhaustion that he couldn't remember half the work he'd done. But he hadn't been too tired to think of Josey. She'd moved into his head like a squatter grabbing an empty cabin without so much as a by-your-leave, and he couldn't work for thinking of her, couldn't eat without picturing her across the table from him, couldn't sleep for dreaming of her. And now he was conjuring her up with nothing more than his thoughts. Hell!

Dropping his pencil, he leaned back in his chair and surveyed her with shuttered eyes that carefully concealed the heat just the sight of her stirred in him. "I didn't expect to see you tonight. Is something wrong?"

It wasn't the most welcoming beginning, and for two cents, she would have mumbled some excuse about needing to see Kat and escaped upstairs. But she had a promise to keep. "No, not really," she said quietly. "I just need to talk to you for a minute. I hope I'm not disturbing you."

If Gable hadn't been fighting the unwanted desire tugging at him, he might have laughed. *Disturbing him?* She'd been disturbing him from the moment he'd first laid eyes on her. And the passage of time wasn't making it any better. Not that he had any intention of admitting that to her. "Have a seat," he said gruffly, motioning to one of the two chairs angled in front of his desk. "What's up?"

Josey hesitated, hating the insecurities that tugged at her. What was it about this man that could send her confidence nose-diving? She could look an expectant mother in the eye and tell her her drug use was putting her baby at risk; she could hold her own with the chief of staff of Mass General and defend a diagnosis. But she had only to be in the same room with Gable to feel like an inexperienced teenager all aflutter over her first crush. Could he see what he did to her? Hear the ragged pounding of her heart?

"Kat stopped by my place on the way home from school today," she blurted out, sinking down into the chair he'd motioned her to. "She needs a special dress for the dance, something more sophisticated than what she would find in Lordsburg or Silver City. She wanted me to ask you if you'd consider letting her go to Tucson."

"With you?"

The question caught her by surprise. "Actually, we hadn't even discussed that, but yes, if she needed me to go with her, I suppose I could."

After the way he'd ranted and raved just weeks ago about how she unduly influenced Kat, Josey half expected him to nix the idea immediately. Instead he picked up his pencil and ground out a staccato beat on the papers he'd been working on when she walked in. And all the while his steady eyes studied her contemplatively.

Feeling like a bug under a microscope, Josey refused to squirm. "She can't go to the dance in just any old dress, Gable. I know this may not seem like such a big deal to you, but to a young girl like Kat, this is more important than grades, or deciding where to go to college, or having her own phone line. All her friends will be there, dressed to the nines. If Kat's dress isn't as pretty as theirs, she'll die of mortification."

Gable tried to remind himself that he and Kat had already discussed this, but when Josey looked at him with pleading green eyes, all he wanted to do was give in to her. Memories flashed before his eyes, faded with time but still achingly poignant... his father standing firm on a decision until his mother talked to him, asking him to reconsider, gently softening him with nothing more than quiet words and the unspoken messages that spilled from her eyes whenever her glance locked with his. Looking back on his parents' relationship, he wouldn't say his mother had been able to melt his father with nothing more than a tender look, but they'd shared a special love, and the old man had never been able to deny her anything.

Even as Gable told himself he was in no danger of following in his father's footsteps where Josey was concerned, he knew he was in trouble—in more ways than one. After he'd recovered his rustled cattle, he'd posted armed guards all over the ranch to make sure his devious neighbors wouldn't be able to cause any more problems. But the search for the cattle had cost them valuable time that they would never get back, and the roundup was still behind schedule. Making the loan payment on time was going to be iffy. It was not a good time to go to Tucson.

Still, he wanted to find a way for him to take both her and Kat shopping. He was losing it, he thought with a silent groan. Well and truly losing it!

"That's almost three-hundred miles, round trip," he pointed out. "Your car's not in any shape for a trip like that, and you couldn't help drive Kat's if you went in hers."

Josey winced. She hadn't realized it was so far. "Maybe one of your hands—"

"I'm shorthanded as it is, Josey. I couldn't justify taking a man away from the roundup just to act as chauffeur for you and Kat."

"But, Gable, she's already found the kind of dress she wants in a magazine and I can guarantee you she's not going to find it anywhere around here. I know this is a bad time and you're under a lot of pressure right now, but she's going to be so disappointed if she doesn't get to do this. There must be a way..."

When she looked at him that way, he would have moved heaven and earth to please her. Scowling at the thought but helpless to deny it, he growled, "I do have some business there I've been putting off, but if I take you, we'll have to go and come in one day. While you two are shopping, I'll get some things we've been needing for the ranch, then come back and pick you up. It'll be a rushed trip, but we can leave at dawn on Saturday, if you like. That's the only day I can get away."

It was his one and only offer. Take it or leave it. The words weren't spoken aloud, but she heard them nevertheless. Her heart pounding, Josey's eyes locked with his and noted the dare he made no attempt to hide. He was giving in, but there were strings. Why hadn't she realized earlier, when she'd told him she could go with Kat, that there was probably a catch? Three hundred miles to Tucson and back, alone with him in the cab of his truck except for Kat. Just the thought of spending that much time with him stole her breath. Too deep, she thought, fighting the attraction that even now was heating the air between them. She was getting in too deep. But it was too late to back out now. Kat would never forgive her if she turned down her only chance to get a dress in Tucson.

"Then I guess I'll see you bright and early Saturday morning," she said, lifting her chin. "I'll let you get back to work and go tell Kat. She'll be thrilled." The matter settled, she sailed out of his office on legs that were anything but steady. What kind of madness had possessed her to ever agree to spend more time with him when she already found it impossible to sleep nights without dreaming of him?

Gable was asking himself the same thing when he and Kat drove over to Josey's early Saturday morning. The day had dawned fair and clear, the slight breeze that rippled over the buffalo grass fresh with morning dew, holding just a hint of the heat that would come with the longer days of summer. Drawing in the scent of it through the open windows of his truck, Gable found his thoughts skipping ahead to the busy streets and shops of the city, the air there singed with exhaust, asphalt and the noise of too many cars and people. His gut clenched. It went without saying that he didn't like the city. Any city. It was too crowded and hemmed in, the pace too maddening and exhaustive. Whenever he found himself trapped between the towering canyons of downtown buildings, he was always ready to chew nails by the time he was able to escape and head home.

He must have been crazy to let Josey talk him into this, he fumed silently as he pulled up in front of her house. Then she was running down the porch steps and sliding onto the seat beside Kat, and suddenly it was hard to think of anything but how much he wanted her. He hardly glanced at her as he mumbled a good morning and put the truck in gear, but much to his irritation, he knew he could have described what she was wearing right down to a *T*. Jeans, a green camp shirt and white sandals that teasingly exposed her pink painted toenails. With Kat seated between them, she wasn't even within touching distance, but suddenly it wasn't the time spent in the city he was dreading but the long drive over and back with Joscy's mere presence teasing his senses. If Kat hadn't been there, he knew he'd have been hard pressed to find a reason not to reach for her and draw her close, she was driving him that crazy. He could see already it was going to be a long day!

At his side, Kat was so excited, she could hardly sit still. "This is going to be so much fun! When do you think we'll get there, Gable?"

His eyes trained on the road, he retorted, "Ten or so. You'll have plenty of time to shop."

At the shortness of his tone some of the light dancing in Kat's blue eyes faded and was replaced by an attack of conscience. "Can we afford this now?" she asked, guilt stricken. "I know you've got the loan payment to make, but I was so excited about the dance, I didn't even think to ask where the money was coming from for my dress. I just assumed—"

Cursing himself for ruining her fun, Gable held the wheel with one hand and slipped his right arm around her to give her a hug. "The cost of one dress isn't going to make or break us, brat. Quite worrying. You can't count pennies and buy yourself a knockout of a dress. And that's what I want you to have, got it? After all, how many times are you going to be seventeen and going to your first big dance? Considering the circumstances, I think we can afford to splurge a little.''

It was just the right thing to say. With a sigh of relief, Kat grinned widely, returned his hug, and settled down to talk fashion. "All right! Then I just may try on every dress in the mall. Josey, what color do you think would be best for me? A lot of the girls are going with pastels because it's spring, but I think I'd look better in something darker. What do you think?''

Her eyes on the rugged line of Gable's profile, Josey hardly heard her. If she'd been sitting next to him, she would have kissed him. With one word, he could have shot down Kat's excitement and ruined the trip for her, as well as the dance she was so looking forward to. Instead he'd shrugged off the worries that had to be heavy on his shoulders and made the day perfect for her. What was she supposed to do with a man such as that? She had a hard enough time fighting her attraction to him when he was being infuriatingly chauvinistic. How was she supposed to resist him when he was being thoughtful and nice and so incredibly sweet?

"Josey? What do you think?''

She blinked and jerked back to awareness to see that both Kat and Gable were staring at her. Mortified color spilled into her cheeks. "What?''

"What color would be best for me?'' Josey repeated. "I know it's spring, but I think I really look better in dark colors.''

"Oh, blue, I think. Sapphire, like your eyes. Or aqua.''

Pleased that she agreed with her, Kat nodded. "Yeah, that would be perfect. But it's got to be slinky. You can't knock a guy's socks off if you're not slinky."

"As long as you don't knock anything else off," Gable warned dryly. "Like his pants."

Startled, Kat blushed fiery red, then giggled. "I'm going to a dance, not an orgy, Gable. No one's going to strip."

His mouth twitched at her laughter, while over her head, his eyes met Josey's. "Glad to hear it. Everyone keeps their clothes on, no one gets in trouble. Isn't that right, Josey?"

Amused in spite of the hot color still firing her cheeks, she met his gaze unflinchingly. "Right. I presume you practice what you preach?"

If she'd hoped to put him on the spot, she'd failed miserably. He only gave her a crooked grin that taunted and teased and warmed her blood as he lifted one shoulder in a careless shrug. "I never kiss and tell. You'll just have to wait until that night and find out for yourself."

So he hadn't forgotten their date. Josey almost groaned aloud at the thought. That's what she'd been afraid of.

The mall was just opening when Gable dropped them at the entrance to one of the more exclusive department stores and gave Kat two hundred dollars. "Try not to spend it all in one place," he advised with a grin. "I'll meet you back here this afternoon at four. Will that give you enough time?"

"Oh, yes, that'll be great!" Kat assured him, stars shining in her eyes as she clutched her purse to her. "I can't wait to get started!"

"Remember, you're seventeen, not twenty-eight, so get something appropriate."

Too happy to let anything rain on her parade, she only grinned and saluted smartly. "Yes, sir. Any other instructions, sir?"

"Behave yourself, brat." He chuckled, then glanced at Josey. "See you later, Doc. Try to keep her in line, will you?"

He didn't give her a chance to answer, but drove away with a casual wave that did something funny to Josey's stomach. Watching his truck disappear from view, she was stunned by the need to call him back. It wasn't as if he'd dumped her in the middle of nowhere, she told herself sternly. She was back in the city, among people and traffic and noise again, right where she belonged.

She should have felt as though she'd just come home, but when she dragged her eyes back to the mall and followed Kat inside, it wasn't the city or the apartment she'd left behind in Boston that came to mind when she thought of the comfort of familiar surroundings, but her grandparents' place.

Stunned, she almost stopped in her tracks in surprise. When had she begun to think of New Mexico as home? Her stay there was only temporary; she had a life to go back to in the east, a career to get back on track. She didn't know if she would ever be ready to go back to the clinic and all the stress that went with it, but there were other options. Before she'd left Boston, she'd been approached by an old friend from medical school who wanted her to go into partnership with him in Chicago. She liked Jonathan, respected his skills as a physician. They would work well together if she wanted to make the move to Chicago. If not, she could open her own office...maybe in Salem....

But her heart twisted just at the thought of walking away from the unexpected peace she'd found in the desert. Even now, she was only two hours away, and already she missed the wide open spaces, the endless vistas that seemed to change hourly with the passage of the sun in the clear sky, the soothing murmur of the wind.

"Okay, where do you want to start?"

Dragging her out of her musings, Kat was as ecstatic as a kid in a candy store for the first time. She could hardly stand still. Josey couldn't help but laugh at her. "This is your day, sweetie. Lead the way."

That was all the encouragement Kat needed. Her eyes sparkling like diamonds, she was off like a shot, drawn to a shop whose window was filled with a rainbow of prom dresses. "Jeez, Josey, look at these! Aren't they gorgeous? They must cost a fortune." Half afraid to look, she peaked at a price tag and dropped it like a hot coal. "Oops! Too much! Maybe we'd better try somewhere else. Like Wal-Mart. I think we're out of our league."

Josey grinned and gave in to the need to hug her. If Gable could see his sister now, he wouldn't worry about her going wild with his money. She might only be seventeen, but she had a good head on her shoulders. "Not so fast. There's a sales rack in the back. Let's check it out."

A dozen or more frilly dresses were crammed onto the rack, but there was only one that was the color Kat was looking for. The minute she spied a bold splash of blue among the pastel skirts of the more traditional dresses, she reached for it. And promptly fell in love. "Oh, God, this is it!"

It was, Josey had to admit, a beautiful dress. Made of a soft, sapphire blue fabric that flowed like water through Kat's hands, it didn't have a single girlish flower or ruffle to distract from its clean lines. The bodice was fitted, the skirt long and fluid, the kind that would whisper with every step taken. It was more sophisticated than the other prom dresses on the rack and Josey wasn't altogether sure

Gable would approve of it, but it was the kind of garment that would look gorgeous on Kat's tall, slender figure.

"Go try it on," she encouraged. "It's perfect for you."

"But how much—"

Josey didn't give her a chance to look at the price tag, but took the dress from her and pushed her gently toward the dressing rooms at the rear of the store. "It doesn't cost a penny to try it on."

"But Gable only gave me two hundred—"

"Right now, we're not buying, just looking. Go!"

Kat went, but only because she couldn't deny herself the chance to try on something so beautiful. Within less than two minutes, she stood in the small cubicle in the dressing room and watched in the mirror as Josey zipped up the back of the dress for her. It fit like a glove.

"Oh, wow!"

Standing behind her, Josey smiled at her in the mirror. "You wanted a dress to knock Matt out of his shoes. You just found it."

Entranced, Kat fingered the silky material as if it was something out of a dream. "It's even slinky. I can't believe it—the very first dress I try on, and it's perfect! How much is it?"

The moment of truth had come. Holding her breath, Josey reached for the tag attached to the back of the bodice and turned it over. Surprised, she laughed. "One eighty-nine! I would have sworn it was twice that much. Sweetie, you're getting this dress!"

"You bet I am," she began, only to stop when she remembered the two hundred Gable gave her was all she had. The smile lighting her face sank like the *Titanic*. "I forgot about tax. And shoes. How can I get shoes if I spend all my money on a dress?"

Disappointment was already clouding her eyes, but Josey had no intention of letting her give up so easily. "You still baby-sit occasionally on the weekends, don't you? Well then, I'll just loan you the extra you need and you can pay me back later."

Kat stared longingly at herself in the mirror, then finally shook her head. "I don't think Gable would approve."

"Then consider it part of my graduation present to you. I probably won't be here in May, so I'll give it to you now. No problem, okay?"

It was the perfect solution, one Kat couldn't resist. Whirling, she gave Josey a fierce hug. "If I could have had an older sister, I would have wanted her to be just like you." As quick as a cat, she whirled again, presenting her back so she could be unzipped. "I feel just like Cinderella getting ready for the ball. Now all we've got to do is find some glass slippers."

The afternoon flew by. The worry of choosing a dress out of the way, they quickly found a pair of dainty high-heeled sandals to complete the outfit, then set out to enjoy themselves. Josey, like Kat, had never had a sister to go shopping with, and together they had a ball. They must have tried on a dozen different dresses just for the fun of it, then, on a dare, Josey agreed to have a complete make-over at one of the mall's exclusive salons, but only if Kat would, too, at her treat. By the time they met Gable at the entrance where he'd dropped them off hours earlier, they both looked like different women.

Restlessly pacing the sidewalk, waiting for them, Gable heard their shared laughter as they walked out of the mall, but when he turned to face them, he found himself confronting two strangers. Two *beautiful* strangers who had the voice of his sister and the woman whose memory had dogged his footsteps all day long. His mind going blank at the sight of them, he simply stared.

Kat giggled, her eyes dancing. "Well, don't just stand there. Say something . . . like how gorgeous we are."

At her side, Josey felt the touch of his hot gaze as if he'd physically reached out and touched her. Her heart skipped a beat, then took up a ragged rhythm that seemed to echo loudly in her ears. "I think he's in shock," she told Kat. "Maybe he doesn't like what he sees."

Oh, he liked it, all right, he thought, unable to drag his gaze away from her long enough to give his sister more than a cursory glance. Too much. If ever he'd had any doubts as to whether he'd misjudged the type of woman Josey O'Brian was, he had his answer now. Never had the differences between them been more apparent. From the top of her elegantly styled curls to the soles of the new, fragile-looking sandals she wore on her feet, she was a lady who would look right at home in New York, Boston, Paris.

Try as she might, though, she would never fit into the harsh, lonely existence of the desert. Her skin was too soft, too delicate for the gritty, hot air that never seemed to stop blowing. The sun would make her old before her time, and the land, unforgiving in its barrenness, would break her spirit. She could wear jeans, even a hat, but changing her clothes couldn't change what she was—a city woman who didn't belong.

But still, he wanted her.

"Earth to Gable." Kat laughed, waving her hand in his face. "Say something!"

"You're beautiful," he growled roughly, jerking back to attention and taking the packages they both held. "Both of you. But you don't need me to tell you that. I'm sure you had every guy you saw drooling over you."

Kat grinned, delighted. "Yeah, we did. It was great!"

Gable only grunted. "I presume you got a dress?"

The male attention they had gotten forgotten, Kat fairly glowed. "Oh, yes! It's awesome! Wait'll you see it, Gable. He's going to love it, isn't he, Josey?"

Josey nodded, unable to manage a word. He'd said she was beautiful, she thought, dazed by the unexpected pleasure that shot through her. Granted, Kat had practically pulled the words out of him, but she didn't need to hear the words to recognize the desire she'd seen flare in his eyes at the sight of her. The heat of that look alone left her throat as dry as the desert.

"Good," he said shortly. "Then it wasn't a wasted trip." His expression once again shuttered, he turned away, avoiding Josey's eyes. "I'm glad you had a good time, but we'd better get going. We've got a long drive ahead of us and I want to stop somewhere and get something to eat. I'm starving."

Moving like someone had lit a fire under him, he hurried them to the truck, carefully piled their packages in the space behind the seat, and started out for home just as soon as they were all buckled in. Stopping only long enough to get gas and a hamburger at McDonald's, they were soon racing east on Interstate 10 toward the rapidly approaching darkness of the night.

For a while, Kat chattered like a magpie, so excited she could hardly sit still. But the exhilaration of the day and the steady hum of the tires on the highway finally caught up with her, and before they were fifty miles outside of Tucson, she was asleep.

In the gathering darkness, the ensuing silence stretched between Gable and Josey like the highway that raced ahead of the reaching headlights of the truck. Sure that he could hear the wild hammering of her heart, Josey was just searching for a way to break the screaming quiet when he did it for her.

"Obviously, Kat enjoyed herself," he said softly, the glow from the dash lights carving the angles and planes of his hard face in deepening shadows. "How about you? Or do I even have to ask? After being out in the sticks for the past six weeks, you were probably thrilled to get back to the hustle and bustle of the city."

His tone, by the time he finished, was jeering, casting disparagement not only on city life in general but anyone who was crazy enough to seek it out. Angled against the door, Kat slumped between them, Josey fought the need to tell him the truth—the energy of the city that she had once thrived on had worn her to a frazzle and she couldn't wait to get back to her own little ten acres in the desert. But he would never believe her, and maybe that was for the best.

"It was good to get back to civilization," she said stiffly. "I hadn't realized how much I had missed just the every-day things I used to take for granted—like bookstores and malls and fast-food restaurants being right around the corner. When I go back to Boston, I'll never take Mc-Donald's for granted again."

The sudden sharpening of his gaze told her he'd gotten the point. She would eventually go home where she belonged. What else was there left to say? Both lost in their own thoughts, they rode the rest of the way home in silence.

Chapter 8

"Watch out, Flynn! Dammit, get out of the way before you get yourself gored!"

At Gable's sudden warning yell, Flynn spurred his horse and just barely sprinted out of the way of the enraged bull that bore down on him and his mount with murder in his eyes. Swearing, he pulled his favorite mare to a stop a safe distance away and glared at the animal with acute dislike. "Damn jerky on the hoof, you mess with me and I swear to God you'll be in the next trailer to the slaughterhouse!"

"That's it, Flynn," Cooper chuckled, "threaten him good. Nothing like a good scolding to straighten up a dumb bull crazy on locoweed."

"Well, it's better than shooting him, which is what I'd like to do," he tossed back angrily. "He almost got me!"

In no mood for any of their bickering, Gable scowled at the both of them. "Save it for later," he ordered, struggling to control his own mount, who was understandably nervous around the unpredictable cattle milling around the north springs. "We've got work to do."

His face set in harsh lines, he eyed the destruction around them and swore in disgust. Fences were down as far as the eye could see, knocked sideways and crooked by cattle so drugged out on locoweed they couldn't see straight. Dammit to hell, where had they gotten it?

Even as he asked the question, he knew the answer. The neighbors plotting to get their hands on the Rawlings's springs.

He should have known something like this was coming, he thought furiously. Ever since he'd got back from Tucson almost a week ago, things had gone too smoothly. There were no more interruptions, no problems, and the roundup had proceded as planned, without a single hitch in the works to slow things down. That alone should have made him suspicious, but he'd been so intent on making up for lost time that he hadn't given his enemies a second thought, other than to keep guards posted around the growing yearling herd in the holding pasture.

But his enemies had been too clever to strike at the obvious. Not content with the problems they'd already caused, the bastards had come up with a new method to hit the ranch—attack it from the inside out. Under cover of darkness, they'd slipped into the pastures furthest from the house and scattered locoweed in strategic places near the springs, then slithered back out like the snakes they were. During the night, the cattle had stumbled across it, eaten the weed, and consequently done enough damage in their crazed state to once again grind all work on the roundup to a halt. He'd be damned if he'd let them get away with it.

"Flynn, take a crew and start working on the downed fences," he said as he dismounted. "Cooper, divide up the rest of the men and send them out to search the other pastures. We'll have to check them all—I wouldn't put it past the bastards to contaminate every inch of land we've got. While they're doing that, I'll go over this end of the pasture, you can start on the northern end. As soon as we finish here, we can start on the other downed fences."

"What about the springs?" Cooper asked as Flynn rode off with a group of men. "If they put it in the water, we're going to have a hell of a mess on our hands."

That was a nightmare Gable didn't even want to think about. Scowling at the clear water that flowed in a bubbling stream through the copse of cottonwoods that shaded the western side of the pasture, he couldn't imagine anyone deliberately poisoning something so pure.

"It's the springs they're after," Gable said flatly. "They wouldn't be stupid enough to ruin them before they even got their hands on them."

Cooper only shrugged, not completely convinced. "I don't think the greedy S.O.B.'s are playing with a full deck anyway, but you're probably right. Just the same, I'm going to check around and make sure nothing got in the water. At this point, we can't be too sure of anything."

"Whatever you do, watch your back," Gable called after him as he cantered away. "These dang-blame cows are crazy as bedbugs right now. Be careful!"

Cooper only shot him a chiding look that told him he didn't need the warning, but Gable wasn't taking any chances. Even under normal conditions, cattle could, without the least provocation, be as skittish as old maids around a lecher. With locoweed in their guts, they were downright dangerous and as unpredictable as hell. He'd already lost cowboys he couldn't replace. He couldn't afford to lose any more.

Keeping one eye on the cattle that were watching him just as warily as he was them, he searched the ground near the springs but found the weed carelessly scattered a short distance away. Cramming it into the plastic bag he'd tied to his saddlehorn when he'd left the house, he swore grimly and moved on through the brush, slowly making his way toward Cooper in the distance, who had already relayed orders to the rest of the men and was searching as diligently as he.

It was tedious work, the kind that required little brain power. The gurgle of the springs called to him, drawing his gaze. Clear and green, the water was the exact shade of Josey's eyes when she'd stepped out of the mall in Tucson and nearly bowled him over.

Stiffening at the thought, he swore and tried to push her out of his head, but it was too late. He hadn't seen her in six days. Six *long* days. But he could remember every detail of what she'd been wearing, right down to the color of her lipstick. And the expensive scents she and Kat had tested at the perfume counter had filled the cab of his truck for days. He hadn't been able to draw in a deep breath without thinking of her, aching for her. Which was why he'd been avoiding her ever since.

But with every passing day, his conscience reminded him that he couldn't avoid her forever. They had a date tomorrow night.

"Gable! Watch out—"

At Cooper's yell of warning, he jerked his head up...just in time to see a crazed cow running right at him with murder in her eyes. "What the—" Swearing, he scrambled to get away, diving for cover, but there wasn't any. Hot, bovine breath struck him. His heart in his throat, he tried to throw himself out of the way, but in the next instant, one of the animal's sharp horns sliced along his ribs. "Aa-argh!"

"Damn, she got you!" Racing toward him hell-bent for leather, Cooper tumbled from his horse the minute he reached him, while the other hands scurried to subdue the frenzied cow. "Are you okay? Let me see."

Hissing a string of unprintable oaths through his clenched teeth, Gable fiercely bound his arms around his ribs in a vain effort to get a handle on the searing white-hot pain. "I'm fine," he finally managed to grit out. "It's just a scratch."

"The hell it is," Cooper growled right back, dropping to his knees in the dirt beside him. "That ain't grape juice squeezing between your fingers. Let's take a look at you and see how much damage she did."

"It's nothing serious," Gable insisted harshly. "It can't be. I don't have time to be laid up now. There's too much to do."

Flynn came riding up at that moment, his face pale, his hair practically standing on end from his wild ride from the far end of the pasture. "Is he okay?" he demanded of Cooper as he threw himself from his horse. "I saw the whole thing but was too far away to warn him. Where's he hurt?"

"My side," Gable growled, cutting off Cooper before he could so much as open his mouth. "And it's no big deal. Clean it up and slap a bandage on it, and I'll be right as rain in no time." The words were hardly out of his mouth when the sticky blood he'd been trying to hide oozed between his fingers and ran down his side.

Cooper didn't wait to see more. Whipping off his own shirt, he wrapped it tightly around Gable's ribs and used the arms to tie it in place. "Help me get him to the truck, Flynn. I'm taking him to Josey."

"The hell you are—"

"You take the left, I'll take the right," Flynn said, ignoring him as he moved into position to help Cooper get him to his feet. "The doc'll fix him up in no time. Thank God she's here. I sure wouldn't want to drive all the way to Silver City with him bleeding like a stuck pig."

"I am *not* going to Josey O'Brian's," Gable stated flatly, infuriated at being ignored. "There's no need to bother the woman for something so trivial."

"Maybe not," Cooper agreed with a wicked grin. "But you're going, anyway. And don't give me that go-to-hell look. You've been as touchy as a peeled rattler ever since you made the trip to Tucson, and unless I miss my guess, you've got woman problems, son. And the only woman you've spent any time with lately is the doc, so she must be the one. It'll do you good to see her. Maybe she can fix up your disposition as well as your side."

"Dammit, Cooper, I'm warning you—"

"Go ahead and warn all you like," he retorted with a chuckle. "In case you haven't noticed, you're not in any shape to throw your weight around. Ready, Flynn? Good, let's go." And without another word, they hefted him to his feet and helped him to the pickup.

Josey was relaxing on the sleeping porch at the back of the house when the doorbell rang. Hurrying to the front door, she pulled it open. "I'm sorry. I was in the back," she began, only to pale at the sight of a bare-chested Cooper supporting Gable, who was as ashen as his blood-splattered shirt yet still somehow managed to glare at her defiantly.

Fear clutching her heart, her first instinct was to reach for him. *Dear God, he was hurt!* But her years of training were already stiffening her spine. All business, she jerked the door open wide and motioned them inside. "Take him through to the kitchen, Cooper, so I can clean him up. How much blood has he lost?"

"I can speak for myself," Gable said harshly, wincing as Cooper eased him down the hall and through the narrow kitchen doorway, lowering him into a chair. "I'm not going to bleed to death, if that's what you're worried about. I probably just need a few stitches."

"A locoed cow got him," Cooper informed Josey as she quickly went to work untying his shirt from around Gable's ribs. "Nicked him with her horn before he could get out of the way. When I saw how bad he was bleeding, I figured you needed to take a look at him."

"He and Flynn are as fussy as a pair of old women," Gable snapped. "You'd think they'd never seen a little blood before."

Hovering over him, Josey pulled away the makeshift bandage to reveal Gable's shirt underneath. It had an eight-inch rip in it and was dark red with his blood. Appalled, Josey tried not to think about what other damage the cow could have done if it had set its mind to it, and glanced up at Cooper. "You were right to bring him here. This is a nasty wound."

"That's what I figured," the younger man said. "Well, now that he's in good hands, I'll leave him to you. I've got to get back to the roundup."

"Get back?" Gable sputtered in surprise. "How the hell am I supposed to get home? Dammit, Cooper, come back here!"

"See you later, big brother." Cooper laughed, giving him a mocking wave. "Maybe if you're real nice to the doc, she'll give you a ride back to the house."

Her head bent, the cloud of her hair falling forward to hide her ashen cheeks, Josey stared down at the gaping wound and felt a trembling deep inside that shook her to the core. Get a grip! she told herself, horrified. He was just another patient and she had a job to do. But when her fingers reached out for the buttons of his shirt, they were anything but steady. If the cow had struck him a little lower, it could have ripped his gut wide open.

Suddenly desperate to get her hands on him and assure herself that he was all right, she tugged at his shirt. "Let's get this off so I can get a look at you."

Her voice was soft and smoky, like something out of one of Gable's dreams. He swallowed, intending to tell her that he certainly didn't need her help to get out of his shirt. She was close, so close he could have buried his fingers in her hair simply by lifting his hand, the fresh tantalizing scent of her filling his lungs with every breath he took, quietly driving him crazy. Suddenly, the rip in his side wasn't nearly as painful as the one in his groin. Muttering a silent curse, he clamped his teeth together and curled his fingers into fists. He would get through this, he promised himself fiercely, without touching her.

But he hadn't counted on the effect her hands would have on him. Her fingers skimmed over him, gently easing the shirt from his shoulders and slipping it down his arms, trailing liquid fire in their wake. Groaning, he closed his eyes.

She froze immediately. "Are you okay?"

Bare-chested, feeling as though his jeans were a size too small and the air he dragged into his lungs too thin, he nodded, tight-lipped. "Just get on with it."

"I'll try not to hurt you," she said huskily, "but I've got to clean it before I can do anything, and that's not going to be a picnic. It looks pretty nasty."

"I'm not going to faint from a little pain," he assured her, then braced himself when her hands moved to the bloody mess at his side.

She couldn't have been gentler as she cleaned and probed the wound, but it hurt nevertheless. A muscle ticking along his granite jaw, Gable squeezed his eyes shut again and sucked in a sharp breath, welcoming the pain, all his concentration focused on the burning heat that throbbed with every graze of her fingers. For a few moments, at least, it took his mind off the heat burning lower down.

"I'm going to give you a shot for the pain," she said at last, "then stitch it up. When was the last time you had a tetanus shot?"

"Six months ago."

"Good, then you should be okay there." While she was talking, she prepared the shot and smoothly injected it, then knelt awkwardly at his side. At his look of surprise, she explained, "I don't have an examining table for you to lay down on, and I can't do this bent over at the waist. This way I'm at eye level with the wound." Carefully testing the jagged tear, she asked, "Can you feel that?"

"Just the pressure of your touch. It's sort of numb." He only wished some of his other body parts were.

She nodded, satisfied, and edged closer. "If you start to feel any pain at all, just tell me. Hold still."

And with that, she began. Unable to tear his eyes away from her, Gable watched her every movement. Wearing green shorts and a white shirt tied at the waist, her hair now pulled back into a ponytail, she looked like a teenager instead of a doctor, but her hands were sure and competent. If she was aware of his gaze upon her, or the fact that she was leaning against his outer thigh, she gave no sign of it. But Gable was. Soft and warm and beauti-

ful, she couldn't take a breath without his eyes drifting to
the gentle rise of her breasts.

Time slipped away and it could have been only minutes, or an hour later when she finished with her handi-
work. "There," she said in satisfaction. "Now I'll just put
a bandage on that and I'm all through." Rising gracefully
to her feet, she retrieved a bandage and a roll of white
gauze from the supplies she'd hastily brought in from her
study. "Normally, a bandage would be enough," she said
as she returned to his side, "but I know you're not going
to let this keep you away from the roundup, so I might as
well wrap you up tight. Stand up and lift your arms."

It was a simple request, her intentions clear. But the
minute he came to his feet, bringing his chest within scant
inches of hers, nothing was quite as simple as either of
them would have liked. Her eyes lifted to his, their heated
depths telling him more loudly than words that the no-
nonsense, professional manner she'd cloaked herself in
from the first moment she'd touched him was nothing but
a front. She wasn't aware of him as just a patient, but as a
man. A man she wanted, whether she would admit it or
not. Like candle wax tossed into the fires of hell, his good
intentions went up in a cloud of smoke. He reached for
her. "Josey..."

Her arms slipped around him, but only to wrap the
gauze around his rib cage, securing the bandage she'd
placed over the wound more firmly in place. His heart
jackhammering, Gable might have been disappointed if he
hadn't felt the trembling of her fingers. Settling his own
hands at her slender waist, he drew her imperceptibly
closer. "Josey—"

"You really should take it easy the rest of the day," she
cut in breathlessly, her eyes studiously trained on the gauze

as she cut and taped the end of it. "You had a close call...lost a lot of blood..."

"Josey...honey, look at me."

Her heart skipped a beat at the roughly growled endearment, and fingers that had only seconds before been sure and confident couldn't seem to hold on to anything. The tape clattered to the floor, the gauze soundlessly following it. Muttering at her clumsiness, she started to bend down to retrieve them.

But Gable had no intention of letting her put so much as another inch of space between them. His hands moved from her waist to her shoulders, drawing her back up. "Leave it," he ordered thickly, and in the next instant, she was in his arms, his mouth hot on hers.

Her head spinning, her heart thundering, Josey swayed against him even as a warning voice reminded her that he was a patient and her behavior was hardly professional. He'd been hurt; she should stop this nonsense at once and take him home.

But her arms, instead of pushing him away, slid slowly up his bare chest to circle the strong column of his neck and hold him tight. Forever. It seemed like forever since he'd held her, kissed her. Yet it had only been days...days in which the need he stirred in her so easily had been building like the gathering winds of a hurricane. And all that time, she'd been waiting, just waiting, for him to pull her into his arms again. Murmuring his name, she crowded closer, unable to get enough of the taste of him.

Gable told himself later that if she'd pushed him away then, he would have let her go. But his name on her lips, a whisper of confused longing, completely undid him. Something twisted in his heart, something he vaguely recognized as tenderness, and just that quickly, the nature of the kiss changed. Leaning back against a corner of the

kitchen table, he pulled her between his spread legs and
slowed the kiss, taking it deeper with nothing more than
the stroke of his tongue, while his hands took a leisurely
journey over her, gentling her, pleasuring her, blindly
committing the flare of her hips, the smallness of her
waist, the soft fullness of her breasts to memory.

Time. Without saying a word, he told her they had all
the time in the world to explore the desire that burned like
wildfire in their blood. There were no ranch hands or
family to interrupt, no anger to fight through. It was just
the two of them, alone, together, giving in to a desire they
could no longer fight. Why had it taken them so long?

"God, lady, do you know what you do to me?"

Wrenching his mouth from hers, his breathing as rough
as hers in the absolute stillness that surrounded them, he
buried his lips against her neck, nuzzling her, and felt a
shiver slide down her spine. His hands tightened reflex-
ively, as if afraid she'd slip away before he could stop her,
just as she had in his dreams. How many nights over the
past few weeks had he awakened to find her gone and fire
raging in his blood? Dammit, he wouldn't let her go. Not
now, not when he finally had her where he wanted her.

Battling the urgency pulling at him, he nipped at her
earlobe, stroked it with his tongue, then abandoned it to
press hot, hungry kisses over her face, her eyes, the stubborn jut of her chin, the sensitive corner of her mouth. But
it wasn't enough. From the moment he'd first laid eyes on
her, some secret part of him had known that nothing short
of all of her would ever be enough for him. And he'd been
fighting it ever since. What a fool he'd been! Covering her
mouth with his, he gave her a hard, thorough, possessive
kiss while the fire in his blood turned impossibly hotter.

Boneless, pliant, her muscles melting one by one, Josey
gasped and clung to him, her breath hitching in her throat.

Somewhere deep inside her, a warning bell clanged loudly, but she couldn't be distracted by it now. She wanted him, his touch, his taste, all of him, she who had never let any man get past the solid barriers that protected her vulnerable heart. Her senses swimming, she struggled with the conflicting urge to laugh, to run, to draw him down to the floor with her and never let go. When he finally let her up for air, she could only hang on to him for dear life, her senses swimming and knees weak as she whispered huskily, "Oh, Gable, I want..."

"I know, honey," he laughed shakily, his arms tightening around her as he tried to hang on to some semblance of sanity. "I want you, too. But if we don't cool down some, I'm going to take you right here on this damn table. And let me tell you, it's damned uncomfortable." Burying his hands up to his wrists in her hair, he tilted her face back up to his. "And that's not what I want for either us. I've dreamed of making it long and slow and hot for you and I can't do that here." Leaning down, he pressed a sweet, tempting, teasing kiss to her mouth, then spoke against her lips. "Where's your room?"

Dazed, a pulse hammering in her throat, her body positively burning for his, she wanted to drown in the hot passion in his eyes and let him take her wherever he wanted. But old insecurities rose up, reminding her that she wasn't what he thought she was—an experienced woman of the world. She could patch him up, bind his wounds, save his life if he needed her to, but she didn't know if she could give him pleasure in bed. And it was only fair that she warn him. Swallowing to ease the sudden dryness in her throat, she tried to find the words. "Gable..."

His mouth wandered to her jaw and then down her throat. "Hmm?"

Helplessly, she tilted her head back. "I—I might not be very g-good at . . . this."

Caught up in the taste of her, he laughed softly. "Are you kidding? You've got me hotter than a two dollar pistol." Nudging aside the collar of her blouse, he started to trace the delicate line of her collar bone with his tongue. "Where's your room, sweetheart? Tell me."

She wanted to. God, how she wanted to! But not yet. "Gable . . . I'm not what you think I am."

The desperation thickening her voice reached him then. Lifting his head, his dark brows snapped together in a frown. If he hadn't known better, he would have sworn her green eyes were dark with fear, which was ridiculous. She had no reason to fear him. "Are you trying to tell me you're not a doctor? Because if you are, I won't believe you. I've seen you in action, lady, and you know what you're doing."

If she could have found the least thing humorous about the situation, she would have laughed. But there was nothing funny about what she had to tell him. "Of course I'm a doctor. It's not that. I—I just thought you should know I'm not that . . . experienced."

There. She'd said it. She should have been relieved, but he didn't make it easy for her. His narrowed eyes studying her as if he could see into her soul, he asked suspiciously, "What do you mean, not *that* experienced? How many lovers have you had? One? two? Less than five?"

Heat flew into her cheeks but she didn't look away. Dragging in a bracing breath, one corner of her mouth curled in a half smile that wasn't quite steady. "How about none of the above?"

None of the above. She was telling him she was a virgin. Shock ripped through him, along with the memory of the stunned passion that clouded her eyes every time he kissed her, as if she were surprised by her body's response to him. He'd known, he thought, shaken. Somewhere deep inside, he'd sensed her innocence, her vulnerability, but he hadn't wanted to believe it. Now she gave him no choice.

His hands dropped from her as if the touch of her skin suddenly burned him. "Why?"

The sudden loss of his touch hurt, but she would have bitten off her tongue before telling him so. Squaring her shoulders, she shrugged, all the while silently praying that he couldn't see how badly she needed him to hold her. "Because there were always other things more important than sex—school, getting my degree, keeping the clinic open. I haven't had the time or energy for anything else."

She reeled off the excuses as if she'd gone over them many times in her head, but there were shadows in her eyes, old hurts that had him studying her with a frown. "Those are reasons for avoiding a commitment, honey, not involvement. Are the men in Boston blind or what? You're a beautiful woman. There must have been someone."

"No—"

She started to turn away, but he stopped her simply by taking her hands, drawing her back to face him. At the pain he saw there, his fingers tightened around hers. "Josey? What is it? Why do I get the feeling you're leaving something out?"

He was probing too much, worrying a wound that hadn't healed and probably never would. Tugging her hands free before he could stop her, this time she managed to turn and step away from him. Suddenly cold, she hugged herself, but it didn't help. "I didn't say I didn't have chances. I just wasn't interested."

"Why?"

She hadn't meant to tell him, would have sworn that she couldn't. But the words just spilled out. "I was afraid."

"Afraid?" he echoed, startled. Whatever he'd expected her to say, it wasn't that. He couldn't picture her being afraid of anything. "Of what?"

"Of being like my mother." Tears blurred her eyes, threatening to spill over as she faced him. "Of falling for a man who's looking for Suzie Homemaker and wanting to please him so badly that I'd take cooking lessons even though I hate to cook. Of needing someone so much that I'd become whatever he wanted me to be, do whatever he wanted me to do, rather than risk losing him."

The memories surged out of her, painting a picture for him of a childhood that must have been confusing and painful and turbulent, of a mother who was so insecure she changed the color of her hair, the style of her clothes, everything... to suit the man in her life. A dozen times Gable wanted to haul her close and stop the words, but the hurt had been building in her for a long time and she needed to get it out. So he did what she needed him to do... he listened. And hurt for her.

At last, she drew in a shuddering breath and raised her chin. "So now you know. I didn't mean to bore you with my life story, but maybe it's best if there are no surprises between us."

Still reeling, Gable could only stare at her. No surprises? She'd been nothing but one surprise after another since he'd met her. If she'd been the women's libber he thought her, the sophisticated city woman who only needed a man for one thing, he could have handled her easily. But she was so much more complicated than that. Now he knew that when she stood toe-to-toe with him defending her rights, she was fighting not only him, but the childhood that had molded her. And when she kissed him and turned so sweet and giving in his arms, a part of her was still struggling with that same childhood and the fear she couldn't let go of, the fear that had kept her from giving herself to a man—*any* man—all these years.

"This changes everything."

He spoke half to himself and looked up to see her eyes flash, her fury swift and indignant. "If you think I told you because I expect something in exchange before I...give myself to you," she sputtered for lack of a better phrase, "then you can think again. I'm not looking for a commitment and neither are you. My virginity isn't for sale."

He laughed and reached for her again, hugging her. "Don't start spitting at me like a wildcat. I never thought it was." No, she wasn't the type of woman to play those types of games. When she gave herself to a man, she'd do it heart and soul. And that was something he had to think about long and hard. A man didn't rush into a relationship like that without knowing where he was headed.

Giving her a swift, hard kiss, he deliberately put her away from him. "I need to get back to the roundup," he said, changing the subject. "Can you give me a lift?"

She almost told him no. He had no business going back to work after she'd just put twenty stitches in his side. And she wasn't taking him anywhere until she knew where she stood with him. But he hadn't asked again where her bedroom was, and she was horribly afraid she already knew. He wanted nothing to do with a virgin. Turning away, she blinked back tears. "Yes, of course. Let me get my purse."

She never knew how many times she dreamed of him that night, but when she woke up at dawn the next morning, she was aching for him. It was going to be a long day. She had hours to get through before she was supposed to pick him up for their date that evening.

Not for the first time, she asked herself why she hadn't just broken it off while she had the chance. He'd been quiet on the way back to the roundup and had made no attempt to touch her. She should have told him then that going out with him wasn't a smart move, and he probably would have agreed. But the words had stuck in her throat.

Because she was falling in love with him.

It came to her like a streak of lightning in the night sky, lighting up all the dark corners of her soul. Stunned, she clutched her pillow to her madly thumping heart. "No!" Her face ashen, she squeezed her eyes shut, closing out the images swirling in her head...her mother—no, it was *her!*—headed for a doomed relationship. Throwing back the covers, she reached for her clothes. She had to find something to do so she would be too busy to think, too busy to hurt.

Like a woman possessed, she threw herself into cleaning the house, and by seven-thirty, she had already scoured the kitchen from top to bottom, then moved on to the bathroom. She was draped over the claw-foot tub and up to her elbows in soapsuds, scrubbing it for all it was worth, when the phone rang.

She would have welcomed a medical emergency just then, anything to fill the long hours of the day that stretched before her, but it was only Kat. "I didn't wake you, did I?"

Sitting for what seemed like the first time in hours, Josey smiled tiredly. "No, of course not. I've been up since dawn. What do you need, sweetie?"

"Actually, I was wondering if you'd come over this afternoon and help me get ready for the dance," she said hopefully. "You could bring your stuff and get ready for your date with Gable at the same time. It'll be fun."

Josey paled, her heart jerking in her breast. "Oh, Kat, I don't know. I have a lot to do—"

"Oh, please don't say no! I've just got to look drop-dead gorgeous for Matt tonight, and I'm not sure I can pull it off by myself. *Plee-ase*, Josey? I don't have anyone here to help me but the guys, and they only grunt and shrug when I ask their opinion about my hair or makeup. Please, I need you."

If it had been anyone else but Kat, she would have turned her down flat. But Kat was . . . Kat, the little sister she'd never had. Her resolves tumbling, reluctant amusement curled her mouth. "Did anyone ever tell you you're a brat, Kat Rawlings? One of these days you're going to meet someone who's not going to let you have your way and it's really going to shake you up. What time did you plan to start getting ready?"

"Four," she replied with a laugh. "Matt's picking me up at six-fifteen."

"Okay." She sighed, giving in. "I'll see you then."

Chapter 9

"Oh, Josey, I'm so glad you're here!" Pushing open the screen door, Kat hurriedly dragged her inside. "I've got a million things to do and I just don't see how I'm going to find the time to get them all done. And I'm so nervous—does it show? I swear I've chewed my fingernails right down to the quick. And my hair, God, Josey, look at my hair! We've only got two hours to make me beautiful for tonight, and I look like the bride of Frankenstein! What am I going to do?"

Josey laughed, her own doubts about the evening pushed aside by Kat's. "First of all, you're going to calm down. Have you had anything to eat today?"

"Eat?" she echoed in a tone that suggested Josey had just asked her if she'd walked on the moon yet. "Who can think about food at a time like this?"

Shooting her a reproachful look, Josey carefully laid her dress out on the couch, set down her makeup bag, and headed for the kitchen. Making herself right at home, she slapped together a sandwich for Kat, then poured her a glass of milk. "Eat," she instructed sternly. "You're not going to be a fun date if you pass out on Matt on the dance floor. Where's your dress? Does it need to be pressed?"

Her mouth full, Kat nodded and forced down another bite. "It must have gotten wrinkled on the way home from Tucson. I was afraid I'd scorch it if I ironed it myself. It's upstairs in my closet."

"I'll get it while you finish eating. And make sure you finish every drop of that milk."

Grinning, Kat reached for the glass. "Whatever you say, Doc."

When Josey came back into the kitchen with the blue dress cradled in her arms, Kat had already set up the ironing board for her and adjusted the iron to delicate. Dutifully following orders, she finished the last of her sandwich and milk as Josey carefully ran the iron over the whisper-soft material of the skirt.

"I still can't believe I found such a knockout of a dress!" Kat said excitedly as she moved to the sink with her dirty dishes. "Matt's going to drop his teeth when he sees me in it!"

"I hope not," Josey chuckled. "But he might be struck dumb. You do look gorgeous in it."

"I know." Her eyes dancing, Kat grinned and reached for the handle to the faucet to rinse out her glass. But when she turned it to cold, only a thin stream of water dribbled from the spout. An instant later, it slowly trickled to a stop. "Oh, no!"

Lifting the iron from the dress, Josey looked up from her task to find Kat staring in growing consternation at the faucet. "What's the matter?"

"There's no water."

"What?" Frowning, Josey set the iron down at one end of the ironing board, well away from the hem of Kat's dress. "Try the hot," she suggested.

But when Kat gave the handle for the hot water a twist, the result was the same. There was no water, at least in the kitchen. Eyes wide with growing panic, she turned back to Josey. "I can't believe this! We don't have any water!"

"Maybe there's just something wrong with this faucet," Josey said, trying to calm her down before she completely freaked out. "Check the bathroom upstairs. While you're doing that, I'll check the fuse box. Where is it? You might have blown the fuse to the well pump."

Kat was already heading for the stairs. "It's in the pantry," she called over her shoulder. "On the left side at the back. You can't miss it."

Taking only a moment to hang up Kat's dress, Josey hurried to the walk-in pantry next to the refrigerator and switched on the overhead light. Spices, staples and canned goods crowded the shelves, partially hiding the fuse box, which was right where Kat had said it would be. Pushing a can of shortening out of the way, Josey stood on tiptoe to study the neatly labeled fuses. The one for the well pump was intact and appeared perfectly normal.

"Well, it's not the fuse," she said, hearing a step behind her in the kitchen. "Did you have any luck upstairs?"

"I haven't been up there," Gable replied, "but if Kat's up there testing the pipes for water, she's not going to find any."

Startled, Josey whirled to find him standing just behind her in the middle of the kitchen. Cooper and Flynn had followed him inside, but she had eyes only for Gable. After his injury yesterday, she knew he had to be sore today, but he obviously hadn't let that slow him down. His boots and jeans were dusty, his hands dirty, the cuffs of his Western shirt rolled back out of the way to his forearms, his hat pushed back from his sweaty brow. Unable to stop herself from taking in every inch of him, she let her gaze roam upward to his weathered face, the granite jaw, the sensuous line of his mouth…and the cold fury burning in his blue eyes.

His words finally registering, her glance pushed past him to his brothers, who were just as dirty and angry, before her eyes snapped back to his. "How did you know there was no water?"

Without a word, he held out a piece of paper she hadn't noticed him clutching in his hand. Boldly scrawled words leapt out at her threateningly.

WATER, WATER EVERYWHERE AND NOT A DROP TO DRINK. NOW IT'S YOUR TURN TO SEE WHAT IT FEELS LIKE TO BE HIGH AND DRY, RAWLINGS. ENJOY.

"I found this attached to one of the windmills," he told her grimly. "Someone had sabotaged it, then used an ax on the metal stock tank the water was pumped into."

Josey paled, her eyes flying to the window over the kitchen sink, where she could just catch a glimpse of the small wooden pump house that supplied water from the well to the house. "Are you saying the house well has been sabotaged, too?"

He nodded. "We just checked it on the way in. One of the belts has been cut."

"It was working fine this morning, so it had to be cut after we left for the roundup," Cooper added, dragging out a chair from the table and collapsing with a grunt of disgust.

"When Kat was here by herself?" Josey asked, horrified.

Flynn nodded, his boyish face set in stern lines. "The bastard was obviously just interested in damaging the well pump, but I hate to think what would have happened if Kat had looked out the window and seen him cutting that belt. She would have come after him for sure and could have been seriously hurt."

"Oh, God," Josey whispered, sinking into a chair across the table from Cooper. Suddenly the attacks against the ranch were turning ugly and striking far too close to home. And Flynn was right. Kat was such a firebrand, she wouldn't have thought twice about confronting someone caught damaging Rawlings property. "I can't believe your neighbors would do this for *water!*"

"Believe it," Gable retorted, tossing the note down onto the table. "After we came across this this morning, we split up and checked every windmill and stock tank on the ranch. They're all out of commission."

"All of them?" she gasped. "But your ranch takes up over a hundred square miles!"

"Whoever did this was thorough," Cooper said tersely. "The only reliable water we have left for the cattle is the springs, which means we either have to move the herd to the western pastures of the ranch or carry water. Either way, it's going to be a hell of a lot of work over the next few days—"

"Nothing!" Kat's wail preceded her, rolling into the kitchen seconds before she charged in behind it, too upset to notice that she was interrupting. "I tried all the bathrooms—" she began, only to break off at the sight of her brothers. "Thank God, you're here! Something's wrong with the well. We don't have any water, and I've got to get ready for the dance. You've got to fix it, Gable."

The dance. He'd completely forgotten it...and his date with Josey. He swore. Hell, what was he supposed to do now? Sweeping off his hat to plow his fingers through his hair, he gave Kat a short accounting of what had happened. "I can't do anything about it tonight, Kat," he said regretfully. "We don't have any spare belts, and it's too late to make it to Pete's place in town to get the supplies we need for the repairs before he closes up shop. You know he's closed on Sundays, so we're not going to have water again until Monday...if we're lucky. I'm sorry, brat, but that's the best I can do," he said regretfully, then waited for her to explode. He didn't have long to wait.

"*Monday!* You can't be serious! I've got to be ready in two hours. *Two hours,* Gable! I've still got to bathe and wash my hair... Oh, God, my hair!" Stricken, her hands flew to her head, tears welling in her eyes as she turned to Josey for help. "What am I going to do, Josey? I had it all worked out. I was going to be gorgeous for Matt, and now I'll have to go to the dance with dirty hair!"

"Don't panic," she told her soothingly, rising to slip a comforting arm around her shoulders. "There's a simple solution to this. You obviously can't stay here without water until Monday, so you'll just have to go to a hotel in town. Instead of picking you up here at six-fifteen, Matt can pick you up there at seven, so that'll give you plenty of time to get ready."

Flynn squirmed at that, but didn't say a word. Instead he and Cooper both shot Gable a questioning look, their doubts about the idea clearly written in their eyes. Swallowing a curse, he said, "We can't afford to be forty miles from the ranch at a time like this. I'm sorry, but it's just too dangerous."

Kat glared at him as if he'd stabbed her in her heart. "So I'm supposed to go to the dance with dirty hair, is that it?

My God, I can't even brush my teeth! How can you do this to me?''

"Dammit, Kat, *I'm* not doing anything to you! I've explained the situation to you. I'm not any happier about this than you are, but there's nothing I can do about it. The ranch is under attack and we can't just walk off and leave it at this time.''

Her arm still around the younger girl's shoulders, Josey felt the tension in her, the hurt anger. "How about my place, then?'' she suggested quickly without thinking. "It's only a mile away, and surrounded on three sides by your ranch, anyway. It would be the next best thing to being at home, and I have plenty of room for all of you.''

"Oh, Josey, that's perfect! Especially since you and Gable are going out tonight, anyway. Give me two minutes to get my things together and I'll be ready." Taking Gable's agreement as a given, she hurried out, practically dancing with excitement.

His eyes on Josey's expressive face, Gable knew the exact moment when she realized that not only had she invited Kat to stay with her, but the rest of the family, as well. Her eyes wide, she glanced at him, her thoughts crystal clear. After their date, he wouldn't just take her home; he'd come inside with her, sleep in one of her beds . . .

All under the watchful, knowing eyes of his brothers. They hadn't said a word, but he caught their amused looks and bit back a curse. His attraction to the lady was no secret, but after the heated moments she'd spent in his arms yesterday, after the way she'd opened up to him, he'd just as soon not stay at her house, chaperons or no chaperons. Especially when he was still grappling with the news that she was a virgin.

Dammit, he didn't even want to think about walking into her house, trying to sleep on a bed under her roof, not when he had trouble looking at the woman without wanting her. But what the hell else could he do? They couldn't stay at the ranch without water, and town was too far away.

His eyes locked with hers. "I hope you know what you're getting yourself into. These guys," he said, nodding toward his brothers, who were grinning like a couple of idiots, "can be real slobs. Feel free to throw them out anytime you get sick of them."

"Hey, who's calling who a slob?"

"I resent that!"

Josey only chuckled, but inside she was shaking. Of the three Rawlings men, it wasn't Cooper or Flynn she was worried about.

Josey had always thought her grandparents' place was huge. With three bedrooms, a sleeping porch, study, living room and farm kitchen, it was certainly too big for just one person, and she'd sworn on more than one occasion that it echoed like an empty barn when she walked down the hall. But the minute the entire Rawlings clan stepped through the front door, the silence of her own singular existence was pushed aside by laughter and the unfamiliar echo of teasing male jibes. For the first time since she'd arrived in New Mexico, it sounded like a home.

Bedlam. There was no other way to describe the next two hours. Kat immediately claimed the only bathroom as her own and didn't come out again for forty-five minutes. The second she was through, it was Josey's turn. Hurrying through a quick shower, she slipped into the delicate pink dress Kat had talked her into buying in Tucson, then grabbed her makeup kit and blow-dryer and rushed down the upstairs hall to Kat's room to help her finish getting ready.

Downstairs in the kitchen, Cooper and Flynn, one of them stuck with watching over the ranch on a Saturday night, good-naturedly argued over who would pull the duty, then tried to draw Gable into the fray. But he had his own date to get ready for and was having none of it. Leaving them to their argument, he escaped upstairs to the bathroom.

The intoxicating scent of Josey's perfume slammed into him the minute he stepped inside. Subtle, sophisticated, it was the kind of fragrance that tugged at a man's senses and haunted his dreams in the dead of night. Leaning back against the closed door, he found himself picturing Josey as she stepped out of the shower, drying herself, dabbing that damnable scent at her throat, her breasts, her—

Hot blood pooling in his loins, he broke off the thought with a growl of disgust. What the hell was he doing? Trying to drive himself crazy? The woman was as innocent as Kat when it came to relationships. A virgin who was tying him in knots and trusting him not to lose his head tonight, to bring her home and retire to her sleeping porch—alone—as though it was something he did all the time. How was he going to get through it without going quietly out of his mind?

Snarling an oath, he moved away from the door and jerked off his clothes, a quick flick of his wrist turning the water to cold the minute he stepped into the shower. An icy spray blasted his hot body, but it didn't help. With every breath he took, Josey's perfume teased his senses, reminding him that only moments before she had stood in the same spot, stark naked.

Needless to say, when he walked out of the bathroom fifteen minutes later dressed in creased jeans and a starched and pressed pale blue Western shirt, he was in a bear of a mood. He had every intention of telling Josey he thought it would be best for both of them if they canceled their plans for the night, but he never got the chance. She was in Kat's room and through the closed door, he could hear the two of them laughing and talking as they got dressed. Disgruntled, he went downstairs to wait.

He was pacing the kitchen, ignoring the needling jibes of his brothers when Kat, ready for her date, shyly stepped into the room twenty minutes later. He nearly dropped his teeth at the sight of her. "My God!"

"Jeez!"

"What have you done to yourself?"

Gable could only stare at her. Caught halfway between adolescence and adulthood, the blue of her dress exactly matching her sparkling eyes, she was the spitting image of their mother when he'd been a boy—young, gorgeous, full of life and mischief, with a figure that wouldn't quit. She'd grown up, he thought, shaking his head in wonder. How had she grown up without any of them noticing?

Confused, wanting back the familiar tomboy who used to ride hell bent for leather with the ranch hands, but so damn proud of her he felt his throat thicken, he looked past her to Josey, only to get hit in the gut with a second shock.

If Kat was young and gorgeous, Josey was riveting. Wearing a simple, pink flowered sundress and white sandals, she wasn't dressed nearly as elegantly as Kat, but she didn't need elegance to steal his breath. Not when she was so delicate, so soft and vulnerable, that he had to fight the need to reach for her and assure himself she was real. God, she was beautiful! And she seemed totally unaware of it. With a smile and a flirtatious remark, she could have had him and his brothers at her feet, but all her attention was focused on Kat and the quiet pride in her eyes was strictly for his sister. What was a man supposed to do with a woman like that but grab her and kiss her senseless?

All a jitter, Kat twirled, holding out the slinky folds of her skirt. "Do I look okay?" she asked anxiously. "Are you sure? You think my dress is okay? And my hair? Josey says it looks really soft and feminine down, but I just know everyone else is going to have theirs up. What if Matt doesn't like it?"

"Then he's a damn fool," Gable replied just as the doorbell rang. "That's probably him now. Good, because I've got a few things I want to say to him."

"Me, too," Cooper said, pushing to his feet. "Like he'd better not touch a hair on her head if he knows what's good for him."

Flynn, as protective as Cooper and Gable, jumped up to join them. "I want to know what the hell his plans are for tonight. If he's even thinking about going parking with her out on that dead end road on his daddy's place, he can forget about it. She's too young for that kind of crap."

The three men, in total agreement, stormed off toward the front door like knights of old defending the suspected dishonor of a princess in distress. Kat, stricken, wailed, "Oh, no! They're going to ruin everything! Josey, you've got to stop them."

Struggling with laughter, Josey said, "Surely they're not serious, honey. They're just a little overprotective right now. They won't say anything to embarrass you."

"Oh, yes, they will! You don't know them. I went on a hayride last Halloween with some kids from school and Cooper and Gable followed behind us on horseback just to make sure none of the guys got any ideas about kissing me. God, I was mortified! Please, Josey, do something. They'll listen to you."

Josey seriously doubted that—Lord, she wasn't even family—but she couldn't just stand there and let them ruin the evening for Kat when only moments before she'd been fairly dancing with excitement. "Come on," she said, and grabbed her camera, which she'd set out on the counter earlier. "I'll see what I can do but don't be surprised if all three of them tell me to butt out."

They hurried into the living room to find that the situation was every bit as bad as Kat had feared. The three hulking men were practically surrounding poor Matt and throwing questions at him so fast, he could only flush and stammer. Stiff and uncomfortable in his rented tux, hot color washing his baby soft cheeks, he looked like a scared penguin in desperate need of a hole to climb in. Wanting to knock the three men's heads together, Josey pulled Kat forward and gave Matt an easy smile as she smoothly introduced herself, stopping Gable in midsentence. "I'm so glad you came early, Matt, so I can get some pictures of you and Kat together. You both look great! I know you're going to have a wonderful time tonight."

"Thank you, ma'am!" he breathed in relief, then his eyes fell on Kat and everyone else in the room ceased to exist. "God, Kat, you're so pretty!"

Cooper snorted at that. "Pretty? She's gorgeous!"

"And she'd better come home looking just like she does now," Flynn added threateningly.

Grinding her teeth, Josey elbowed them both out of the way and pushed the young couple together so she could get a picture. "Smile," she said cheerfully. "That's it. Great! Now let me get one of each of you by yourself, and then you can be on your way. You don't want to be late."

Dwarfed by the towering Rawlings men, she flitted among them like a butterfly among redwoods, taking control of the situation simply by ignoring them and acting as if they were harmless. Gable let her get away with it until Kat and Matt were just about to escape out the front door. "Have fun," he called after them. "And behave yourselves."

Or else.

The words weren't spoken, but Matt obviously heard them. He paled slightly and almost tripped over the threshold. "Yes, sir! We will, sir! I promise," he assured him in a voice that had a tendency to break. "G-good night."

Indignation sparking in her eyes, Kat sent her three brothers a furious glare and hurried out, pulling Matt after her. There would, Josey decided, be hell to pay when she got home. And whatever grief she gave her three brothers was no more than they deserved. Whirling to face them, Josey scowled at the lot of them. "I can't believe you did that! You had that poor boy scared to death!"

Unrepentant, Cooper only grinned. "Good. Now he'll think twice before he lays a hand on her." Glancing at Gable, his brows knit in a sudden, fierce scowl that was belied by the mischief dancing in his eyes. "Don't think Kat's the only one on the hot seat tonight. What are your plans for the evening?"

Gable's lips twitched. "I haven't the foggiest. The lady asked me out. For all I know, she could be thinking about going parking on that dead end road on Matt's daddy's place."

"Oh, no," Flynn retorted, just barely suppressing his laughter as he turned on Josey. "We'll have none of that, young lady. You're supposed to have fun tonight, but you'd damn well better behave yourself. You got that? We expect you both to return just the way you left."

"Or else," Cooper added. "Have we made ourselves perfectly clear?"

Josey felt the revealing heat climb in her cheeks but found it impossible to hold back a grin. Rogues, she decided. They were all three heart-pounding, breath-stealing rogues. And more than a handful for any woman who knew her way around men.

But she didn't. She was out of her league and smart enough to know it. Old insecurities stirred to life, tying her nerve endings in knots, and suddenly it was a struggle to keep her smile in place and her tone light and teasing. "Jeez, guys, I'm shaking in my shoes. Are you sure you don't want to come with us and act as chaperons? I may lose my head completely once I'm alone with him."

"I don't think that'll be necessary," Gable drawled dryly. "Let 'em get their own dates."

"Easy for you to say," Cooper retorted. "One of us has to stay here and hold down the fort."

"Yeah, and since I'm the youngest, I shouldn't be stuck with all that responsibility," Flynn added triumphantly. "See you later, Coop."

"Hey! Now just a damn minute—"

Gable didn't wait to hear more. Urging Josey toward the front door, he called back over his shoulder, "See you later, guys. Don't wait up." They never even noticed.

Gable knew she expected him to take over control of the date at that point, but he was sure she would be more comfortable if she was calling the shots. So within minutes, they were on their way to Lordsburg in Josey's Jeep. Comfortably ensconced in the passenger's seat while she drove, he studied the delicate lines of her profile as she stared straight ahead at the road. Without his brothers there to add teasing laughter, they were surrounded by a silence that was as deep and consuming as a black hole, but

Gable never noticed. With her attention focused on her driving, he could indulge his need to just look at her.

As if she read his thoughts, she shot him a quick look, found his eyes on her, and abruptly leaned forward to turn on the radio. "Would y-you like to listen to some music?"

"Only if you want to," he said quietly. "I'm fine."

With a flick of her wrist, she filled the quiet with a familiar country tune of love and heartache and might-have-beens. But the words had hardly registered when her hand shot out and switched off the music. Just that quickly, the silence returned, this time awkward and tense.

Gable lifted a brow in surprise. He started to ask her what was wrong with the music, but she didn't give him a chance. Hastily rolling down her window, she lifted her face to the cool night air and breathed it in as if she'd just found an oasis in the desert. "It's getting a little s-stuffy in here, don't you think?" she choked.

His gaze narrowed, studying her in the growing darkness. "Are you all right?"

If he hadn't been watching her so closely, he would have missed the telltale tightening of her fingers on the steering wheel and the sudden stiffening of her shoulders. "I'm a little... nervous," she admitted, just when he was beginning to wonder if she was going to answer him. "I told you I wasn't very good at this."

The husky, whispered admission struck Gable right in the heart. If any other woman had told him such a thing, he would have accused her of pulling his leg. But this was Josey, sweet, innocent, incredibly delightful Josey. And she had so little faith in herself as a woman, she had no idea how good she was at stirring up a man. He wanted to tell her, to pull her into his arms and soothe her, but she was already as skittish as a filly around a mountain lion.

If he made the mistake of moving so much as an inch toward her, she'd probably drive them right into a ditch.

Resolving to set her at ease, he settled more comfortably in his seat and half turned to face her, his back wedged against the door. "You call this nervous," he teased, his grin flashing in the darkness. "When I was in high school, one of my friends set me up with a blind date straight out of a nightmare. Turned out the girl was the football coach's daughter and she was trying to make her old boyfriend jealous. And I was the bait."

Her nervousness forgotten for the moment, she gasped, "Oh, no! What happened?"

Able to laugh about it now, he chuckled. "We went to a party, and her boyfriend was there, of course. She told me if I didn't hang all over her when he was looking, she was going to tell her daddy that I couldn't keep my hands off her."

"My God, what did you do?"

"Well, I had two choices. I could either go along with her and lose my self-respect, or tangle with her daddy. If I'd chosen the first one, I'd have had to tangle with *my* daddy when he found out about it, and believe me, I didn't want to do that." His smile turned wistful at the thought of his father, but he only shrugged and continued. "So that really only left me one choice. And if I was going to have to face her old man, I was going to do it on my terms. I left the party and went back to her house to tell Coach Scofield exactly what his baby girl was up to. Thank God he knew what a brat she could be. When she finally got home from the party, we were both waiting for her. What followed was not a pretty sight."

Josey laughed, the lighthearted sound washing over Gable like spring water, flooding his senses with warmth, making him ache. Finally she was talking to him as easily as she did his brothers, telling him stories from her own

school days, her nervousness pushed aside by the fond-
ness of her memories. He should have been pleased. They
would both enjoy the evening more if they could just laugh
together. Instead, he found himself struggling again with
the fires she always seemed to touch off just under his skin.
He wanted, needed, to hold her. Badly.

But she was a virgin, an innocent fighting her fears, her
past. And that stopped him cold every time he thought
about it. She was vulnerable, and the last thing he wanted
to do was hurt her. She deserved to be courted with time
and patience and gentleness by a man who had nothing but
commitment on his mind, by a man who could show her
that she was in no danger of following her mother's ex-
ample because she was strong and independent and perfect the way she was. The thought staggered him. He
should have been running, he should have been avoiding
her like the plague. But all he could think about was getting close to her.

The nightspots in Lordsburg were few and far between—a few bars that drew local cowboys like flies, a
handful of adequate restaurants and the only real night-
club between Las Cruces and Tucson—the Château. The
decor was Spanish in style and a long way from the Swiss
Alps, but the food was good, and there was actually a live
band on Saturday nights. With nowhere else to go, Gable
and Josey, along with what seemed like every other adult
in the county over the age of eighteen, ended up there for
dinner and dancing.

The place was hopping, the music loud, the dance floor
crowded. Seated at a booth right off the parquet floor,
Josey had just given her order to the waiter when Gable
seconded it, then grabbed her hand. "Come on, let's
dance."

It happened so fast, she didn't even have time to think about protesting. He only had to take two steps and turn and his arms closed around her as the band slid gracefully into the strains of a slow, lilting love song. Her heart in her throat, Josey closed her eyes on a silent moan. This wasn't fair, she wanted to cry. The magic that always weakened her knees whenever he touched her was back, this time stronger than ever as he pulled her against the hard wall of his chest and swayed to the romantic music.

Trying to hang on to her common sense, she held herself stiffly in his arms. "Maybe we shouldn't be dancing," she choked. "Your wound—"

"Is just fine," he assured her huskily, chuckling softly. "I've got a good doctor. She patched me up real good and didn't say a thing about not dancing. Relax, honey, you're doing just fine."

How was she supposed to fight it, fight him, after that? He held her as though she were something fragile, delicate and so incredibly precious that she wanted to cry. Murmuring his name, knowing she was making a mistake but no longer caring, she slipped her arms around him and crowded closer with a sigh. Home. Why did it always feel as if she had come home whenever he held her?

Gable felt the exact moment she gave in and very nearly groaned aloud. This was stark, raving madness. He should take her back to their table and end the evening as soon as possible. But he couldn't bring himself to release her. What else was new? he thought mockingly. She'd knocked him for a loop from the beginning and he had a feeling when he was old and gray and a hundred and six, he still wouldn't be able to resist her. He wanted to show her, teach her, everything. God, why hadn't he taken her some place more private?

Chapter 10

In a world of their own, they danced one dance after another, lost to everything but the enchantment they brought to each other. Given the chance, Gable would have kept her in his arms all night, but then the band took a break. Watching her, he knew the exact moment she realized that they were one of the last couples on the dance floor and drawing more than one look of amused speculation. Hot color flooded her cheeks. "Oh! I—I guess we should return to our table."

She would have bolted then if he hadn't stopped her just by twining his fingers with hers. "Not so fast, lady," he growled. "There's no hurry."

"But our food—"

"Was delivered three songs ago and is probably stone cold by now, anyway." Pulling her back in front of him, his eyes gazed down intently into hers. When was the last time just looking at a woman, dancing with her, had given him such pleasure? "I—"

"Hey, man, I didn't expect to see you here tonight. Heard you had more trouble out at your place today. How's it going?"

Gable swallowed a curse of frustration and glanced up to find John Stinson and his wife standing in front of them, the older man's round, florid face lined with concern. He stiffened. He'd once considered him a friend, but now he knew better. In front of his wife and half their neighbors, Stinson might say all the right things, but he hadn't had much to say when some of the missing cattle from the Double R were found on his land. In fact, he hadn't bothered to offer a single excuse.

No, John Stinson was no friend of his, but Gable couldn't cut him dead, not when his wife was with him. Isabelle Stinson was an innocent bystander in all this and a hell of a nice lady. How she'd ever hooked up with John, God only knew.

His mouth tight, his eyes unwelcoming, Gable unbent enough to smile at Isabelle and introduce her to Josey. But when he turned back to his former friend, his jaw was as hard as granite. "It's nothing that we can't handle," he said, referring to the trouble John had mentioned. "Just some problems with a couple of windmills. By Monday, everything will be back in working order."

"Good, good, glad to hear it," John enthused. "You know what you're doing, of course, but I'm worried about you, Gabe. Nobody can suffer the kind of setbacks you and your brothers have over the past few weeks without feeling the pinch in your pocketbook . . . especially when you got a big loan payment coming due. If I were you, I'd be sweating bullets right about now, yessiree, Bob. Coming up with that kind of money is no easy task."

Gable scowled. From the way Stinson talked, he knew just exactly how much it was going to cost to keep the ranch, and that was something no one but he and his brothers were supposed to know. So who the hell had been talking at the bank? "We'll manage," he said tightly. "You don't need to be concerned."

"But I am," John said, slapping him on the back as though they were still the best of friends. "We go back a long way, and I'm honor bound to help you out if I can. So if it looks like you're not going to make that payment, you come to me, you hear? You lose the Double R to the bank, you'll have nothing to show for it, but I'd give you fair market value, of that you can be sure. I couldn't rest easy at night knowing that you didn't have enough of a stake to start over somewhere else."

Gable just stared at him. Hypocrite, he thought angrily. How the hell could Stinson look him in the eye and not choke on the line of baloney he was feeding him? Did he think Gable was a complete idiot? "Thankfully, that won't be necessary, John," he said coldly. "My brothers and I have everything under control, so there's no reason for you to lose any sleep over us. We're going to make that loan payment just fine."

Smart enough to know when he was pushing his luck, John made a quick excuse about needing to get back to their table and hurried off with his wife in tow. Standing stiffly at his side, Josey burst out, "I don't believe that man! Does he actually think you would sell so much as a rusty nail to him after he helped rustle your cattle?"

"Thinking has nothing to do with it," Gable said, settling his hand at the back of her waist to guide her back to their table. When she only snorted, he couldn't help but laugh. "No one's ever accused John of being overly bright. He wants the springs, so he's going after them. To a man like Stinson, that means doing whatever has to be done."

"But he's got to know you're on to him," she said as she slid into the booth on one side while he took the other. "My God, you all but accused him of stealing your cattle when we found them hidden in his back pasture and he didn't blink an eye! Any idiot could figure out that he's the last person you'd go to for help when you know he's trying to ruin you!"

His feet tangling with hers under the table, Gable leaned back and grinned at the way her green eyes shot hot sparks of indignation at him. Lord, she could be a firebrand when the mood struck her! It wasn't the first time he'd seen her in a temper, of course, but usually her eyes were flashing at him, not *for* him. He liked the difference, he decided. He could fight his own battles, but having her in his corner wasn't half bad, especially when his mind teased him with all the other ways the two of them could enjoy her frustrated energy.

For now, though, he contented himself with watching the color rise in her cheeks. "You give John too much credit," he chuckled. "He's two steps down from an idiot and motivated by greed. If he's the brains behind this conspiracy, then we've got nothing to worry about."

"But you don't think he is, do you?" she asked shrewdly.

His smile died. "No. Someone a heck of a lot more cunning than John and the others we know about organized the attacks on the ranch. I've just got to figure out who it is and hope I'm smarter than he is."

Over the next hour, however, they discovered that John Stinson wasn't the only one with nerve. During the course of their cold meal, three other ranchers, all supposed friends of the Rawlings family, came up to their table and expressed concern over the trouble brewing on the Double

R. Not a one of them left without offering to buy the ranch should Gable and his brothers decide to cut their losses and sell.

After Joe Patterson made his pitch and walked away, Gable took one look at her face and knew she was about to explode. Under other circumstances, he would have been, too, but he was enjoying her too much to let outsiders spoil the evening.

"Come on," he said abruptly, throwing some money on the table and taking her hand. "Let's get out of here."

Josey opened her mouth to protest—she was the one who had asked him out, so she should pay—but the passion flaring in his eyes turned the words to dust on her tongue. Her heart beating to the rhythm of the love song the band was playing, she followed him out into the night.

The drive home was as different as night and day from the trip to town earlier in the evening. This time Gable drove, all his awareness tied up in the woman at his side. She sat too far away, hugging the passenger door, but he could feel her gaze on him and the sudden apprehension that gripped her now that they were alone again. He wanted to tell her that she had nothing to fear from him— he would never do anything to hurt her—but he had a feeling words would never be enough. Instinctively, he reached for her hand. Just as soon as they left the lights of town behind them and the highway was a dark, empty ribbon ahead of them, he tightened his fingers around hers and tugged her across the bench seat until she was pressed close to him from hip to knee. At her start of surprise, he half expected her to pull away, but then her fingers linked with his, and the breath he hadn't realized he was holding shuddered out. Nothing had ever felt so right in his life.

The miles flew by too quickly, and all too soon he was pulling up in front of her house. He cut the engine, and for a long moment neither one of them moved while the silence, rife with anticipation, deepened. Someone had left the porch light on, and inside, either Cooper or Flynn was probably sprawled on the living room couch watching TV, waiting to tease them about their hot date that was ending at the unheard-of early hour of eleven o'clock.

Frowning at the thought, Gable glared at the light shining in the living room, and, just for tonight, wished his brother to the farthest reaches of the universe. The only time he seemed to have Josey all to himself was when they were on the road driving to and from town or to and from his neighbors' ranches in search of his cattle, and dammit, it wasn't enough. When had he begun to need more?

Releasing her hand, which he hadn't been able to resist pulling to his thigh sometime during the drive, he turned to her. "I'd just as soon not have my brother as an audience," he said huskily, slipping his arm around her, "so I'm going to kiss you good night out here." His free hand moved to her chin, nudging it up until he could look down into her eyes. "Any objections?"

She didn't answer him; she couldn't. But, oh, how she wanted him! Her heart in her eyes, she brought her mouth to his with a sigh that came all the way from her soul.

Magic. From the moment her lips touched his and he closed his arms around her with a groan, the magic of the night spilled over them like falling stardust. There was no past to haunt them, no old hurts to rise up between them and destroy the moment, no one to interrupt what they had both been waiting for all night. There was only the two of them, locked in an embrace that neither wanted to end.

She opened to him like a flower, sweet and moist and so hungry, she shook Gable to the very roots of his being. She was a virgin, he tried to remind himself, an innocent who didn't know what she was inviting by turning boneless in his arms and pressing wantonly against him, her tongue teasing and seducing as it danced into the hidden recesses of his mouth. His breathing harsh, he buried his face against her neck, struggling to hold on to reason, but her skin was so soft there, he couldn't think straight. He pressed a kiss just under her ear and then in the hollow of her throat, drawing a murmur of pleasure from her. Any minute now, he promised himself, he was going to come to his senses and stop this before it got out of hand. But not just yet. He just needed to hold her a little bit longer.

Then she moved against him, whispering his name, and his good intentions flew right out the window. With a will of their own, his hands roamed over her back, sliding over the thin material of her dress, measuring the flare of her hips, the smallness of her waist, before gliding around her ribs to her midriff, hesitating just beneath her breasts. He didn't want to scare her off, but God, he needed to touch her! Giving in to temptation, he closed his hand over her fullness and she cried out in surprise, melting against him, stealing his breath as she arched against him.

A groan ripped through Gable. For one long agonizing moment, he tortured himself with the feel of her breast filling his palm, his fingers making short work of the scooped neckline of her dress. Soft. God, she was soft, and so damn responsive! By the glow of the porch light, he could see the paleness of her skin, the dusky rosiness of her nipple, a sight no man but him had ever seen—

A virgin, he reminded himself again, cursing the fates. Why did he seem to forget that every time he touched her? She was driving him out of his mind, and he knew it was only a matter of time before he gave in to the needs tearing at him and made love to her until they were both too weak to move. But he'd be damned if the first time would be in the front seat of her grandfather's old Jeep. She deserved more than that.

"Honey, we've got to stop."

On fire for him, Josey looked up at him as if he spoke in a foreign tongue. "Stop?" she murmured. "Oh, no, don't. This feels so good. I never knew—"

The admission was almost his undoing. His body hard and hot, he captured her face in his hands and chuckled ruefully. "You do know how to pick your moments, lady." Needing to taste her one last time, he pressed his mouth to hers, then forced himself to set her from him while he still could. Quickly, before he could change his mind, he rearranged her clothes and tried to smooth her hair back into some semblance of order. But when he'd finished, her mouth was still swollen from his kisses and her cheeks prettily flushed, and it was all he could do not to reach for her again.

"Come on," he rasped, fumbling for the door handle. "We may as well go inside."

Josey would have given anything to slip around to the back door and escape to her room without Cooper or Flynn spotting her. She didn't have to glance in the mirror to know that she looked as though she'd just been thoroughly kissed, and she was in no mood for any of their wisecracks. Her senses were in a turmoil, her heart beating crazily, her body burning deep inside. But Gable was a step behind her as he followed her up the porch steps, and she refused to run like an embarrassed teenager. After all, this was her home and she had nothing to be ashamed of. In spite of that, hot color stained her face and throat as she opened the front door and stepped inside.

But she saw in a glance that the house was deserted. Kat wouldn't be home for several hours yet, and both Cooper and Flynn were gone. Surprised, she walked over to the lamp that had been left burning by her grandfather's easy chair and found a note from Cooper.

"'Flynn won the night off in a game of blackjack,'" she read aloud to Gable. "'I think the little fart cheated, but the bottom line is he's gone to town and probably won't be back till dawn. He never did know when to come home. I've gone to take a quick run around the ranch to make sure everything's locked up tight, but don't wait up for me, either. There's a hot poker game in the bunkhouse tonight and I'm feeling lucky.'"

So they were alone.

The realization hit them both at the same time. Josey looked up from the note and couldn't have known that her green eyes were dark as emeralds and filled with an unconscious longing that hit Gable right in the gut. She didn't say a word; she didn't have to. Every instinct Gable possessed urged him to go to her, to take her in his arms and finally give in to the craving that had been tearing them both apart for longer than either wanted to remember. It was what they both wanted, what they ached for...

But she was an innocent, he reminded himself. She'd waited a long time to give herself to a man, and he needed to stop and think about what he was getting into before he found himself in over his head. All he could think about was making it perfect for her. He wanted to woo her with candlelight and romance, then seduce her with the needs of her own body and seep her in pleasure. Hours, he thought with a silent groan. He wanted hours with her, but that was a luxury they didn't have.

Still, he couldn't make himself walk away from her. Not this time. "This isn't want I wanted for you, honey," he said hoarsely, fighting the need to eliminate the distance between them. His face hard with the strain, he made a silent promise that he wouldn't rush her. The decision was hers and she had to know what to expect. "Kat will be home in less than two hours."

Her heart swelled, hot tears stinging her eyes. How could she have ever thought she couldn't love this man? He could have had her in his arms, his bed, with nothing more than the touch of his hand. Instead he was giving her a chance to think, to halt the madness between them before it went any further. But it had been too late for that weeks ago.

"I don't care," she whispered, letting the note drop carelessly back down to the table as she stepped toward him. "We have right now, and that's enough for me. Make love to me, Gable. Please. I need you."

The simple admission drove the air right out of his lungs. He reached for her, unable to stop himself. "Josey, honey..." In the next instant, he swept her up in his arms and started up the stairs, startling a gasp from her. "I'm not taking any chances on anyone walking in on us," he said thickly. Carrying her as if she weighed no more than a feather, he strode down the upstairs hallway to her bedroom, nudged the door open with his shoulder, then kicked it shut behind them. "I want you too much to have to worry about interruptions."

Leaning back against the door, he cradled her close, content, for the moment, just to hold her. In the darkness that surrounded them, he could see her eyes widen with surprise and laughed softly. "What did you expect?" he teased. "For me to rush you right into bed before you could even catch your breath?"

Her grin sheepish, she nodded. "Something like that. We only have so much time—"

"And I mean to make it feel like all night," he promised huskily, lowering his mouth slowly to hers. "Let me kiss you, sweetheart. Right now, that's all I want. A simple kiss.''

His lips settled on hers as lightly as morning dew landing on the grass, asking nothing more than she let him gently explore the secrets of her mouth. Slowly, languidly, with the gentleness she so effortlessly pulled from him, he tenderly feasted on her, nibbling at the sensuous curve of her upper lip, the maddening fullness of the lower, sliding his tongue along the tempting seam between the two, focusing all his attention on the heat that throbbed there.

She whimpered, a small revealing sound he was sure she wasn't even aware she made, and clutched at him as her head fell helplessly back against his shoulder, her neck suddenly boneless. Instinctively, Gable's hands tightened on her, the fires burning under his skin urging him to take her to the bed now and lose himself in her. Only this first time wasn't about him, but her, and he wanted so much more for her than a quick loving. Stamping down the flames licking at him, he eased his grip on her, his control rigid as he let his mouth wander to the sweet sensitive spot where her neck met her shoulder. At her shudder, he smiled against her silken skin, loving the taste of her. Yes! This was what he wanted for her...mindlessness and a passion so deep she lost herself in it.

''That's it, sweetheart,'' he said softly, murmuring encouragement as he slowly eased his arm from her legs and let her slide down the length of him. Too late, he realized his mistake. Pliant, she settled against him, her hips cradling his arousal, and it was all he could do not to carry her to the bed then and there. He groaned, unable to stop himself from pulling her snug against him.

He heard her breath catch in her throat, felt the sweet heat of his own name whispered against his neck as she buried her face against him, and almost went up in flames as her hips nudged his. "Yes!" he said fiercely, but when she moved again, he had to stop her. "I thought I could take this slow and easy, but you're damn near burning me up," he said with a shaky laugh. Taking her hands, which had slipped to his waist, he placed them on his chest. "Unbutton my shirt, sweetheart."

She blinked, her fingers already toying with the first button. "You want me to undress you?"

Grinning at her surprised tone, his eyes locked with hers. "Mmm-hmm. There's a lot more to making love than what happens in bed. Let me show you."

And with no other warning than that, he reached for the zipper to her dress and slowly began pulling it down. He felt her stiffen, heard her breath hitch, and smiled down at her with eyes that were scorching in their intensity. "Easy," he whispered. "I just want to touch you. You're skin is like silk, did you know that? So incredibly soft. You don't know how many nights I've dreamed of just running my hands over you."

With nothing more than his husky words and the tantalizing sweep of his fingers, he seduced her. Her dress parted down the back, and with a murmur of pleasure, he charted the new territory like an explorer traveling undiscovered territory, learning every inch of her. Not content to just touch her, he rubbed and stroked and fondled, nudging the bothersome material out of the way and mesmerizing her with hands that knew just where to linger and caress.

Gasping, her senses swimming and her blood hot, she felt her knees turn to water and she forgot all about unbuttoning his shirt. "Gable!"

The cry was hardly out of her mouth and he was sweeping her up into his arms and carrying her to the bed, the need to love her just then tearing at him like sharpened talons. His face hard with desire, his eyes never leaving her naked body gleaming in the darkness, he hurriedly tugged off his boots, then attacked the rest of the buttons on his shirt with fingers that were anything but steady. Stunned, he tried to think of the last woman who had made him tremble, but he couldn't come up with another name, another face. Only Josey. God, she was beautiful! And if he didn't have her soon, he was going to go quietly out of his mind!

Flinging the last of his clothes away, he came to her then, naked but for the bandage wrapped around his chest, slipping into the bed with an urgency he couldn't control. Slow down, a voice in his head ordered, reminding him of her innocence. Now, more than ever, she needed his control.

He tried to give it to her, but he hadn't counted on Josey.

She wanted him. She was a doctor, she knew the physical and biological facts about the birds and the bees, but nothing in her experience had ever prepared her for this. How could she not have known that there was a hunger such as this? A need that made any other seem insignificant in comparison? She wanted to laugh, to cry, to soar with the wonder of it. Of him.

Her breath tearing through her lungs, she reached for him the minute the mattress gave with his weight, a sigh of unadulterated pleasure rippling through her as his arms surrounded her and his hot skin slid along hers. Yes, this was what she'd needed and hadn't even known, his weight pressing her down into the sheet, his legs nudging hers open so he could settle against her. Her fingers itching to touch him, she learned his body as he had learned hers, letting her hands wander over him, skimming gently over his bandaged-covered wound, glorying in his strength, the hard, whipcord lean length of him and the groans she so easily pulled from him.

"Honey, you're driving me crazy!" he growled against her mouth, giving her a scorching kiss that left them both breathless. "We were going to take this slow and easy, remember?"

But he couldn't. The fire burning hotter and hotter in his blood, he found it harder and harder to hang on to his control. He ached and only she could make it better. Her name a groan on his lips, his hands raced over her, craving the closeness he denied them both. Then her fingers slipped past his waist, his hips, until they closed around his arousal, and what he knew about desire shattered.

Control forgotten, the pressure building in him until he was crazy with it, he slid his hand down the length of her, over the gentle curve of her stomach, to the very core of her, seeking her readiness. At his gentle touch, she went wild, arching under him, her hips blindly moving against his. It was too much. With a single, smooth motion, he thrust into her, and nearly lost it all when her tight heat surrounded him.

Groaning, he squeezed his eyes shut and held himself perfectly still, promising himself he could at least give her body time to adjust. But every second cost him, and within a heartbeat, his muscles were shaking with the strain.

When he opened his eyes, it was to find Josey smiling up at him, her heart in her eyes and a look of wonder lighting her face. He'd never seen anything so beautiful in his life. Unbelievably, a chuckle rose up in him and he grinned. "Hold on, sweetheart. The best is yet to come." With a single stroke, he set the fires in her raging out of control.

Before the sun peaked over the horizon at dawn, Gable and his brothers were already up and dressed and ready to return to the Double R to get an early start on all the work they'd had to put aside yesterday. The ravages of a late night showed on all their faces, but no one seemed inclined to talk about the successes or disappointments of the previous evening. And that was just fine with Gable. Long after he'd slipped away from Josey's bed, then sat up waiting for Kat, he'd lain on the bed on the sleeping porch and stared out at the night, unable to close his eyes without having images of the loving they'd shared rise up before him.

Even now, hours later, the emotions she'd pulled from him staggered him. How could she have taught him so much about making love when *she* was the innocent? Yet that was exactly what she'd done. She'd gone into his arms and given him...everything. Lord, she was something! Her trust had humbled him, her generosity stunned him, her passion fired him in a way no other woman ever had. He'd lost himself in her, in the taste and smell and soft heat of her, and it was only when he'd had to force himself to leave her bed that he'd realized that a measly two hours with her was never going to be enough. That realization had kept him awake for hours.

What the hell was he going to do now?

Standing at her bedroom window watching Gable as he drove off, Josey hugged herself and asked herself the same thing. If she lived to be a hundred, she would never forget last night. Bubbling with emotions, she'd lain in bed after he'd left her, hugging her pillow and wishing it was him. Then Kat had rushed in after the dance, too excited over her date with Matt to notice her distraction, thank God! While the girl had dreamily given her a minute-by-minute account of her fantastic evening, Josey had tried to give Kat her full attention, but all she could think of was that she'd shared something with Gable, a wonder, a joy that she'd never expected to share with any man . . . all without a single promise or word of love spoken.

Even now, she told herself that the magic they'd found together didn't have to end after just one night. After all, there was no law that said she *had* to return to Boston. She could stay in New Mexico, set up a rural practice. . . .

And change your life to accommodate the new man in your life, a man who had never once mentioned the future, a voice in her head finished for her. *Just like your mother.*

She paled at the thought, pain squeezing her heart. Was that was she was doing? Looking for ways to follow in her mother's footsteps after all these years of deliberately avoiding them? No! she wanted to cry. But she could feel the truth in the pounding of her heart and the sting of the tears that flooded her eyes. She hadn't just given him her body and her innocence last night, she'd given him her love. And right or wrong, it was too late to take it back.

The sun was just setting when the Rawlings men returned late that afternoon. Tired and dusty and sweaty, they trailed in one after the other through the back door, with Gable taking up the rear. For most of the day, Joscy had worried about what she would say to him when she saw him again, how she would face him in front of his family when she was full of doubts and insecurities and in desperate need of his arms around her. But when the screen door slammed behind him and he was suddenly in front of her, his eyes as wary as she knew hers must be, she didn't give a hang about the watchful eyes of his brothers. Unmindful of the flour coating her hands from the chicken she and Kat were frying for supper, she stepped toward him, her only thought to reassure them both that they hadn't imagined the wonder of the night before.

She opened her mouth, a shy greeting hovering on her tongue, but then the phone rang. Kat, who had been waiting all day to hear from Matt, snatched it up, but the call was for Josey. Disappointed, she held the phone out to her. "It's somebody named Jonathan, calling from Chicago. You want to take it in here or the study?"

She hesitated, aware of Gable's sudden stiffness and the hard glint that invariably came into his eyes whenever something happened to remind him that she did have another life in the city. But she had nothing to hide. She could talk to whomever she wanted to.

"I'll take it in here," she said, wiping her hands on the dishcloth. "Why don't you mash the potatoes? Everything else is almost done, and as soon as I finish here, we can eat." Taking the phone, she smiled. "Well, hello, stranger. How's life in Chicago?"

"A heck of a lot more exciting than it is out in the sticks where you are." He chuckled. "When are you going into practice with me, sweetheart? I could really use an extra pair of hands right now."

Her smile still intact, Josey almost groaned. Why hadn't she taken this in the study? Turning her back on the rest of the room, she said, "I don't know, Jonathan. I know I'm leaving you hanging, but I still need a couple of weeks to make a decision. I know we'd work well together..."

"But you're still not sure if you can bear to leave that precious clinic of yours," he finished for her, his tone laced with amused resignation. "Come on, Josey, you said yourself that place was running you right into the ground. Why would you want to go back there where you're overworked and underpaid? I promise you you'll never have that complaint with my OB/GYN practice. It's a first-class operation. What do you say?"

Her gut clenched just at the thought of delivering another baby, of possibly losing one again. "I need more time, Jon. After everything that happened, I'm just not ready."

Gable watched her turn away from him, her tone lowered as she talked about leaving, and had to fight the urge to break something. *Fool!* he berated himself. *Idiot! You fell for a pair of laughing green eyes and let yourself forget what she was. A city woman who made it clear from the beginning that it was only a matter of time before she returned to a life you want no part of. You've already been through this once.* How the hell could you let this happen to you again?

Bitterness turning his eyes to slate, he glared at her slender back, at the apron tied at her waist, the hair that was pulled back out of her way in a ponytail while she cooked, the camp shirt and well-washed jeans that covered the soft, sensuous curves he had charted with his hands and mouth last night. Dressed as she was now, she could have easily passed for a ranch wife on any ranch in the state. Natural, her face free of makeup, there was no artifice to her, not even a hint of sophistication. She looked and acted as if she belonged there, in his world, in his life, as if she never intended to leave. Dammit, she'd even hung out a shingle! He'd spied it yesterday when he'd turned into her drive.

But it was all just window dressing. That's all it had ever been, and like a backward cowhand who didn't have the sense to know better, he'd been taken in, he thought angrily. When he thought of the way he'd had to tear himself away from her last night and the countless times he'd had to fight the urge to come in early today, just to see her, he wanted to throw something. How could he have been so blind? Last night had changed nothing. She would one day soon return to Boston. And by God, she wasn't taking his heart with her when she left!

Turning his back on her, he moved to the sink and washed up, deliberately closing his ears to the softly murmured conversation going on behind him. "Are you through with those potatoes yet?" he asked Kat, the rhythm of the masher hitting the pot grating on his nerves. "Cooper, Flynn, clean up, then set the table. Let's get this stuff dished up so we can eat. It's been a long day."

At his harsh tone, his brothers and Kat glanced at each other in surprise. Arching a dark brow at him, Cooper drawled, "No longer than any other day after a late night. Something wrong, big brother?"

"Not a damn thing," he snapped. "I'm just tired and hungry. You got a problem with that?"

"Whoa," Cooper said, holding up his hands like a victim held at gunpoint. "I don't know what's eating at you, but I'm pretty damn sure I didn't have anything to do with it. And neither did Kat or Flynn. Now, you want to start this conversation over or just forget it?"

Heat climbing up his neck, Gable swore under his breath. Cooper was right. He was acting like a jackass. "Sorry. My mistake. Let's forget it, okay?"

The others nodded, but tension still fairly hummed on the air. Flynn looked inclined to make a comment, his gaze whipping from Gable's stony face to Josey's turned back, but a warning look from Cooper effectively silenced him. With a shrug, he walked over to the sink to wash up.

By the time Josey hung up after convincing Jonathan she really wasn't sure what she was going to do yet, the table was set, the food dished up and it was time to eat. Quickly slipping into her chair across from Gable, she apologized. "Sorry. You shouldn't have waited for me. Please, go ahead and eat."

"Hey, no sweat," Flynn said with an easy grin. Always the daredevil, he shot a mischievous look at his older brother. "Gable was ready to chew wood, but we managed to keep him from gnawing on a table leg."

Gable took the platter of chicken as it was passed to him, his narrowed eyes shooting a warning at Flynn, but he only grinned, unrepentant. "Course, I'd be a bear, too, if I knew I was the one who had to start repairing all those well pumps tomorrow," he confided to Josey. "We've all got our specialties, and Gable's just happens to be machinery. Man, I don't envy him all that work."

Surprised, Josey glanced at Gable, but he hadn't looked at her since she'd gotten off the phone, so she turned back to Flynn. "Surely he's not going to repair all the pumps by himself."

"Well, he does need a second pair of hands," Cooper admitted, his own eyes gleaming as he caught on to Flynn's game. "The only problem is, we don't have a second pair to spare. You know how shorthanded we are and the deadline we're under. We can't afford to take anyone else off the roundup, not if we want to make that loan payment on time."

Not slow on the uptake himself, Gable's narrowed gaze bounced between his brothers. "That's enough," he warned.

Flynn didn't spare him a glance. "You'd sure be a lifesaver if you could lend a hand, Josey. We'd pay you, of course. We couldn't ask you to work and not pay you anything."

Stunned, eyes wide, Josey unwittingly stepped into the trap of letting him distract her with the mention of payment. "You will not! I'm not going to take money for helping you—"

"It'll be work," Cooper cautioned her, grinning when Gable swore under his breath, "so don't be so quick to turn the money down. Oh, it won't be anything you can't handle—holding a wrench, handing Gable tools—that type of thing, but you need to wear your oldest jeans. And a long-sleeved shirt. It's still spring, but that sun can get hot when you're out in it all day long. Better bring a hat, too."

"But—"

"She doesn't have to do this," Gable said harshly. "I'll find a way to manage just fine on my own."

Kat, deceptively innocent, entered the conversation for the first time. "What's the matter? Don't you want Josey's help?"

Dammit, what was he supposed to say to that when four pairs of eyes were turned on him accusingly, waiting for his answer? "I never said that. Of course I can use the help..."

"Good," Flynn said smugly, his grin broad. "Then it's settled. Now, wasn't that easy?"

Chapter 11

"Hand me the wrench. No, not that one! The open-ended one."

Josey gritted her teeth at Gable's terse tone and handed him the wrench he pointed out with his chin. "Now what?"

"Just hold it a second, will you? And don't let go of the pliers, dammit! Watch what you're doing!"

"I'm trying!"

"Well, try harder."

His eyes on his hands and the pump they were repairing out in the hot sun, he didn't see the temper that flared in Josey's eyes or the hurt she had no intention of letting him see. Work, he told himself. If he could just concentrate on what he was doing, he could forget that she was crouched so close to him at the base of the sabotaged windmill that her legs brushed against his every time she moved. And it was driving him half out of his mind!

Cursing his brothers for interfering in something that was none of their business, he ground out, "There. Hold it. I'm just about finished."

The new part in place, he sighed in relief as the wind caught the windmill and started it pumping again. Picking up his tools, he headed for his truck. "Let's get on the next one," he told her, without bothering to see if she was following. "The day's already half gone."

Hands on her hips, Josey blew her hair out of her eyes and stood her ground, scowling at his retreating back. From the moment he had picked her up four hours ago, he'd been throwing out orders like a drill sergeant, snapping at her one minute, then giving her the silent treatment the next. Whenever he'd deigned to look at her—and those times had been few and far between—his blue eyes had been as cold and unrelenting as a stranger's. If she hadn't known better, she would have sworn he couldn't possibly be the same man who had made such tender love to her Saturday night.

"Thank you, Josey," she mimicked. "I don't know what I'd do without you, Josey. I know you could be home drinking iced tea right now and I really appreciate you sweating out in the hot sun with me. Dammit, Gable, what's your problem?"

He turned then, but only because he couldn't walk away from her mockery. From twenty feet away, his razor-sharp eyes drilled her. "The only problem I've got is another ten windmills to repair. If you're not getting the thanks you want, then I'm sorry. I haven't got time to fall all over you in gratitude. Are you coming or not?"

"That depends," she retorted quietly. "I never said I wanted gratitude. But I would like some acknowledgment that you're even aware that I'm here." Unable to stop herself, she stepped toward him. "What's wrong, Gable?

You've been giving me the cold shoulder ever since we made love, and I don't know why. What have I done?''

A muscle ticked along his jaw at the sound of the hurt lacing her voice, but he steeled himself against it. *She* was the one who had hurt him by making him forget who and what she was. That wasn't a mistake he intended to make again. "We didn't make love," he told her icily. "We had sex. There's a difference."

The barb drove home like a well thrown lance, stabbing her in the heart. She gasped, the blood draining from her cheeks. Hurt, like hot oil, gushed through her, scalding her and almost driving her to her knees. When Molly had lost her baby because of a mistake she must have made—though for the life of her Josey didn't know what she could have done differently—she'd held the sobbing woman as she had cried for her lost child, sure she could never again feel that kind of pain. But that couldn't touch the agony that squeezed her heart now. Because she'd made the mistake of letting herself love him.

Unshed tears stinging her eyes, she turned and began walking away from him, across the pasture before she was tempted to ask what she could do to make things right between them again. Her grandparents' place was less than a mile away, cross-country.

"Where the hell do you think you're going?" he demanded, thunderstruck.

She never checked her stride, never even cut him a glance. "Home."

A short, pungent oath scorched the air. "Dammit, Josey, come back!"

One foot in front of the other, she told herself, stiffening her trembling legs. If she could just manage to put one foot in front of the other, she could make it home without breaking down. *Then* she could cry. "No, thank you," she called back coldly. "You've made it quite clear you don't need me, so I'll leave you alone." And without another word, she topped a small rise and disappeared over the other side.

Furious with her and himself, Gable wasn't fit to shoot the rest of the day. Alone with his conscience, he managed to repair the house well pump and three others, but he had too much time to think. He didn't like himself right then, didn't like what he'd done even though he knew a quick ending was better for both of them than a slow, agonizing death to a relationship that was fated to go nowhere. But hurting her had never been his intention.

The image of her reproachful eyes haunting him with every beat of his heart, he told himself he was glad there was no longer any reason for his family to impose on Josey's hospitality now that they had water at their house. But the lie stuck in his craw and he was in a foul mood when he finally pulled into his own yard at dusk.

Cooper and Flynn, looking as tired as he felt, were waiting for him on the front porch. He frowned at the pair of them. "What are you two doing out here?" His eyes flew past them to the house, to the darkened windows. "What's wrong now?"

"Nothing. It's just been a hell of a day and we thought we'd go down to the Crossroads and have a few beers," Flynn said, naming a small beer joint ten miles away. Conveniently located at the intersection of two busy country roads, it was a popular hangout mainly because it was smack-dab in the middle of cattle country. At the end of a hard day, tired cowboys from every ranch in that area of the county could be found there, enjoying a game of pool, burgers that were unapologetically greasy and beer. "Wanna come with us?"

"Where's Kat?"

"Over at Patty Carlson's house," Cooper said. "They've got a big history test tomorrow and are going to stay up half the night studying. Which means we're batching it tonight. And I don't know about you, but I sure as hell don't feel like cooking."

"Me, either," Flynn added with feeling. "A grease burger and a couple of beers, that's what I want. You gonna clean up or go as you are?"

With Josey's image hovering just on the edge of his awareness, waiting to taunt him the minute he was alone again, it was a decision Gable didn't even have to think about. Maybe a couple of beers would help him forget. It certainly wouldn't hurt. "Let's go."

They went in Cooper's truck, the three of them packed in the cab like sardines, but the ride was a short one. And, as expected, the place was overflowing. Cooper and Flynn immediately spied friends and drifted away, which was just fine with Gable. Grabbing himself a bar stool, he ordered a beer and seriously set his mind to forgetting that he'd ever met a woman named Josey O'Brian.

But a single beer didn't help. Neither did half a dozen. Disgusted, he decided to order something stronger. Slapping money on the bar, he motioned for the bartender. "Give me a whiskey."

By the time his brothers dragged him outside hours later, his head was buzzing and his legs were unsteady, and he was sure he couldn't see straight because he was so damn mad at Josey. What did it take to get the lady out of his head?

"Jeez," Flynn growled as he struggled to squeeze in beside him. "I didn't know you were going to get bombed out of your mind. How many did you have?"

"None your bizness," he slurred, hanging on to the door as Cooper pulled out of the parking lot. "Dropme at Jozee'z."

Cooper and Flynn exchanged glances. "I don't think so," Cooper said flatly. "You're in no shape to go calling on a lady."

"I'mnotdrunkdammit!"

"No? You look pretty soused to me," Flynn said bluntly. "You show up at Josey's like this, she'll throw you out on your ear."

"You can see her tomorrow," Cooper added. "After you sober up."

Swearing, Gable fumbled for the door handle. "I'll see 'er tonight. Lemme out. I'm gonna walk."

Flynn grabbed him just in time, cursing his stubbornness. "Damn you, Gable, it'd serve you right if I let you fall out on your head! Not that it would hurt you. You always did have a head like a rock. Take him to Josey's, Coop. If you don't, he'll probably just jump in his truck the minute we get home and drive over there, anyway, and he's got no business being behind the wheel in the condition he's in."

Cooper didn't like it any more than Flynn did, but trying to reason with his older brother wasn't getting them anywhere. Muttering under his breath about pigheaded jackasses, he pulled up in front of Josey's house ten minutes later and left the motor idling as Gable stumbled from the truck. "If she bites your head off, you've got no one to blame but yourself," he warned. "And we're not sticking around to pick up the pieces. You can walk home. Maybe the exercise will clear your head."

All his concentration focused on the porch steps before him, Gable only waved him away. "Fine. Go home. Know what I'm doin'."

Swearing, Cooper took him at his word and drove away, shaking his head over his stupidity, but Gable was too busy negotiating the steps to notice. Finally reaching the top one, he moved toward the front door with the rolling gait of a sailor who suddenly found the deck heaving beneath his feet. Frowning, he stared down at his boots, wondering what was wrong, but then he spied the doorbell, glowing like a beacon in the night. It took him three stabs with a wavering index finger before he finally found it and leaned on it.

Sound asleep, Josey bolted up at the first jarring ring of the doorbell. Her heart in her throat, she stared wide-eyed at the luminous dial of her bedside clock, but it was a long moment before her eyes focused enough for her to read it. Two o'clock! Who would be ringing her doorbell at this hour of the night?

"Dammit, Jozee! Open up!"

At the sound of Gable's bellow, she stiffened. What was he doing here? Had something happened at the ranch? Suddenly remembering the sabotaging of the wells and Gable's prediction that the men who were after the Double R would stop at nothing to get what they wanted, she paled, her imagination already picturing him hurt. Strangling on a soft cry, she snatched up her robe and practically ran down the stairs, turning on lights as she went.

"'Bout time," he grumbled, scowling as she dragged open the door. "Wanna talk t'you."

Startled, Josey fell back a step as he stumbled in, her eyes taking a quick inventory of him, searching for some type of injury. His cheeks were flushed, his eyes glazed, his balance off and his hair was standing on end. But it wasn't until she caught the whiff of whiskey on his breath as he lurched toward her that she realized he wasn't hurt. He was drunk!

The weight of his arms settled heavily on her shoulders in a haphazard hug that nearly buckled her knees. Stunned, she tried to jerk free, but he had her effectively pinned against him from chest to knees. "Dammit, Gable, let go! You're drunk!"

"Damn right," he growled. "'S your fault."

"Mine?" Stung, she pulled her head back enough to frown up at him. "How do you figure that? I wasn't the one who held the glass to your lips."

"Couldn't get you out of my head," he admitted with an honesty that he would no doubt regret later. His eyes, when they fastened on hers, were accusing. "You weren't suppos'd to be like Ka-ren."

Josey stilled at the mention of his ex-wife, hurt tearing through her that he could think she was anything like the woman who would have used him and his family to get what she wanted out of life if he hadn't stopped her. "I'm not," she whispered, stricken. "I'm not anything like her."

"I thought you were different—gonna stay." He snorted at that, the sound jeering. "But you're a big city doctor. Gotta go where the bucks are. And Jon'than, whoever the hell he is. Climb that ladder of success. Whatsamatter? You too good for us?"

"No, of course not—"

"Yes you are," he argued sadly. "Don't care anymore. I'm gonna kiss you anyway."

"No—"

Tangling his fingers in her hair, he dragged her mouth up to his and cut off her protests with a hot, hungry kiss that fairly shouted possessiveness. At the first touch of his lips, Josey stiffened, her jaw clenched. No! she cried silently, fighting the pull he had on her heart. She wouldn't let him do this to her. He couldn't compare her to his ex-wife one minute, then kiss her as though he couldn't get enough of her the next.

Tears burning her eyes, she stood utterly still, refusing to struggle, telling herself she could do this. She could resist him. She had to. But then he lifted his head and gave her a reproachful look. "Open your mouth, honey. Lemme kiss you right."

"No, I don't want you—"

He didn't wait to hear more. Swooping down, he took her mouth as if he were starving for the taste of her, his tongue slipping inside to tease and plunder and seduce, refusing to allow her to remain impassive. Whimpering, Joscy clutched at him, trying to hang on to reason, but at the first slow glide of his tongue, she was lost...lost to the hurt he could so easily bring her, lost to common sense, lost to everything but the heat of him pressed against her, weakening her knees, and the fire he'd lit in her blood so easily.

Her hands, ignoring the dictates of her brain, roamed over him, sliding over the soft cotton of his shirt, measuring the hard wall of his chest, the breadth of his shoulders, the powerful muscles of his arms. So strong, she thought, entranced. She always forgot how strong he was until she touched him. Lean and solid and as tough as a weathered cedar fence post, he had the ability to make her feel things that no other man had, things that she'd never thought she wanted to feel...delicate and feminine and protected. When had she come to need that from him?

Caught in the joy of finding herself back in his arms, she didn't realize that he was leaning heavily against her until he jerked his head back suddenly and they both almost fell. "Gotta sit...down," he gasped, and blindly reached out with one hand for the couch three feet away.

Dazed, her heart ricocheting in her chest, Josey quickly slipped her arm around his waist. "Here...let me help you. Another step and you're there."

He would have made it, but suddenly the starch in his knees gave out, and like a felled tree, he started to topple. Somewhere on the edge of his polluted consciousness, he heard Josey's startled cry as she tried to catch him, but he was too heavy for her. Through blurred eyes, he saw the approaching couch rise up to meet him, and, in the next instant, he was flat on his stomach, his face buried in one of the flowered cushions that Josey hastily stuck under his head. Groaning, he closed his eyes and clutched it, his eyes suddenly so heavy he couldn't keep them open. "Gimme a minute," he slurred. "Need to rest...my eyes."

Her hands on her hips, her body still tight with need, Josey stared down at his prone form stretched out before her and tried to tell herself this couldn't be happening. He couldn't be falling asleep on her couch after just kissing her senseless.

But he had. As relaxed as a child who had suddenly run out of gas after a hard day of serious play, he lay unmoving before her, his breathing slow and easy and peaceful. Not so much as an eyelash twitched.

Fighting sudden tears, she shoved at his shoulder. "Wake up, Gable! You're not staying here tonight. Do you hear me? Go sleep it off somewhere—"

The phone rang, startling her and drawing a look of stunned disbelief from her. She didn't believe this! What was wrong with everyone tonight? It was after two in the morning, and her house was busier than the emergency room at Massachusetts General! Didn't anyone sleep anymore?

Snatching up the phone, she said tersely, "O'Brian residence."

"Dr. O'Brian? Thank God!" an unfamiliar male voice breathed in her ear. "Please, you've got to help my wife. I don't know what to do and we'll never make the hospital in time—"

The caller was frantic, rushing his words together so that Josey could hardly understand him. Her problems with Gable forgotten, she said soothingly, "Calm down, Mr.—"

"Lopez," he said shakily. "Juan Lopez. I'm sorry, doctor. Of course you don't know me. I'm a ranch hand on the Double R. My wife—"

"What about your wife? What's wrong?"

She could almost hear his effort to maintain control, but at her quiet question, words bubbled out of him like an overflowing fountain. "The baby's coming. And Rosa knew, she knew all evening she was having pains and she didn't tell me. She thought it would go away—the baby's not due for another six weeks—but now the pains are two minutes apart and the hospital is too far away and I didn't know what else to do but call you. Please, Doctor, you've got to come!"

Josey blanched. Another baby coming too soon, its parents expecting her to save it. No! she wanted to cry. She couldn't. Not yet. Losing Molly's baby had almost destroyed her. If she lost another one...

She shied away from the thought, unable to even think about what such a loss would do to her. "What about your wife's doctor, Mr. Lopez?" she asked huskily, her fingers tightly gripping the phone. "Have you called him?"

"He thought we still had six weeks, so he went to California for a convention. And there's no way his partner in Silver City can get here in time. Please, Dr. O'Brian, will you come?"

No! She couldn't take the chance. But how could she turn her back on someone who needed her so badly? "Give me directions to your house, Mr. Lopez," she said quietly. "I'll be there just as quickly as I can."

The night that followed was one of the longest of Josey's life. Only by closing off all her emotions could she get through it, but still the strain ate at her, tightening her nerves until they were as taut as the strings of a tennis racket. Finally, at four-fifteen in the morning, Elizabeth Josephine Lopez came into the world with a lusty cry, drawing a sigh of relief from her mother and tears of joy from her father. The baby appeared healthy and perfectly formed, but Josey still couldn't let go of her fear that the minute she relaxed her guard, something would go wrong. As soon as both mother and daughter were cleaned up, she followed them and the new father into Silver City to the hospital, where they were checked out again and pronounced in perfect health.

Josey accepted the parents' heartfelt thanks with a smile that didn't quite reach her eyes. Bone weary, afraid she would shatter if she let go of her control long enough to share their joy, she wished them good luck with their new baby and hurried out of the hospital, the long drive home still in front of her. By the time she finally stepped onto her own porch again, hours after she'd left, dawn was a brightening promise on the horizon that she was just too tired to appreciate.

Rubbing at the headache that beat in her temples like a sledgehammer, she focused all her thoughts on the next twelve hours of uninterrupted sleep she was going to get and pushed open her front door...only to stop at the sight of Gable standing directly in front of her, looking incredibly handsome with his hair tousled and his jaw darkened with a night's growth of beard. She'd completely forgotten she'd left him sleeping on her couch.

Conflicting emotions hit her from all sides, buffeting her, tearing her apart. She wanted to turn on her heel and walk out without a word, to run into his arms and beg him to hold her, to unload on him every doubt and past hurt that had flailed her for the past four and half hours. But in the end, she couldn't manage to do anything but whisper his name.

In a single glance, he took in her tiredness and the medical bag clutched in her hand. "What happened?" he demanded sharply. "Where have you been? I just spent the last ten minutes turning the place upside down looking for you. Has someone been hurt?"

"I delivered Rosa Lopez's baby this morning, then followed her and Juan into Silver City to make sure everything was okay." Setting her bag down on the entrance table, she started to move past him. "I didn't think to leave you a note. Sorry."

Her cool apology cut him to the quick, and without stopping to think about it, he reached out and grabbed her arm. Her eyes flew to his, their sudden wariness telling him that a hell of a lot more had gone on here last night than he remembered. "No," he said gruffly. "I'm the one who should be apologizing. I don't remember much of what happened last night, but I know I must have acted like an ass for you to look at me like that. Did I hurt you?"

"No!" She tugged against his hold. Couldn't he see that she wasn't in any shape for this kind of discussion now? "Please, I'm tired. Can we do this later?"

"I *did* hurt you." He swore, wanting to kick himself, the headache throbbing at his temples suddenly turning into hammer blows. "What happened?" he demanded, moving his hands to her shoulders to hold her in front of him. "What did I do?"

"Nothing—"

He might have believed her if she'd looked him square in the eye, but she wouldn't. Capturing her chin, he gently tilted her head up. "If nothing happened, you wouldn't be so anxious to get away from me," he pointed out shrewdly. "Tell me, Josey. What did I do to hurt you?"

He wasn't going to let her go until she told him—she could see it in his eyes. Feeling as though she was going to shatter at any moment, she blurted out, "You said I was like Karen. That I was only interested in money and success and thought I was too good for you."

She couldn't have surprised him more if she'd socked him in the eye. "I told you about Karen?"

"No, Kat did. You just said I was like her, and I'm not, dammit!"

No, she wasn't, he admitted. She was turning out to be everything he'd thought Karen was when he first fell in love with her, and it scared the hell out of him. The defenses he'd built against her were falling one by one, and there didn't seem to be anything he could do about it. "I'm sorry," he said quietly. "On your worst day, you couldn't be like Karen if your life depended on it. You just haven't got it in you. I know that, but I was jealous . . ."

The admission stunned her. "Of who?"

"Jonathan." He spit the name out as if it was a curse. "You'd never even mentioned the guy before and suddenly he was calling you, trying to talk you into leaving. I was furious. I couldn't believe you'd just walk away after the night we'd had together."

"But I didn't."

A half smile, crooked and wry, turned up one corner of his mouth. "That fact didn't register when I was drowning my sorrows at the Crossroads. I'm sorry, sweetheart. I never meant to hurt you."

Whatever reaction he had been expecting from her, it wasn't the tears that welled up in her eyes and spilled unchecked over her lashes. With a strangled cry, she launched herself into his arms, shudders racking her slender frame. After everything that had happened, she just couldn't hold in her emotions any longer. "Oh, Gable, hold me!"

Alarmed, he dragged her closer. "Hey, what's wrong? I said I was sorry!"

Her face buried against his neck, she held him tighter. "I know. It's not you...it's just everything. The baby—"

"It's okay, isn't it?"

Her tears drenching his shirt, she nodded. "She's beautiful!"

That announcement came out as a wail, confusing him even more. "And that's why you're crying? Because she's beautiful?"

"No. I mean, yes. I—I'm just so glad she's okay!"

He frowned, his fingers smoothing her hair back from her damp cheek as he cradled her against him. "Well, why wouldn't she be okay? You were there to make sure there weren't any problems, weren't you? How could something go wrong when you were right there?"

His easy confidence in her, given without the least hesitation, was her undoing. Clutching him, tears rolling down her cheeks, she choked, "Sometimes it doesn't matter if you're right there. Things can still go wrong."

Weeping, she burrowed against him and told him of the baby she hadn't been able to save in Boston. From the moment the cord had prolapsed, the baby had had only minutes before its air supply was cut off, and by the time Molly had come into the clinic, it had been too late. Logically Josey knew she'd done everything humanly possible, but the loss of that one little innocent life had haunted her, weighing her down, until one day she'd simply reached the limit of her endurance and had fallen apart from the strain. *That* was why she'd come to New Mexico, because she'd needed a complete break from Boston, from medicine.

"Oh, God," he whispered, his arms tightening around her as remorse squeezed his heart. "Then Kat got sick and you got dragged into taking care of her... of all of us. Honey, I'm sorry—"

"No." She pulled back slightly, her eyes, red from crying, lifting to his. "Don't apologize. You didn't know, and I wanted to do it. I was starting to miss medicine, but I wasn't ready to jump back in with both feet and go back to Boston. That's what I told Jonathan. We went to medical school together and he wants me to give up the clinic and become his partner. But I like the rural practice I've got going right now. It's nothing like working in a clinic and I've really enjoyed it."

"Until last night."

She didn't bother to deny it. "I knew I couldn't run from the past forever," she admitted huskily. "And last night it caught up with me. I'd been avoiding pregnant women ever since I left Boston, but I couldn't let Rosa down when she had no one else to turn to."

So while he'd been passed out on her couch, she'd faced her past and her fears all alone. Silently cursing himself, Gable brought his hand to her cheek and gently wiped her tears away with the pad of his thumb, a protectiveness he hadn't allowed himself to feel for a long time clutching his heart. "Once you spit in the eye of a dragon, you never have to fear that dragon again," he murmured, just barely resisting the urge to draw her back against him. She was tired, the adrenaline that had kept her going for hours now draining away to leave her standing before him like a wilted flower. Placing his hands on her shoulders, he turned her toward the stairs. "Come on, I'm putting you to bed, then I'm getting out of here so you can get some sleep."

Her limbs suddenly weighted with the exhaustion that she'd been ignoring all night, she let him gently compel her up to her room simply because she didn't have the strength to stop him. "I don't need any help," she protested weakly. "I know you've got to get to work..." Suddenly remembering she hadn't seen his truck outside when she'd driven up, she stopped just inside her bedroom door. "How did you get here last night? Your truck—"

"Cooper dropped me off."

"Then I need to drive you home."

She started to turn back toward the stairs, but he stopped her before she could take more than a step, pulling her back into the room and quietly shutting the door. Shadows engulfed them, soft and still and quiet. "Relax, sweetheart. I can take care of myself. As soon as you're in bed, I'll call one of the guys to come and get me. Now what drawer do you keep your nightgowns in?"

Her mind fuzzy, Josey couldn't follow the jump in the conversation. Frowning, she stared up at him, confused. "My gowns?"

A half smile curling one corner of his mouth, Gable only shook his head and turned away. "Never mind. I'll find them."

Crossing to the old-fashioned chest-on-chest, he realized he'd found her nightclothes in the second drawer from the top when he suddenly sank his hands up to his wrists in batiste, satin and silk. He almost groaned at the feel of the soft garments against his skin. Hurriedly, before the erotic images forming in his head could take hold, he pulled out a pink batiste nightgown and turned back toward Josey, who hadn't moved so much as an inch.

"All right, sweetheart," he said gruffly, tossing the gown over his shoulder as he reached for the buttons on her blouse. "Let's get out of these clothes, into your gown and then into your bed. You look like you're out on your feet."

"Gable—"

"Shh," he admonished softly, quieting her. "All you have to do is just stand here and let me take care of you."

His attention focused on her blouse, he watched his hands move from one button to the next and told himself he could do this. After everything she had been through, it was the least he could do for her. But when his hands pushed her unbuttoned blouse from her shoulders and let it drop to the floor, his hands suddenly weren't quite as steady as they needed to be.

With the blinds closed and the sun just peaking over the horizon, the light was dim, the shadows soft, revealing. She stood before him in nothing but jeans, her bra and tennis shoes, but Gable couldn't drag his eyes away from her. Even with her eyes swollen from crying and her face pale with exhaustion, she had a quiet, subtle beauty that tugged at him, wrenching his heart.

Another time, another place, he would have been pulling her down to the bed, his need for her more than he could bear. But then tenderness engulfed him, dampening his passion and with a sigh that was her name, he reached for her, not to love her, but to care for her, to pamper her. Effortlessly, he unhooked her bra and let it slide to the floor. In the next instant he dropped to his knees at her feet and untied her shoes.

Impossibly moved, Josey felt the helpless tears fill her eyes again and could do nothing to stop them. "Gable, please..."

"Lean on me, sweetheart, and lift your foot. That's it."

Her hand resting on his shoulder, she balanced on first one foot, then the other as he pulled off her shoes. Then he was standing again, his fingers at the snap of her jeans, the rasp of her zipper a soft growl in the throbbing silence. Bemused, she stared down at his dark brown hair, nearly black in the dusky light, as he bent to work her jeans down her legs. Unable to resist temptation, she smoothed the dark strands back from his brow, loving the thick, silky texture against her sensitive fingertips as he helped her step out of her jeans.

Startled, his eyes flew to hers, the heat that flared in the light blue depths warming her inside and out. His fingers suddenly still on her ankle, she saw him swallow before he managed to say hoarsely, "Honey, I don't think it's a good idea for you to touch me right now. I'm hotter than a firecracker with a lit fuse and you're in no shape for anything but sleeping."

The admission pleased her, thrilled her. But he was right. Reluctantly her hand fell away from him. "Sorry."

His smile was crooked, rueful. "Don't be sorry. Believe me, I want you to touch me...just not right now."

He stood, then, and tugged her nightgown over her head, sighing in relief as the delicate material covered her from her neck to her ankles. Before he could be tempted to take it off, he scooped her up and settled her in the middle of the bed with the sheet pulled up to her chest. "Go to sleep," he said gruffly, and leaned down to brush a kiss on her brow.

"Stay with me a while," she whispered. "Just for a few minutes," she insisted when he started to object. "Until I fall asleep."

His body tense and hot, his arms longing to hold her, he couldn't deny her. "Just for a little while," he agreed, and moved to the small, overstuffed chair next to the window.

He'd hardly sat down when her eyes drifted shut and her breathing slowed. Soundlessly, Gable rose to his feet and crossed to the foot of the bed and stared down at her. He had a million things to do, but still he wanted to stay, to lie beside her as she slept and just hold her. Weeks ago, he would have laughed at such foolish sentiment, but he was no longer the cynic he'd once been. Josey had changed him. Ignoring his blustering attempts to scare her off, she'd pushed and prodded her way into his life and his heart, and nothing was ever going to be the same again.

Chapter 12

Later, Gable never knew how he found the strength to leave her. The roundup was winding down, the final loan payment was due in two weeks and there was the sale of the yearlings to arrange, as well as their transportation to ranches in northeastern New Mexico, where the cows would grow fat from summer grazing. But it was Josey who filled his thoughts during the long day, Josey who distracted him still later at supper as his brothers discussed the trouble they expected to encounter when they tried to move the cattle next week.

The food like sawdust on his tongue, he didn't hear a word that was said until Cooper swore in exasperation and reached over to punch him. Jerking to attention, he drew back and scowled at him in reproach. "What the hell was that for?"

"For daydreaming when we've got a crisis on our hands," he retorted. "In case you've forgotten, there are six men out there after this ranch. We know about Ham-

ilton, Mitchell, Stinson and Hopkins. That leaves two unaccounted for, which means an attack could come from
anywhere. And there will be an attack of some type,'' he
warned. ''After all the trouble our dear, sweet neighbors
have gone to so far, they're not going to stand idly by and
watch us ship enough yearlings out of here to make the
loan payment. Things could get ugly.''

Cooper wasn't telling him anything he hadn't already
thought of. ''Then we'll just have to make sure we're prepared,'' Gable said grimly. ''I'll notify the sheriff—''

Flynn's snort told him what he thought of that. ''A hell
of a lot of good he's going to do us. He was useless last
time.''

''Which is why we're not going to sit on our hands and
expect any real help from him,'' Gable retorted. ''We'll set
up a decoy, and everybody will have guns. Nobody's
stopping us from making that loan payment.''

The plans for the movement of the cattle complete, Gable should have retreated to his office after supper to do
some much needed paperwork. But the task held no ap-
peal for him and before he quite knew how it happened, he
was in his truck and headed north...toward Josey's. He
told himself it wasn't because he couldn't stay away. He
was just being neighborly. When he'd left her this morning, she was physically and emotionally exhausted, and he
was concerned about her. He'd just check on her, make
sure she was recovered, and be on his way.

But when he knocked on her door a few minutes later,
he could hear the sound echo through the empty house. He
frowned, glancing back over his shoulder to where her Jeep
was parked in its usual spot out front. She had to be
around here somewhere.

''Josey?''

Finding the front door unlocked, he strode inside and did a quick check, but found no sign of her. Wandering to the back of the house, he stepped onto the screened sleeping porch, but here, too, there was nothing but the silence that always accompanied the end of the day. Starting to get concerned, he was scowling at the long shadows cast by outbuildings when he suddenly noticed the barn door was open. In a dozen long strides, he was across the yard.

The relief that coursed through him at the sight of her fussing over some new kittens drove the air right out of his lungs. She was coming to mean too much to him, he realized, stunned. The lighthearted greeting he'd planned stuck in his throat, and he couldn't do anything but stare at her, drinking in the sight of her.

"Gable!"

Spying him in the open doorway, she scrambled up, her heart thundering in her chest, a kitten cradled to her breast, a slow smile of welcome skimming across her mouth. Long after he'd left her this morning, she'd dreamed of him, then awakened to think of nothing but his gentleness with her. He cared about her. Sometime during the middle of the afternoon, the realization had hit her right between the eyes, so obvious she'd almost missed it. A man didn't treat a woman the way he'd treated her this morning if he didn't care for her.

Wanting to walk into his arms, she stroked the kitten she held one last time, then returned it to its mother, a tattered stray that had showed up on her doorstep soon after she'd moved in. "Delilah had her kittens this morning and I was just checking to make sure everything was okay," she told him as she turned back to him with a rueful smile. "It's been a fruitful day."

With the open doorway behind him, his face was in shadows, but she could feel the touch of his eyes searching her face as if he had never seen her before. Surprised, she started toward him, her smile slipping a little. "There's nothing wrong at the ranch, is there? Everybody's okay?"

"Everybody's fine," he said quietly. "How about you? You were out like a light when I left this morning."

Hot, hazy images from dawn wrapped around her, warming her until a flush rose in her cheeks. Her eyes locked with his, he didn't make a move to touch her, yet she still felt his hands on her, slowly moving over her until her clothes just seemed to melt away.

Her heart thudding in her chest, she swallowed, forcing moisture into her suddenly dry throat as she tore her gaze from his and moved to step around him. "I—I'm fine. Why don't we go inside? I made some tea earlier—"

But he didn't want tea, he didn't want anything but to unload his feelings on her and let her know once and for all what she was doing to him. Stepping in front of her, he cut off her escape. "We have to talk, Josey. Now."

She didn't have to ask about what, she could see the answer in the sudden passion burning in his eyes. "All right," she said with a calmness that was only skin deep. "Go ahead."

But the calmer she got, the more agitated he became. "I know you don't intend to stay forever, and I swore I wasn't going to do this," he growled as he reached for her. His hands closing around her upper arms, he gave her a small shake of frustration. "Do you have any idea what I've been going through? I don't even know myself anymore and it's all your fault! Jealous—dammit, I don't get jealous! And I haven't had too much to drink at the Crossroads in ten years! I can't work for thinking about you. And sleep? God, that's a laugh! How can I sleep when you're always in my head, my dreams? It's got to stop! Do you understand me?"

He was furious by now, but Josey couldn't hold back the beginnings of a smile. Oh, yes, she understood, all right. She knew exactly what he was going through because she'd gone through the same thing...until she'd finally quit fighting it and admitted to herself that she loved him.

Her eyes shining with love, she risked snapping his control and grinned. "So what do you want?" she asked huskily. "Just tell me."

"Dammit, lady, haven't you heard a word I said?" he roared. "I want *you!*"

If she hadn't been aching to be in his arms, Josey would have laughed. God, she loved him! "I'm right here," she said simply, slipping her arms around his neck, her eyes daring him. "What are you waiting for?"

For a stunned moment he just stared at her, sure his frustration had warped his hearing. But she was melting against him, her mouth already lifted for his kiss. Groaning her name, he snatched her against him.

He told himself to go slow, to make it good for her, but desire swept through his blood like a forest fire fanned by an unceasing wind, and before he could catch his breath, he could feel himself going up in flames. Shuddering, he struggled for control, but the battle was lost before it began.

"Josey." Her name a chant on his lips, he dropped frantic, hungry kisses on her upturned face, the curve of her cheek, her brow, the pulse hammering in her throat. Desperation tore at him, and he knew she could feel it, taste it, but he couldn't slow down. His hands raced over her, fighting under the tails of her shirt and the waist of her jeans, searching for the remembered silkiness of her skin. He had to touch her...*now.*

Her senses spinning, Josey felt him all but rip her shirt from her, and gasped. "Inside," she breathed against his mouth. "Let's go inside the house."

"Here," he groaned against her ear, nipping at the sensitive lobe as he slid his hands to her bottom to pull her up flush against him, letting her feel his hardness. "I want you right here."

Urgency firing her blood, she pulled at his clothes with unsteady fingers, the need to have his hot, naked skin sliding against hers more than she could bear. "The corner," she whispered, lifting her mouth to his for a hot, desperate kiss. "There's a pile of hay in the corner. Hurry."

Gable needed no second urging. Taking his eyes from her only long enough to find the hay she'd mentioned, he lifted her up until she could wrap her legs around his waist, lowered his mouth to hers again, and headed blindly for the corner. When he dropped to his knees in the mound of sweet-smelling hay, she was still in his arms, her legs tight around him in a grip that nearly drove him out of his mind.

The last of the afternoon sunshine streamed through the narrow gaps in the siding of the old barn, painting warm strips of light across the dirt floor and picking up minuscule particles of dust that floated in the air. But it could all have come tumbling down around his ears for all the notice Gable gave it. Every sense he had was finely attuned to the woman who dragged him down into the hay with her, her hands frantically working at buttons and snaps and zippers. He couldn't touch her, kiss her, love her, fast enough.

His breath catching, he tore at his clothes without taking his mouth from hers, then started on the buttons of her blouse. But his fingers were shaking, making the task impossible. Muttering a curse, he sent the buttons flying with a downward movement of his hands, drawing a laughing gasp from her that only fired him on. Urgency gnawing at him, he attacked her tennis shoes and jeans, sending them flying without a thought to where they landed. He needed her so badly he was about to burst with it and nothing else mattered.

Only when he had her nearly naked, her bra and panties shielding the last of her secrets from him, did he hear the voice of caution thundering in his head for him to slow down. His heartbeat roaring in his ears, he stared down at her, transfixed. God, she was lovely! In the gathering twilight her skin was pearly, her green eyes dark and stormy with desire. Sweet Lord, he thought, his hand trembling as he traced a line from the pulse pounding at the base of her throat to a point between her breasts, then over her navel and belly, down still further to the damp heat of her. This was only the second time she'd lain with a man and both times were with him. Tenderness spilled into him. Was this all he could give her? Wham, bam, thank you, ma'am?

"I didn't mean to rush you," he murmured, slipping his fingers beneath the elastic of her panties to explore her softness with a slow, gentle touch. "I keep forgetting how new you are to this."

Josey arched under his hand, a strangled cry escaping her. She wanted to tell him that she didn't feel new to this, to him, at all, but his fingers had need coiling in her so tightly, she couldn't manage the words. His touch was so right, his nearness so natural, the beat of his heart so perfectly aligned with hers that she felt as if they'd lain just this way down through the ages, finding each other and loving each other again and again and again. And in this lifetime, she'd waited far too long for him.

She moved against him, his name a plea on her lips, her hands hungry for him, her body straining for the release only he could give her. "Now!" she cried, panting. "I need you now!"

"Sweetheart—"

Her fingers found him then, curling around him, stroking him, teasing him until he was half mad with pleasure. He groaned, his control shattering. In the blink of an eye, he stripped the last of her clothes from her. She was still gasping when he settled between her thighs and thrust into her, setting a pace that sent them both skyrocketing into oblivion.

When she floated back to earth, she found herself still cradled in his arms, his face buried against her neck, the weight of him against her sweet and comforting in the gathering shadows that surrounded them. Smiling into his hair, she sighed...and drew in the scent of him mixed with hay and twilight. It was a scent she didn't think she would ever forget.

He stirred then, easing to his side and taking her with him, his hands starting another slow journey over her as he smiled down into her face. "You're good for me, lady," he growled. "Even when you're driving me crazy."

She arched a brow at him, impishness dancing in her eyes. "This was just a tumble in the hay," she teased, drawing a groan from him. "You ain't seen nothing yet, cowboy."

"That's what I'm afraid of." He laughed, tightening his arms around her. "Every time I hold you, it's harder to let you go."

The admission surprised her as much as it did him, reminding them both that they'd avoided any mention of the future as carefully as if it were a land mine. Her smile fading, she laid her palm against his cheek. "Stay the night."

He wanted to, only God knew how much! Regret darkening his eyes, his hand covered hers. "I can't. We ship the cattle out next week, and we're expecting trouble. Cooper and Flynn and I hammered out a plan over supper, but there's still a lot of work to do to get things ready."

"Trouble?" she echoed, alarmed. "You mean violence?"

He shrugged. "Since we don't know everyone we're dealing with, it's hard to say. But I'm not underestimating anyone. Mitchell and the rest of them know if we sell the cattle and make the loan payment, their chances of getting their hands on our water are lost forever. We plan to be prepared for anything."

"Then you'll need a doctor," she said, terrified at the idea of him hurt. "If someone decides to get rough—"

"Forget it," he said, cutting her off. "This could get nasty and I don't want you anywhere within miles of it. Understand?"

His tone was unbending, his eyes hard. Her chin up, Josey stared back at him just as stubbornly. "Your chauvinism is showing," she warned softly. "I'm a city girl, remember? I can take care of myself."

"Maybe you can in Boston," he retorted, "but this ain't Bean Town, lady. As long as you're here, you're mine, and I'm taking care of you. You got that?"

"No—"

He cut off her protest with a hot kiss that stole the words right off her tongue. His hands sweeping over her, he rolled to his back, dragging her on top of him, stirring her senses again. She tried to hang on to reason, but he knew her body too well now. With a touch, a stroke, he had her hot and aching and melting against him, their argument forgotten.

A week later, on the day the yearlings were to be transported, the Rawlings brothers and their cowboys were at work hours before dawn. Two different fleets of trucks had been leased and had to be loaded, one with the cattle that would be sold off to yearling ranchers in the northeastern part of the state, the other with decoy stock that would be used to mislead their greedy neighbors. To the untrained eye, it looked like mass confusion in the dark. Cattle bawled and shied away from the loading ramps, while cowboys swore and pushed and prodded until they got the stubborn animals on the trucks. It was tiring, frustrating work, especially in the middle of the night, but fatigue was pushed aside by the sense of urgency that crackled on the air. If there was going to be trouble, the men from the Double R were ready for it.

"Okay, that's it," Gable said as the last yearling was loaded. "You boys ready?"

Cooper and Flynn nodded. Since they were the ones who usually delivered the cattle to the yearling ranches, they would lead the fleet of decoy trucks over their usual route—north to Lordsburg and then northeast to Interstate 25. Gable and a handful of gun-toting cowboys would drive the trucks with the real yearlings east, over a less traveled route that would eventually take them to El Paso, where they would hit a smaller highway and turn northeast.

"Yeah," Cooper said, the lines of his lean face grim in the pre-dawn light. "We got the easy part—anyone tries to stop us will just find six trucks half full of old steers tough as leather. You're the one who could run into trouble. Keep in touch over the CB, okay?"

"Keep tuned to Channel three," he said. "I'll let out a holler if something goes wrong. Let's go."

Everyone already knew who was going where, who was driving, who was riding shotgun. Moving to the head of the line of trucks loaded with yearlings, Gable made sure everyone was in their respective places before climbing into the cab of the front truck. The motor was already idling, the diesel ready to go. Buckling in, he reached for the release of the emergency brake—

Without warning, a battered yellow Jeep streaked down the road and pulled over into the grass of the shoulder right in front of him. Stunned, he watched Josey step out, her medical bag in her hand as she hurried toward him.

"Dammit to hell!" Biting out an oath, he unsnapped his seat belt, but before he could jump down from the cab of the eighteen-wheeler to confront her, she was opening the passenger door and climbing in. "You want to tell me what the hell you think you're doing?" he demanded, glaring at her with hostile eyes. "I thought I told you you couldn't go along on this little jaunt."

"Too bad," she retorted defiantly, settling her bag between them. "Kat told me where you were doing the loading, so here I am. I can either ride with you or take my own car, but either way I'm going."

Through narrowed eyes, Gable studied the stubborn set of her jaw, the rebellious flash of her eyes, and just barely managed to hang on to his temper. "Dammit, Josey, we're not going on a picnic! This could get nasty. Maybe the men in Boston take a woman with them to a fight, but not here. We protect our females from that sort of thing, so get in your Jeep and go home. Now!"

"No." Her jaw set stubbornly, she fastened her seat belt with a calmness that set his teeth on edge. "You're wasting time. Why don't you put this baby in gear and let's get out of here? You've got some cattle to deliver, remember?"

He was, he promised himself, going to throttle her when this was over. Swearing, he put the truck in gear and pulled out onto the road.

For the next hour, they traveled over little used roads, the trail of trucks stringing a train half a mile long behind Gable as he followed the eastern route he and his brothers had marked out on the map days ago. They hadn't passed another vehicle since they'd left the ranch, and if there were any unseen eyes out there keeping track of them, they weren't doing it over the CB. He'd run through all the channels without hearing a peep out of anyone except Cooper, who'd reported that he and the other trucks with him were being tailed, just as expected. So far, however, no one had made any attempt to stop them.

The plan was working smooth as silk and their unsuspecting neighbors were following the wrong trucks, obviously waiting for the right place to make their move. When they did, they'd discover their mistake too late to do anything about it. Another five miles and he and the rest of the men with him would turn onto a state highway that would take them right into El Paso. Once they made that turn, no one in his right mind would try to stop them. The state highway was heavily traveled, and men who usually did their sabotaging dirty work in the dead of night didn't like witnesses.

But still, Gable couldn't shake the niggling thought that things were going *too* smoothly. He kept waiting for the other shoe to drop, and until it did, he'd be as jumpy as a flea on a hot rock.

Josey, sensing his uneasiness, felt her own nerves coil into knots. "We're over sixty miles away from the ranch. Surely you don't have to worry about anything happening out here in the middle of nowhere."

Not wanting to alarm her, he shrugged in apparent un-
concern. "Did I say I was worried? I told you all along
there wasn't going to be any trouble, but you wouldn't listen. You've been watching too many old movies, honey.
This isn't the Wild West anymore."

"Then how come you're carrying a gun?" she retorted.
"Or do your men always ride around the countryside
armed to the teeth?"

"No, of course not—"

His eyes on the winding road in front of them, he broke
off with a curse as he topped a small rise and suddenly
found himself bearing down on two pickup trucks barri-
cading the road. Swearing, he slammed on the brakes, almost locking them up, as the trucks behind him followed
suit. For a minute, he was sure they were going to jack-
knife, but he cursed a blue streak and finally managed to
bring the truck to a grinding halt. And not a moment too
soon. The pickups, abandoned by their drivers when it
looked as though he wasn't going to be able to stop, were
less than a foot from his front bumper.

His heart slamming against his ribs, his eyes flew to
Josey. "Are you all right?"

Shaken, her seat belt biting into her shoulder and across
her hips, she nodded. "My blood pressure's probably off
the chart, but I'm fine. How about the others behind us?
Did they all manage to stop in time?"

Gable looked out his side mirror and saw his furious
cowboys spilling from the trucks, spoiling for a fight. He
didn't blame them. Whoever planned this fool stunt could
have killed them all. "I didn't hear any crashes so they're
all apparently okay. Get on the CB and notify Cooper
where we are. Then switch to Channel 19 and put out an
emergency call for the state troopers."

He grabbed the rifle he'd stashed behind the seat and pushed open the door, his face set in hard, unyielding lines. Josey paled, her heart in her throat. "Oh, God, do you really think you need that?"

"Take a look," he said grimly, nodding at the men who were emerging from the sides of the road where they'd hidden, most of them with rifles in their hands. "I'm sure as hell not stepping out there unarmed."

"But—"

"I know what I'm doing, Josey. Do as I told you and leave the rest to me and my men."

Fury burning in his gut, he jumped down from the truck and faced the entire group of conspirators for the first time. Just as he'd expected, Carl Hamilton, Roy Mitchell, John Stinson and Ben Hopkins were there... along with Joe Patterson and Tom Hardy, the missing two, and as much his friends as the others, he thought, fighting rage. They were all men he had considered friends for most of his life. He'd gone to school with some of them, hung out with some of their sons, shared a few beers and a game of pool at the Crossroads with most of them. And now he was staring down the barrel of their guns.

Reminding himself that one wrong move could lead to bloodshed, he stood unmoving as his men lined up protectively behind him. Struggling to hang on to his self-control, his eyes narrowed as Joe Patterson stepped out in front of the others to confront him. Why hadn't he suspected the older man sooner? The Pattersons had been complaining about the Rawlings's ownership of the springs for three generations. And if anyone had the brains to organize a conspiracy of this magnitude, it was Joe. He'd always been wily as a fox.

Standing his ground, Gable met Patterson's defiant glare with one of his own. "I should have realized you had a hand in this. It's got your name all over it."

"You're damn right," the older man replied. "Your family's been hogging the best water in the state for over a hundred years. It's time you shared with the rest of us."

"I did share," Gable retorted coldly. "I shared with all of you, carted water at my expense to every one of you and made sure your cattle got through the worst of the drought. But it wasn't enough for you, was it? You wanted it all."

The hard look he shot the lot of them had them looking at their boots in shame, unable to look him in the eye. All except Patterson. "Because you had it all!" he tossed back angrily.

Gable bit back the need to tell him that his family had been sweating and dying on the Double R seventy-five years before the Pattersons had even thought about leaving the east, and they weren't giving it up for anyone. That would only escalate the tension. "This isn't going to accomplish anything but land your butt in jail, Joe," he said stiffly. "The state troopers will be here any minute. Clear out before they get here and we'll forget this ever happened."

"Maybe he's right, Joe," Tom Hardy said, his doubts clearly written on his unlined, boyish face. "This isn't turning out as easy as you said it would, and I don't want any trouble with the law. I got a wife and kids—"

"Shut up!" the older man snapped. "You're not chickening out now, you hear me? We got to stand together..."

But Tom wasn't the only one with doubts; some of the others glanced at each other, reconsidering, and that was all the encouragement Gable needed. Stepping across the

no-man's-land between his men and Patterson's, he headed
for the two pickups blocking the road. "Then you'd better stand on the side of the road, Joe, because I'm moving
these trucks and coming through."

"The hell you are!" Snarling an oath, he took a step
toward Gable, intending to cut him off, but Tom Hardy
was there before him. "Get out of my way," he raged at
the younger man. "I mean it, Tom! I came here to stop
him and that's just what I'm going to do."

"No—"

"Yes, goddammit! Now move!"

Tom moved, but only to grab the pistol the older man
was waving wildly about. "Damn you, Joe, put that thing
away..."

"Watch it!"

"Be careful! It's load—"

His back to the struggle as he headed for the pickup
blocking the right lane of the road, Gable heard his men
come to attention. Someone shouted an order for the conspirators to drop their guns, but with a loud retort, the
pistol exploded, cutting off the order that came too late.

Fire, as hot as the flames of hell, shot through Gable's
back and exploded out his chest. Stunned, he staggered to
his knees, his hand moving to his chest. Blood. It gushed
through his fingers. With a clatter, the rifle he held fell to
the ground.

"Gable! Oh, God, no!"

Josey's scream penetrated the buzzing in his ears, but he
couldn't answer her for the pain that squeezed his chest.
Without quite knowing how it happened, he found himself flat on his back staring up at the cloudless sky. But his
eyes, feeling as though they were weighted with lead, refused to stay open.

"Gable? Oh, God, they've killed him!"

"No, ma'am. He's breathing. Here, let me help you."

At the panic in Josey's voice, Gable forced his eyes open to find her and Slim, one of his most loyal hands, leaning over him, their faces ashen. His teeth clenched against the white-hot burning in his chest, he forced a grimace of a smile. "'S not so bad, sweetheart. Just a...a flesh wound."

He saw her gaze drop to his bloody chest, where her fingers were frantically trying to stop the bleeding, but then she looked him right in the eye and lied. "You're damn right it's just a flesh wound. I'll have you patched up in no time."

"Somebody help me get him in a pickup," Slim ordered, glancing over his shoulder to where the rest of the Double R men were relieving the now subdued conspirators of their weapons.

"Dammit, move!" Josey snapped. "We've got to get him to the hospital!"

Gable would have laughed at the way she had men jumping into action, but it hurt too much. Damn, what a woman! Then Tom Hardy stepped forward to help Slim lift him, and pain shot through him at the first movement. His breath hissed through his clenched teeth, while the shadows closing in on him thickened and darkened. He tried to call out a warning, but before he could open his mouth, the blackness consumed him whole.

"Easy," Josey breathed, scrambling up on the lowered tailgate to help the men slide him into the bed of the truck. "Don't hurt him."

"He's passed out, ma'am," Tom Hardy pointed out regretfully. "Maybe it's better that way."

So desperate to staunch the flow of blood seeping through her fingers that she hadn't noticed Gable's silence, she glanced up and found Tom was right. Gable's head slumped to the side, his face as pale as death. He lay unmoving, his breathing shallow. She could lose him, she realized, terrified. Even with all her skill, she could lose him right here in the middle of nowhere.

No! Furiously blinking back the tears stinging her eyes, she said thickly, "Whoever's driving, let's get the hell out of here. We don't have any time to waste."

Tom Hardy didn't have to be told twice. He sprinted around to the front of the pickup, but before he could start it and drive off, Ben Hopkins stepped forward. "We never intended for this to turn out this way, Dr. O'Brian. You've got to believe us! There wasn't supposed to be any bloodshed."

"Tell that to Gable," Josey retorted icily. "He's the one lying here in his own blood."

"I will," he promised. "But right now, I think we can do more for him by seeing that Joe's turned over to the state troopers when they get here. And you don't have to worry about the cattle. You can depend on us to make sure that they get to the yearling ranches as scheduled."

Josey just stared at him, hysteria tugging at her. She didn't give a hang about the cattle or empty promises made by a man who only moments ago had been conspiring with Gable's other neighbors to steal his heritage right out from under him. But Gable would care when he pulled out of this. And he would pull out of it, she told herself desperately. He had to!

"That's not necessary," she said, turning his offer down flat just as two state troopers drove up in separate cars with sirens screaming. "If you want to help, just stay out of the way. Gable's men can deliver the cattle."

The man had the grace to blush. "If that's the way you want it—"

"No, that's the way *he* would want it," she cut in. Glancing at Slim, who still hovered nearby, she said,

"You're in charge, Slim. Get on the radio and tell Cooper and Flynn what's happened. Then see that the cattle get delivered."

He nodded. "You can count on it, Dr. O'Brian. Hold tight and I'll get you an escort to the hospital."

Within seconds they were racing down the highway, with a state trooper in the lead, toward Las Cruces and the closest hospital. The drive only took twenty minutes, but it was the longest twenty minutes of Josey's life. The sun beating down on them and the wind whipping them, she did everything she could for Gable, but she was horribly afraid it wasn't enough. He was slipping away, she thought with a silent cry, the wind tearing the mumbled prayers from her lips before they were half formed. Oh, God, she couldn't lose him! Not now. Not when she was just beginning to understand how much she loved him.

God, what a fool she'd been! She'd been so worried about following in her mother's footsteps that she'd actually convinced herself that returning to Boston was still an option. The beat of Gable's heart faint but steady under her hand, she would have laughed at the thought if she hadn't been afraid that she wouldn't be able to stop. No, there would be no returning to Boston, no setting up practice with Jonathan. Like her mother, she was letting her heart make decisions for her, but suddenly she understood why her mother had found it impossible to walk away from love. She could practice medicine anywhere, but she was a one-man woman, and there would never be any other man for her but Gable Rawlings.

Chapter 13

Within fifteen minutes after they'd reached the hospital, Gable was prepped and taken into surgery. Walking the hall outside the operating room, Josey hardly noticed the shocked looks she drew. Her hair wind-whipped, her clothes dark with Gable's blood, she could have passed for an accident victim herself, but all she cared about was Gable. He'd been so pale, so still, when the nurses had wheeled him away from her, it had torn her apart to let him go. God, what was she going to do if he didn't make it?

Whirling away from the thought, she glanced at the clock and paced again, hugging herself against the worry that chilled her from the inside out. Ten minutes passed. Then another thirty. She would have sworn it felt like half a day.

"Josey! Thank God!"

"Is he all right? Slim called us on the CB and told us what happened. Is he still in surgery?"

"We got here as soon as we could. What do the doctors say?"

Kat, Cooper and Flynn rushed toward her, their faces lined with worry, their questions hitting her from all sides. Suddenly the slim control that had kept her moving during the past forty minutes snapped. Tears welled in her eyes and she could do nothing to stop them. "The bullet hit him in the back," she choked, wiping at her wet cheeks, "and exited through his chest. Close to the heart. He lost a lot of blood, but I don't think it hit a major artery."

Kat swayed. "Oh, God!"

Her own confidence wavering, Josey squeezed her hand and tried to reassure her. "The doctors are doing everything they can for him, honey. And he's strong. He has that in his favor."

"You're damn right," Flynn retorted huskily. "He's tough as an old boot. He's not going to let a little thing like a bullet bring him down for long."

Cooper nodded, unable to push any words through his suddenly tight throat. Since their parents had died, Gable had always been the rock of the family, the one who was there through thick and thin for all of them, the one they all turned to. He'd only been twenty-three when he'd taken over the ranch and the family, yet he'd shouldered the responsibility without a word of complaint...even when that responsibility had led to the breakup of his marriage. How many other men would have done that for his younger brothers and sister? He couldn't die! Unable to sit still, Cooper turned away and, like Josey, began to pace.

Time dragged. Flynn swore the clock over the double doors that led to the operating room had stopped, but it just moved with agonizing slowness. Disgusted, he went down to the cafeteria and brought back coffee for everyone, only to have it sit on the tables in the waiting room and turn cold. And still the clock hardly moved.

When the surgeon finally walked out of the operating room thirty minutes later, tiredly rubbing the back of his neck, Josey's heart stopped in her breast. Then he looked up and grinned, and her knees almost buckled. "He's okay? He's going to make it?"

"Probably live to be at least ninety," the older man chuckled as she collapsed into a chair. "He's a lucky son-ofagun, that's for sure. How he managed to take a bullet that close to his heart without it hitting anything vital, I'll never know."

"Thank God!"

Cooper and Flynn let out a shout of relief and snatched Kat close, the three of them just holding each other for a long time, their eyes all misted with tears. Josey felt her own eyes sting. Cooper, seeing her blink rapidly, pulled her from her chair into the group hug, telling her without words that they already considered her a part of the family.

She almost broke down then and there. She loved Gable with all of her heart, but he'd never once mentioned the future to her. Just because she'd decided to stay in New Mexico didn't mean that she could necessarily expect any kind of permanent relationship with him. Oh, he wanted her, but he'd also never made any secret of how he felt about city women. And she couldn't change what she was. His family might accept her with open arms, but would he?

"Josey said there was only two reasons for you to get out of bed—to go to the bathroom or get out of the house if it was fixing to burn down around your ears. That does *not* include work!"

"Josey said you might feel depressed after you got home, even though you pitched a fit to get out of the hospital. Quit worrying, okay? The cattle have already been sold and the loan payment made. Joe Patterson's in jail and he won't be getting out anytime soon. Stinson, Hopkins and Mitchell are out on bail for criminal mischief— they'll probably get off with probation and community service. We still haven't figured how Tom Hardy and Carl Hamilton got talked into joining the others, but their hearts were never in it. And since you decided not to press charges against them, they're falling all over themselves trying to apologize. We're not going to have any more trouble, so relax and take a nap. We've got everything under control."

"Dammit, Gable, you just spent four days in the hospital! How many times do we have to tell you, you're supposed to take it easy? The only way Josey was able to get you released so quickly was by promising that you would stay in bed and rest. You haven't been out of the hospital eight hours and you're already rushing your recovery. Give me those ledgers."

Gable glared at Kat's retreating back as she walked away with the ledgers he'd snuck downstairs to steal when no one was watching and just barely resisted the urge to throw something. He was going crazy just lying here twiddling his thumbs! He admitted he was still weak but, dammit, he wasn't completely helpless. It wouldn't hurt for him to catch up on some paperwork while he was just lying there. And the minute Josey stuck her pretty little nose through the front door, he was going to tell her that!

But he had hours to wait. His brothers and Kat checked on him throughout the day, watching him like a hawk, using Josey's instructions to try to keep him in line. By the time Flynn brought him a tray with his supper, he was

ready to climb the walls. He took one look at it and shot
him a hard look. "What's this?"

Flynn grinned. "What does it look like? Supper."

Gable's glance was withering. A light meal of broiled
chicken and rice, with a pale-looking pudding on the side,
was not his idea of supper. With a scowl, he pushed it
away. "Bring me some steak."

"Not on your life. Josey said—"

Gable swore, cutting him off. "Josey said this and Josey
said that. If she's so interested in my health, where the hell
is she? Huh? I haven't seen hide nor hair of the woman in
days!"

"Why don't you ask her yourself?" Flynn retorted, his
eyes dancing as he cocked his head and listened to the
sounds drifting upstairs. "I think she just walked in the
door."

"Well, it's about damn time," he grumbled. "Josey!
Dammit, lady, get up here! I've got a bone to pick with
you."

He knew she heard him; he'd bellowed loud enough to
rattle the walls, but he knew better than to expect her to
come running at the snap of his fingers. She took her own
sweet time getting there. Impatience tugging at him, he
wanted to shake her when she finally stepped into the
doorway to his bedroom. Casually dressed in a sleeveless
white cotton shirt and flowered skirt, her legs were bare,
pretty sandals on her feet. She looked good enough to eat.

Especially when she grinned at him impishly. "You
rang?"

"You're damn right," he grumbled. "Do you know
you've incited this whole family to mutiny?"

Unrepentant, she leaned against the doorjamb, green
eyes dancing. "Poor baby. Someone had to see that you

took care of yourself, and I was just the person to do it. Any other complaints?''

Devouring her with his eyes, he could think of a dozen. She was too far away, and, dammit, he'd missed her. She'd saved his life, but the dark circles under her eyes told him she cared more than she'd admitted. If he'd thought he could get away with it, he would have jumped out of bed and snatched her into his arms, or better yet, pulled her into bed with him. But Flynn was watching them as if they were the main characters in a soap opera, and it irritated the hell out of him. What did it take for a man to get some privacy in his own home?

Glaring at his brother, he arched a brow. ''Do you mind?''

The brat only chuckled. ''Not at all.''

''Flynn—''

''Okay, okay,'' he laughed at the warning tone. ''I'm going. I know when I'm not wanted.'' Picking up the tray of untouched food, he headed for the door. ''Maybe you can sweet talk him into a better mood, Josey. He's been as touchy as an old bear all day.''

''So I hear,'' she said, strolling over to the bed and picking up Gable's wrist to take his pulse. Under her fingers it was strong and steady, and at the moment, racing...whether with temper or in response to her touch, she wasn't quite sure. Over their hands, her eyes met his. ''It's a good thing you weren't ever in the service. You're lousy at taking orders.''

''I like giving them better,'' he said with an arrogant honesty that made her laugh. ''Sit.''

She merely arched a brow. ''I'm not a dog.''

''Believe me, lady, I know that,'' he said, chuckling, and took matters into his own hands by twisting free of her professional touch and capturing her fingers in his. He felt her start, saw awareness spring into her eyes, and tugged her down beside him.

Her heart starting to pound crazily in her breast, Josey tried to tell herself that this was a mistake. He'd just had surgery four days ago, and she had no business sitting so close to him when all she wanted to do was go into his arms and assure herself that he was really all right. "I don't think this is a very good idea—"

"Then don't think," he said thickly, pressing a kiss to the delicate skin of her inner wrist, surprising them both with the romantic gesture. He watched her wet her suddenly dry lips, her gaze fixed on his mouth, and felt his body tighten. "I thought you'd be packed and on your way back to Boston by now."

Surprised, her eyes jerked to his. "Why?"

"Because you came here for peace and quiet, and that's the last thing you got. Patching up cowboys, delivering babies and getting caught in the cross fire of a gun battle over water rights can hardly be considered restful. I wouldn't blame you if you wanted nothing more to do with the Wild West."

This was the time to tell him she wasn't leaving. Her heart in her throat, she drew in a deep breath and braced herself as if she were stepping off the edge of a cliff—which she very well could be doing if she had misjudged his feelings for her. "Actually, I've decided to stay," she said in a rush. "There's a shortage of doctors, and I think I could do a lot of good here. And even with the occasional standoff between cowboys, it's not as stressful as working the clinic in Boston."

"Is that the only reason you're staying?" he demanded, his eyes sharp and probing. "Because you like the work?"

She hesitated, overcome with a sudden shyness, but her eyes were bright with love as they lifted to his. "No." Dragging in a bracing breath, she took her courage in her hands and said, "I love you, and there's no way I can go off and leave you even if you don't love me in return. I know how you feel about city women, but this is my home now, and I was never like Karen—"

She was chattering, afraid to let him get a word in edgewise, afraid that he'd answer her declaration with a silence that would speak louder than words. So he did the only thing he could to shut her up. He pulled her into his arms and covered her mouth with his, silently, tenderly, telling her that there was no need for her to be nervous. He adored her.

When he lifted his head eons later, she was in bed with him, stretched out next to him, and neither of them remembered how she had gotten there. And neither cared. "Do you think I'd let any other woman put me through this kind of torture if I didn't love her?" he murmured against her sweet mouth, stealing another kiss. "God, lady, you've been driving me crazy! I was so afraid you were going to leave, and I was wondering if I was going to have to hog-tie you to this bed to get you to stay. You're going to marry me."

She had to smile, his tone was so fierce. "Are you asking me or telling me?"

"Trouble," he groaned. "I knew you were trouble the moment I laid eyes on you."

Taking her hand, he pressed a kiss to it, then dragged it down to his heart and held it there. The wicked humor that had been dancing in his eyes only moments before was gone. In its stead was a vulnerability that she'd never thought to see.

"Marry me," he whispered. "That's a request, not an order. I can't give you big city lights and sophistication, but I can give you enough babies to fill every room in this house—if that's what you want—and more love than you ever dreamed possible. Marry me, sweetheart. I swear you won't regret it."

Regret it? she thought, impossibly moved. How could she regret it when he offered her things she'd never expected to have in this lifetime? Tears spilling down her cheeks, she brought her mouth to his. "Yes," she whispered against his lips, her heart pounding in time with his. "Yes to the babies. Yes, I'll marry you. I love you."

His arms tight around her, he kissed her until they were both breathless, then kissed her again, happiness churning in him until he wanted to laugh and shout and dance with it. Josey Rawlings, his lady, his love, his wife. Damn, he liked the sound of that!

* * * * *

Look for more fun with the Rawlings family as Cooper, Flynn and Kat find romance and adventure in upcoming stories from the WILD WEST series!

HE'S AN

AMERICAN HERO

He's a cop, a fire fighter or even just a fearless drifter who gets the job done when ordinary men have given up. And you'll find one American Hero every month, only in Intimate Moments—created by some of your favorite authors. Look at what we've lined up for the last months of 1993:

October: GABLE'S LADY by Linda Turner—With a ranch to save and a teenage sister to protect, Gable Rawlings already has a handful of trouble...until hotheaded Josey O'Brian makes it an armful....

November: NIGHTSHADE by Nora Roberts—Murder and a runaway's disappearance force Colt Nightshade and Lt. Althea Grayson into an uneasy alliance....

December: LOST WARRIORS by Rachel Lee—With one war behind him, Medevac pilot Billy Joe Yuma still has the strength to fight off the affections of the one woman he can never have....

AMERICAN HEROES: Men who give all they've got for their country, their work—the women they love.

IMHER06

TAKE A WALK ON THE
DARK SIDE OF LOVE WITH

October is the shivery season, when chill winds blow and shadows walk the night. Come along with us into a haunting world where love and danger go hand in hand, where passions will thrill you and dangers will chill you. Silhouette's second annual collection from the dark side of love brings you three perfectly haunting tales from three of our most bewitching authors:

Kathleen Korbel
Carla Cassidy
Lori Herter

Haunting a store near you this October.

Only from ▼ *Silhouette*® where passion lives.

Silhouette Books has done it again!

Opening night in October has never been as exciting! Come watch as the curtain rises and romance flourishes when the stars of tomorrow make their debuts today!

Revel in Jodi O'Donnell's STILL SWEET ON HIM—
Silhouette Romance #969
...as Callie Farrell's renovation of the family homestead leads her straight into the arms of teenage crush Drew Barnett!

Tingle with Carol Devine's BEAUTY AND THE BEASTMASTER—
Silhouette Desire #816
...as legal eagle Amanda Tarkington is carried off by wrestler Bram Masterson!

Thrill to Elyn Day's A BED OF ROSES—
Silhouette Special Edition #846
...as Dana Whitaker's body and soul are healed by sexy physical therapist Michael Gordon!

Believe when Kylie Brant's McLAIN'S LAW —
Silhouette Intimate Moments #528
...takes you into detective Connor McLain's life as he falls for psychic—and suspect—Michele Easton!

Catch the classics of tomorrow—*premiering* today—
only from ❦ *Silhouette* ─

INTIMATE MOMENTS®
Silhouette®

If you enjoyed NIGHT SHIFT and NIGHT SHADOW by Nora Roberts, you'll be sure to enjoy this dramatic spin-off.

When the informant Colt Nightshade had been chatting to was shot, Colt hardly blinked—though he did wish he'd gotten more information. But when an overbearing, red-haired lady cop started giving him hell for interfering, Colt sat up and took notice. Lieutenant Althea Grayson wanted answers, but Mr. Nightshade had a few questions of his own to ask....

You first met Althea Grayson as Boyd Fletcher's partner in NIGHT SHIFT (IM #365). Now you can find out the secret lurking in Althea's past while getting your hands on the irresistibly charming Colt Nightshade in NIGHTSHADE (IM #529), available in November at your favorite retail outlet.

ROMANTIC TRADITIONS

Marriages of convenience, secret babies, amnesia, brides left at the altar—these are the stuff of Romantic Traditions. And some of the finest Intimate Moments authors will bring these best-loved tales to you starting in October with ONCE UPON A WEDDING (IM #524), by award-winning author Paula Detmer Riggs.

To honor a promise and provide a stable home for an orphaned baby girl, staunch bachelor Jesse Dante asked Hazel O'Connor to marry him, underestimating the powers of passion and parenthood....

In January, look for Marilyn's Pappano's FINALLY A FATHER (IM #542), for a timely look at the ever-popular secret-baby plotline.

And ROMANTIC TRADITIONS doesn't stop there! In months to come we'll be bringing you more of your favorite stories, told the Intimate Moments way. So if you're the romantic type who appreciates tradition with a twist, come experience ROMANTIC TRADITIONS—only in

INTIMATE MOMENTS®
Silhouette®

INTIMATE MOMENTS®

Silhouette®

You met them this month and learned to love them! They're the Rawlings family of New Mexico!

If you liked GABLE'S LADY (IM #523), don't miss his siblings' stories:

COOPER: He loves the ranch and his work there, but he's restless and the whole family can see it. Their solution: he needs a wife.

FLYNN: He's a lovable flirt who likes women too much to settle for just one.

KAT: She's always been her brothers' little sister, but now that she's grown up—watch out!

Look for their stories as Linda Turner's exciting saga continues in

Coming to you throughout 1994...only from Silhouette Intimate Moments.

WILD1

SILHOUETTE® Shadows™

NEW! FOR NOVEMBER

IT ALL BEGINS AT NIGHT....

The dark holds many secrets, and answers aren't easily found. In fact, in some cases the truth can be deadly. But Silhouette Shadows women aren't easily frightened....

Brave new authors Cheryl Emerson and Allie Harrison are about to see how scared *you* can get. These talented authors will entice you, bemuse you and thrill you!

#19 TREACHEROUS BEAUTIES by Cheryl Emerson
Widowed Anna Levee was out to discover who had mysteriously murdered her brother. Trouble was, the best suspect was slowly stealing Anna's heart. What if Jason Forrester decided he wanted her life, as well?

#20 DREAM A DEADLY DREAM by Allie Harrison
Kate McCoy assured herself it was just a dream. The erotic fantasies she remembered were strictly her imagination. But when Jake Casperson knocked on her door, Kate discovered her nighttime visions were about to become reality....

Pick up your copy of our newest Silhouette Shadows books at your favorite retail outlet...and prepare to shiver!

SILHOUETTE.... Where Passion Lives

Don't miss these Silhouette favorites by some of our most popular authors!
And now, you can receive a discount by ordering two or more titles!

Silhouette Desire®

#05751	THE MAN WITH THE MIDNIGHT EYES BJ James	$2.89	☐
#05763	THE COWBOY Cait London	$2.89	☐
#05774	TENNESSEE WALTZ Jackie Merritt	$2.89	☐
#05779	THE RANCHER AND THE RUNAWAY BRIDE Joan Johnston	$2.89	☐

Silhouette Intimate Moments®

#07417	WOLF AND THE ANGEL Kathleen Creighton	$3.29	☐
#07480	DIAMOND WILLOW Kathleen Eagle	$3.39	☐
#07486	MEMORIES OF LAURA Marilyn Pappano	$3.39	☐
#07493	QUINN EISLEY'S WAR Patricia Gardner Evans	$3.39	☐

Silhouette Shadows®

#27003	STRANGER IN THE MIST Lee Karr	$3.50	☐
#27007	FLASHBACK Terri Herrington	$3.50	☐
#27009	BREAK THE NIGHT Anne Stuart	$3.50	☐
#27012	DARK ENCHANTMENT Jane Toombs	$3.50	☐

Silhouette Special Edition®

#09754	THERE AND NOW Linda Lael Miller	$3.39	☐
#09770	FATHER: UNKNOWN Andrea Edwards	$3.39	☐
#09791	THE CAT THAT LIVED ON PARK AVENUE Tracy Sinclair	$3.39	☐
#09811	HE'S THE RICH BOY Lisa Jackson	$3.39	☐

Silhouette Romance®

#08893	LETTERS FROM HOME Toni Collins	$2.69	☐
#08915	NEW YEAR'S BABY Stella Bagwell	$2.69	☐
#08927	THE PURSUIT OF HAPPINESS Anne Peters	$2.69	☐
#08952	INSTANT FATHER Lucy Gordon	$2.75	☐

	AMOUNT	$ _____
DEDUCT:	10% DISCOUNT FOR 2+ BOOKS	$ _____
	POSTAGE & HANDLING	$ _____
	($1.00 for one book, 50¢ for each additional)	
	APPLICABLE TAXES*	$ _____
	TOTAL PAYABLE	$ _____
	(check or money order—please do not send cash)	

To order, complete this form and send it, along with a check or money order for the total above, payable to Silhouette Books, to: *In the U.S.*: 3010 Walden Avenue, P.O. Box 9077, Buffalo, NY 14269-9077; *In Canada*: P.O. Box 636, Fort Erie, Ontario, L2A 5X3.

Name: _____

Address: _____ City: _____

State/Prov.: _____ Zip/Postal Code: _____

*New York residents remit applicable sales taxes.
Canadian residents remit applicable GST and provincial taxes.

SBACK-OD

Silhouette